REMEMBER ME?

AMANDA RIGBY

B

First published in Great Britain in 2021 by Boldwood Books Ltd.

Copyright © Amanda Rigby, 2021

Cover Design by Head Design Ltd

Cover Photography: Shutterstock

Every effort has been made to obtain the necessary permissions with reference to copyright material, both illustrative and quoted. We apologise for any omissions in this respect and will be pleased to make the appropriate acknowledgements in any future edition.

A CIP catalogue record for this book is available from the British Library.

Paperback ISBN 978-1-80280-422-5

Large Print ISBN 978-1-80280-418-8

Hardback ISBN 978-1-80280-417-1

Ebook ISBN 978-1-80280-415-7

Kindle ISBN 978-1-80280-416-4

Audio CD ISBN 978-1-80280-423-2

MP3 CD ISBN 978-1-80280-420-1

Digital audio download ISBN 978-1-80280-414-0

Boldwood Books Ltd
23 Bowerdean Street
London SW6 3TN
www.boldwoodbooks.com

We dedicate this book to Christina Phillips

1

Hepworth Preparatory School nestled in fifty acres of rolling hills in the Leicestershire countryside, a bleak collection of red brick buildings that had been patchworked together over time. It had once been a boarding school, populated by the under-achieving male offspring of the local aristocracy, but in more recent times, and thanks to a recently appointed head teacher, their common entrance exam pass rate had soared, ensuring they'd become the co-ed school of choice in the area.

Still bloody cold, though.

Despite the daffodils that were covering the far field, Paul Henderson rubbed his hands together and glared at the radiator clinging to the wall for dear life. It was a relic from the Victorian era and served as a stark reminder that, despite all the improvements, funding was an issue. But he couldn't complain. Unlike the sea of teachers who flocked to Hepworth hoping to use it as a springboard to move them up the ladder, Paul had no intention of leaving. For the last eight months he'd been acting Deputy Head and the Board of Governors would be making his position official in a matter of weeks. And rightly so, since he'd spent countless hours overhauling some of the antiquated, inefficient systems his predecessor had left behind, turning chaos into order.

There was a low hum of conversation, and he scanned the room. He'd split his year eight class up, and given each group a locked box, which had six different padlocks on them. The codes for each lock could only be found by solving the problems on the worksheets he'd handed out. In his experience, it managed to engage even the most resistant pupil.

He walked around until each group had managed to open their boxes, pride and excitement gleaming on their faces. And they said maths couldn't be fun.

They were still discussing the results when the final bell for the morning's session cut through the room.

Wwwwwwwaaaah.

Voices rose in the room next door, accompanied by the scraping of chairs, but none of his students stood up. They knew better. He wasn't a strict teacher in the way that some of his colleagues were, but he demanded discipline and made sure his classes knew it. They all waited as he walked back to the desk.

'Tonight, I want you to write about three things you learned today.'

'Thought this was meant to be a maths class,' someone grumbled from the back.

'I could always give you some quadratic equations,' Paul suggested, which earned him a laugh. He grinned and waved them off. 'Get out of here before I change my mind.'

They didn't need to be told twice. The class stood, accompanied by the squeal of chair legs being dragged against the cold tiled floors, and the students spilled out into the corridor. He should bring them back in and make them leave in a more orderly manner, but he didn't.

Today was special. Jenna had reached the vital twelve-week

stage in her pregnancy. She'd had a scare early on when she thought she might be losing the baby, but that had been a false alarm. According to the midwife, everything was progressing well.

On the way home he would stop and collect the gold necklace he'd ordered. It was a simple design with a tiny golden daisy hanging off it. Jenna often said she didn't like flashy jewellery, which was good since his teacher's salary would already be stretched with the arrival of the baby, but he wanted to give her something to let her know how he felt.

Meeting Jenna had changed his life. She was smart, funny, sexy. And soon to be the mother of his child.

He crossed the courtyard that linked his block to the administration office, and almost ran into Tim Barnes, the head teacher, who was flanked by two of the school governors. They were all dressed in suits, no doubt on their way to yet another meeting with someone from the Department of Education.

'Sorry.' He held up his hands by way of an apology.

'My fault. We've had someone from the local radio station trying to interview parents,' Tim said, running a hand through his thick dark blond hair, while the two governors looked steely-faced. Paul sighed. It had been like that ever since Eric Chambers, a senior teacher, had been filmed swigging from a vodka bottle by one of the year six girls during the journey to Kimbolton School for a netball tournament. The video had quickly found its way to the Internet and the damn thing had gone viral.

Two weeks later, Eric had been suspended and most of the television crews had disappeared from the front gates, but there was still far too much interest in Hepworth.

'You'd think they would've given up by now,' Paul said.

Tim grunted. 'We can only hope. Anyway, we won't keep you. We've got a one o'clock.'

'Of course,' Paul said as they hurried off. He continued through to what had been dubbed the 'new court'. A circular garden surrounded by brick buildings, propped up by Doric pillars.

'Excuse me, sir.' One of his pupils appeared from behind him.

'Yes, Henry?' He glanced down at the young boy.

'I won't be at school next week and my mother asked if there's any work I should be doing, so I don't miss out.'

Missing school? They normally didn't countenance time off during the term if it could be avoided.

'Where are you going?'

'Hospital.' Henry grimaced. 'I'm having my tonsils out.'

An operation. That explained it.

'Don't worry about the work, there will be plenty of time to catch up. You'll need to rest after.'

Henry was an excellent student and was earmarked for an academic scholarship at his next school. His parents were driven, and it was typical that they would want him to continue studying even though he'd been in hospital.

'Thank you, sir.'

'I'm surprised you're not having the operation in the school holidays. Or did the doctor want it carried out immediately?'

'I can't. We'll be in France.'

Paul choked back a reply. Considering the parents wanted him to do well, their priorities appeared somewhat misguided. Not that they would place the blame on themselves. They believed that as they'd paid for their child's education, the onus was on the teaching staff to ensure their child performed to their expectations. Still, Henry was a good kid, and Paul knew better than anyone that you couldn't pick your parents.

'I hope it all goes well. I'll see you when you get back. Off you go.'

Paul sighed and headed for the staff room, where he grabbed himself a coffee and walked to a chair in the corner. It gave him a view of the entire room, yet was away from the hub, which meant he could separate himself from the usual staffroom gossip, which inevitably involved venting frustrations at certain pupils.

He retrieved his phone and opened up the article he'd been reading on baby buggies. Jenna had been keen for one she could use while jogging, but he wasn't convinced the vibrations would be good for the baby. The research confirmed it.

He could just see her teasing smile as she told him he was being overprotective.

Guilty as charged.

He was going to make sure his child had every advantage in life. Everything that he'd never had. He took a sip of coffee and was about to pull out yesterday's tests that still needed marking when a notification blinked up from his social media feed. Nicole Williams.

The low chatter of the room fell away, and the light seemed to fade to black as he stared at the screen.

Not possible.

He pressed on the notification and his ex-fiancée's feed flashed up. In the corner was a familiar photo of her. It was one he'd taken in Greece, back when they were still together.

Back when they'd been in love.

Before it all turned to hell.

I've had enough of Australia. I'm back. Can't wait to catch up with all of my old friends.

No. That couldn't be right.

His pulse thudded in his ears, so loud it gave him a headache.

Paul dragged his finger across the screen to refresh it. The message blinked back at him. It had been posted at 12.35.

Was this some kind of joke? The room started to spin as a comment flashed up in reply.

About time! It's been two years. First round of drinks is on you for clearing off without telling anyone.

It was from Barb. Paul vaguely recalled she used to work with Nicole and was a right bitch.

A second comment appeared. His mouth was dry, and he chugged back the coffee, instantly regretting it as it scalded his throat. Then a third comment. More friends excited at the prospect of seeing Nicole again.

Except that was impossible.

No one was going to be seeing Nicole again, because she was dead.

And he should know.

Because he was the one who'd killed her.

2

It was an accident. Of course it was.

Paul wasn't evil. He was one of the good guys.

Six years working at Hepworth, spending his spare time refereeing rugby matches and accompanying students on trips. Ensuring that every kid who crossed his path knew they were special. That they had potential. That they shouldn't be judged because of past mistakes.

And it had all come crashing down thanks to Nicole Williams.

No, wait. That wasn't fair. It had been different back then.

They'd first met at one of those dreadful university parties. Everyone had been dressed in togas, getting drunk on cheap wine and talking about Voltaire as if they'd been intimately acquainted. It hadn't helped that Paul had come wearing a sheet with a white vest underneath, not ready to display his chest. He hadn't been as fit back then and was self-conscious of his teenage fat. He'd been woefully out of place.

Then Nicole had floated in, all long dark hair and even longer legs that were brown from a summer in Norfolk. She was so out of his league that it hadn't occurred to him to talk to her, but a

person had bumped her, and she'd landed on him, simultaneously sending him crashing to the floor *and* covering him in wine.

Somehow, they'd ended up in her apartment – yes, even as a
first year she'd had a flat rather than a crappy dorm room that
smelled of cabbage and socks. Instead, an expensive cello was
propped up in the corner and the walls were filled with original
artwork, and a huge bookshelf was bursting with an eclectic
range of reading material. Perfect for an art history major.

There had also been vodka. The kind that lived in a freezer
and was often seen on VIP tables at the London clubs Paul never
went to. Three shots and they discovered they both had a deep
and never-ending love of Humphrey Bogart and Casablanca. Five
shots and they both confessed to going naked in public. Nicole's
was at a French chateau during a game of strip poker, and Paul's
had been while skinny-dipping as a thirteen-year-old.

At seven shots they realised they were both orphans.

In that moment, a bond had formed between them. Born of
vodka fumes, but strong enough to last. A secret language of
scars, abandonment and trauma that only the two of them could
speak. They'd waited ten years to get engaged but, when they did,
Nicole had thrown herself into the planning, including a date at
the impossible-to-book church. He hadn't been surprised that
she'd managed it. Nicole had always been excellent at getting
what she wanted.

And getting rid of what she didn't.

It was a week before the wedding when he'd found out about
the abortion.

About how she'd murdered his baby. The wine in his belly
had churned, threatening to fight its way back out as a low buzz
hummed in his ears.

'Don't look at me like that,' she'd protested, glossy hair falling
round her face as she'd screwed up her mouth the way she did

when she didn't get her own way. 'I didn't kill anything. You have to see that the timing is all wrong. I'm trying to get my career back on track, and I can't do that in a bloody maternity dress. It wasn't alive. I terminated a pregnancy, it's different.'

But it wasn't. Not to him.

Nicole, out of anyone, should've understood. She knew what his life had been like. What happened to unwanted kids. Hell, she'd been one of those kids too. The buzzing had increased, and the room had blurred. Like he was pressed behind a plastic bubble, separate from the world.

When things came back into focus, everything had changed. He was suddenly standing by the door, his hands clenched so tightly that his knuckles had turned a terrible blue-white colour.

And Nicole was lying sprawled on the floor, the heel of her shoe snapped. How many times had he told her that they were dangerous? That at five foot ten she didn't need to wear heels.

There wasn't even any blood. Just a tiny purple bruise, blooming out against her porcelain skin.

He'd run to her, steps heavy and sluggish as he pushed through the invisible waves of energy that pulsed through the room. Vertigo made him sway as he dropped to his knees and checked her pulse, her nose, her mouth, but there was nothing. No. No. No. She couldn't be dead. They were meant to have been getting married. His beautiful bride.

He should've called the police. An ambulance. Anyone. With clumsy hands he'd snatched up his phone, his chaotic thoughts trying to work out what had happened.

Had he pushed her, or had she fallen?

That's what the police would ask. What if they didn't believe him? After all, they'd never believed him before. Not back then. Police didn't believe people like him. They looked at him and saw what the social workers had seen.

You're nobody. Nothing.

Heat throbbed in his brow. His life would've been ruined. All because of one mistake. Just like he'd always told his students. One lapse in judgement shouldn't dictate a person's entire future. And so he'd made the decision.

He'd taken her to the one place no one would ever look, and he'd buried her deep. It wasn't like in the films. She'd been impossibly heavy to lift despite her slim build, and his muscles stung from the digging. Dirt had been everywhere as he'd rolled her body into the hole. He'd left her in the tight red dress she'd been wearing. It was now ripped and stained, and he'd stripped her of all jewellery that might identify her, but at the last minute he'd slipped a gold crucifix round her neck.

Neither of them was religious but Nicole had found it tucked behind a coffee shop sofa and had refused to hand it in. She'd laughed and said that if someone was foolish enough to lose it, they needed to learn a lesson. She'd never worn it, since pious wasn't really her style, but somehow it seemed fitting.

Then he'd had to explain to everyone where she'd gone. Thankfully she'd always used the same password for everything, so he could get into her phone.

He'd played the jilted groom. It hadn't been hard. The guilt had formed hard knots in his gut, making eating impossible, while his sleep was filled with nightmares.

But now... two years later, he had a life he'd never envisaged having. He was happy again. In love.

If the truth came out, everything would be ruined. It would make what had happened to Eric Chambers seem like a walk in the park. It wouldn't just be his life. It would affect Jenna and his unborn child, too.

His throat tightened and knuckles whitened as he fumbled around in his briefcase for the vial of pills he kept hidden in the lining. He tried not to take them any more. After all, he was going to be a father. But he knew what happened if he let the pressure build up too much.

The two pale blue tablets were cradled in the palm of his hand. The pathway to clarity.

His hand shook as he swallowed them, chased by a gulp of water. They did nothing to ease his pounding brow, but they would. He willed them to work faster as he tried to focus on his thoughts.

There had to be a logical explanation. A hacker, or one of her friends had somehow logged in.

But why?

Was it a coincidence, or did they know something? Either way, he needed to get the post down before anyone else saw it. He entered Nicole's account details and hit enter. A small wheel turned on the screen.

Access denied.

He tried again, but it was the same. He clicked on the button to reset the password, but the words *incorrect email address* stared him in the face.

He tried to reset the email, but it didn't work. Maybe he should contact the help desk? Did they even have help desks any more? What if they wanted identification? He rubbed his chin as the bell rang.

He let out a shaky breath and put away his phone, before heading to his next class.

The rest of the afternoon went by with agonising slowness, an hour teaching and a further hour discussing the maths exam with a colleague. It wasn't until he finally retreated into his office and closed the door that he allowed himself to let go of the forced smile he'd worn.

Like everything in Hepworth, the offices were decorated in a traditional style with gold-framed oil paintings and heavy wooden desks, all to radiate the idea of tradition and wealth. Unlike most of the teachers, Paul hadn't added his own touches. There were no potted plants or children's artwork, no personalised coffee cups or mementoes.

As far as he was concerned, things like that were clutter, distractions. All designed purely to stop someone from doing their core job.

All that covered his desk was a computer, and his journal, which was filled with meticulous notes. Usually, he relished the time after classes to catch up on everything before going home to Jenna. But he couldn't go anywhere until he'd worked out what was going on.

He steepled his fingers together. What was he always telling his students?

Identify the problem. Review what they knew, develop a plan. And then solve it.

So, what was the problem? He reached for the journal and began to jot things down. Was it that Nicole was back? No, because that was impossible. He'd seen her broken body. Dragged her through the fields. Covered her in soil. Nicole was dead. And besides, if she really was still alive, then why had she waited two years to come back? It didn't make sense.

But it also didn't change the fact that someone had activated her account.

Which meant someone might know his secret.

He'd identified the problem.

There was a knock on the door, and he swore as he closed his journal and pushed it to one side.

'What?' he said in a sharp voice, his mind still whirling.

'I wanted to see if you'd finished for the day?' Alison poked her head round the door, a surprised expression on her face. 'Am I interrupting?'

'No,' he said quickly as he took a deep breath. He needed to calm the hell down. Losing control wouldn't help anyone. 'Come in.'

'You sure?' She double-checked, her gaze raking over him.

'Yes.' He nodded as she finally stepped into the room. They'd both started at Hepworth in the same term and had become friends. At first sharing a pint while coming up with strategies to control classrooms and get parents onside, but after he'd found her in the school car park being groped by another teacher, and he'd managed to pull the prick off her, their friendship had deepened.

Over the years, they'd been there for each other. She'd been a shoulder to cry on when Nicole had 'left', and he'd been a friend to her after her long-term partner, Rob, had taken a job on the Isle of Wight and not asked her to go with him.

Alison awkwardly dropped into one of the leather chairs that were designed to remind parents why they spent so much money sending their kids to the school. She had long legs, made strong from years of horse riding. Her mouth was wide and firm, eyes like amber chips, and dark hair that was currently filled with highlights. Jenna often said that Alison was attractive but to Paul she was simply one of the few people in the world whom he could trust.

Her brows knitted together. 'You look pale. Has something happened to Jenna?'

'The morning sickness has been brutal, but the books all say that will ease soon.' He forced a smile. She was the only person he'd confided in about the pregnancy, but even then they didn't discuss it much. 'We've hit the twelve-week mark today, which hopefully means she won't miscarry.'

Understanding lit her eyes. 'Ah, that's why you were looking so distracted.'

Not exactly. 'I don't want to jinx anything.'

'You won't, idiot. It's going to be fine.' She rummaged through her bag, withdrawing a bag of crisps. She opened it up and offered him one. He shook his head. She'd always been able to eat whatever she'd wanted and remain slim which was a source of envy to many of their colleagues, who often passed comment on it. 'Are you going to start telling people?'

'I think so.'

Jenna's family would be thrilled but, as for him, he had no one to tell. His parents had died in a car crash when he was eight, and the foster family he'd been placed in six months later had sent him back to Arlington, a hellhole of a residential home in Bradford, after a year. He doubted they even remembered who he was, let alone gave a shit about his life.

'That makes sense.' Alison grabbed a handful of crisps from the packet. 'Plus, it means I'll finally be able to go shopping. I've wanted to buy things from the moment you told me.'

'Al, it's still too early,' he said, familiar dread gathering in his gut. He'd assumed he would be worried about his child from the moment it was born, but it had happened as soon as Jenna had greeted him at the door, clutching the pregnancy test, with tears of joy glistening in her eyes.

'Fine. I'll wait a bit longer,' Alison conceded before catching his gaze. 'But you need to stop worrying. You and Jenna are going to be amazing parents.'

'Thanks,' he said as she tugged at the heavy gold signet ring on her index finger. It was a tell of hers. One she used whenever she felt nervous or uncomfortable. But usually she only reserved it for people she didn't know very well. Which meant—

Hell.

She'd seen the post.

He rolled his neck, trying to ease the building pressure.

'Is that why you're really here?' he finally spoke. 'To see if I knew about Nicole?'

A guilty flush rose up her neck and she let out a long sigh. 'I was hoping you *hadn't* seen it,' she admitted, searching his face for clues. He swallowed. What kind of clues did she want to see? That he was on edge that his ex might be back in the country? Or that he was so blissfully happy with Jenna that Nicole's appearance meant nothing to him?

Or both? He finally settled on the latter.

'That makes two of us,' he said, careful to keep his voice even.

'Did you have any idea she was coming back?' She sounded cautious. Like an archaeologist carefully brushing away soil, not sure what was going to be underneath.

'God, no.' Paul shook his head. At least this was one reaction he didn't have to fake. 'How about you?'

'No. I don't tend to read her posts. Not after what she did to you,' she said, once again twisting the ring on her finger. She sucked in a breath and studied him, as if weighing up her words. Then she gave him a cautious smile. 'You never really talk about the night she walked out on you... but I know it ended badly. So... how are you feeling?'

Paul raked a hand through his hair and turned away. What a bloody mess. How was he meant to answer her? Tell her the truth? That whoever this was, it wasn't Nicole? Tell her that he was scared shitless because someone knew what he'd done, and that they could ruin his life at a drop of a hat?

Except it was bad enough that one person knew what had happened, he could hardly tell Alison as well.

'I feel indifferent,' he said at last. 'My future's with Jenna and the baby. I have no desire to ever see Nicole again.'

Alison let out a breath, as if relieved he'd given her the right answer. He couldn't blame her. From her point of view, she'd supported him through a devastating break-up, and he doubted she was in a hurry to do it again.

'Good. I'm glad to hear it. After what she did to you. Leaving you for a job...' She trailed off, as if not wanting to remind him about what had happened when Nicole had suddenly packed her bags and headed to Australia to take a new position.

He swallowed. That part had been almost true.

After her bohemian days at university, where she'd devoured her art history, Nicole had done a full pivot and trained to become an accountant. She was a high-flyer and had worked her way up to being a Chief Financial Officer in less than a decade. But she'd lost her job several months before the *accident*. It wasn't until afterwards Paul discovered an offer letter from an Australasian company to move to their Sydney office. He'd known nothing about it.

The second secret she kept from me.

Not that what he'd done was justified. He knew that better than anyone. He'd paid for it for a long time. Every night he'd wake up from blood-soaked dreams, guilt clinging to him like heavy roots, trying to drag him down into the same dirt grave he'd dug for Nicole.

He'd walked around for months with bags under his eyes, and shoulders weighed down with leaden weights. No more than what he deserved; he'd tell himself. It hadn't been hard to act the poor, devastated fiancé. It was a role he'd expected to play for the rest of his life. Then he'd met Jenna.

The woman who gave him a reason to live again.

The buzz of Alison's phone cut through his thoughts.

She glanced at the screen. 'Shit. I'm meant to be in the hall. I'm still covering Eric's science club.'

'What a mess. At least the press are leaving us alone now.'

'I can't believe none of us knew Eric had been coming to work drunk every day for the last four years. Still, I guess it's good it happened.'

'Good?' Paul blinked, momentarily pushing his thoughts of Nicole aside. 'The whole school's been plunged into a scandal. How is that good?'

Alison coloured. 'That came out wrong. I meant that he has a wife and kids, and at least now his secret is out, he can start getting the help he needs. We all have to face our demons sooner or later. This way he might actually save his marriage as well.'

'I suppose,' he said as her alarm went for a second time. He made a shooing motion with his hands and plastered on a smile. 'You better go, but I'll see you Monday. Have a good weekend.'

'I will,' she said, leaving his office and heading in the direction of the hall.

Paul rubbed the tight spot at the back of his neck as he picked up his phone again. The post was still there. It now had fifteen new comments. And hell... next to each entry was a reply. The air pushed out of his lungs.

Can't wait to see you too, Gigi. And you'd better bring along that perfect husband of yours. I still think about your wedding day. So great.

Debs, we are going to party so hard.

Tabby Cat, I hope that great jazz club we discovered on the Kings Road is still there.

On and on the comments went. Nicole's friends from work and university. And each one was individually answered. Despite the amphetamines, his brow began to pound again and this time he reached into the bottom drawer of his desk, where his predecessor had left a bottle of gin. Not Paul's drink of choice, which was why he'd hidden it from sight. There was an empty coffee cup on his desk, and he poured in two fingers of alcohol. Not enough to make him drunk, or stop him from driving home, just enough to give him some relief from the two questions burning through his brain.

Who was doing this and what did they want?

Three Holloway Drive wasn't the kind of place Jenna ever envisioned herself living in. For a start, it was on one of those estates where all the houses looked the same, but the residents prided themselves on how different they were because of their unique brass taps and brightly coloured splashbacks. No. In her mind she was going to live in a tiny cottage with eighteenth-century ceiling beams that were too low for the room but so full of history and stories that one didn't mind the eccentric quirks. She would have chickens in the garden and a riot of spring flowers growing everywhere.

Paul's house was none of those things. He'd bought it straight off the plan after Nicole had fallen in love with it. Not in love enough to buy it with him, though, which is why he still lived there. While it was lovely to have a clean bathroom, and bedrooms that didn't get covered in mould or a chimney that coughed clouds of smoke into the room, it wasn't quite how Jenna imagined raising her children.

Then again, she'd never imagined having children with

anyone like Paul. Not because she didn't love him. Rather it was the opposite.

People like Paul didn't usually notice women like her. That's why she'd wanted the cottage, so it could be a prop to make her interesting. Desirable. Visible. *Oh, yes,* people would say: *Jenna Reynolds lives in that marvellous cottage. It's quite extraordinary how she keeps the garden so beautiful while taking care of the twins and working full time. What an absolute diamond.*

But somehow, even without the cottage Paul *had* seen her, in a way that the rest of the world had not. And so, when he'd first suggested she move in with him, it didn't occur to her to say she didn't like modern houses or sleek kitchen counters. After all, she had Paul, which meant she no longer needed anything else.

She drained the glistening parcels of ravioli, watching as they slithered about like freshly caught fish. She'd made the pasta sheets herself and stuffed them with Paul's favourite Portobello mushrooms and blue cheese, all to celebrate the good news. Not that she'd be able to eat it. She hadn't been able to keep down more than a few pieces of dry toast and weak tea since she'd conceived.

Still, the doctor said she'd soon start feeling better. Even if it lasted the entire pregnancy, she didn't care. They were having a baby. She finished with the pasta and reached for the crushed tomato sauce she'd made, timed to be ready for when Paul walked in the door.

Except that had been ten minutes ago.

The joys of living with a teacher. At Hepworth there was always a chance he'd be late. Dragged into some last-minute meeting or other, but usually when that happened he'd call or text.

Unless he was stopping to get something with which to celebrate.

The smile she'd been wearing all day returned.

Her phone buzzed and she eagerly snatched it up, expecting to see Paul's name on the screen, but it was her older sister, Lucy. Jenna pressed her lips together. She wanted to answer. Especially now that she was past the twelve-week mark and could officially tell her family about the pregnancy. But to do that might also raise the question she'd been dreading.

When are you getting married?

It was the only fracture in her otherwise perfect relationship. It was something she longed for. After all, Lucy had tied the knot five years ago to her childhood sweetheart, while next week their parents were celebrating their fortieth wedding anniversary.

Then there's me.

Both her mother and Lucy were tall and slim, with ebony hair and matching almond-shaped eyes, always immaculately groomed, and calm under pressure. Unlike Jenna, who was small, with a spare tyre round her waist and auburn hair that had a tendency to frizz. She was the complete opposite of her family.

And of Paul's ex-fiancée, Nicole.

Jenna gnawed on her lower lip. Nicole was the woman who'd walked out on Paul a week before their gigantic wedding. The wedding that had left him humiliated and unanchored. The wedding that had turned him off marriage for life. She *did* understand but unfortunately her sister didn't, and Lucy had taken to making little digs at Paul whenever she could. This forced Jenna to constantly juggle her family and Paul, trying to keep them both happy, while at the same time wondering if it was so wrong that she wanted the same thing everyone else had?

Her phone rang again, but she ignored it, not ready for another argument. She'd have to tell her family at some stage about the baby, she just needed a little bit more time.

The familiar beep of the garage door opening up dragged her

back to reality and Jenna smoothed down her skirt as the car door closed. Tap, shuffle, scuff as Paul walked across the concrete floor, past the neatly stored gardening tools, the emergency chest freezer and her own little car.

Click, click as he turned off the garage lights and simultaneously locked his car, and then he was in the hallway. Oh, how she loved the sounds of him moving round the house with his methodical, careful steps. Warmth cocooned her.

'I'm in the kitchen,' she called out, even though the clip, clip, clip of his leather brogues told her he was coming to find her. She bit down on her lip as she gave the ravioli one final inspection.

Until she'd met Paul, her cooking skills had consisted of boiling an egg and making jacket potatoes. But when she'd discovered that Nicole – as well as being beautiful, successful, and smart – had been known for her famous dinner parties, Jenna realised her days of eating like a broke student were over, and she'd spent their first two months secretly watching as many YouTube cooking tutorials as she could.

If the way to a man's heart was through his stomach, then she was going to pave the road in Instagram-ready creations.

He stepped in and smiled, his gaze first sweeping across her face and then drifting down to her stomach. His dark hair was tousled from the blustery May winds outside, but his mouth was warm on her neck as he wrapped his arms round her waist.

She leaned back into the press of his body. His breath fanned her skin and familiar heat spread through her.

Sometimes she still had to pinch herself that he was hers.

They'd met eighteen months ago, when he'd attended a suicide prevention seminar she'd arranged. She'd trained as a social worker but now worked at a charity where she did everything from fundraising through to event planning. She'd been standing at the back listening to the speaker when he charged in, late. He glanced at her, and she shushed him with her finger on her lips. He'd given her the most contrite smile and stood beside her until the first break, when he could take his seat. But not before he'd suggested they sit together for lunch after the morning session.

It was like they'd known each other forever. He was so handsome, with thick brown hair, wide blue eyes and a chin dimple that endlessly fascinated her. When he'd called the next day to ask her out on an official date, she'd almost wept with delight.

'Something smells good.' He spun her round and kissed her. His mouth tasted of breath mints and coffee and was soft against hers. 'I thought we'd agreed you would take it easy. Especially when you can't even eat it.'

'Did I not tell you about the foot massage you'll be giving me later?' she said in a teasing voice, but instead of giving her one of his lazy smiles, his mouth puckered into a frown. A moment later it was gone.

'If it's a foot massage you want, then a foot massage you shall have.' He planted another kiss on her forehead before untangling himself and walking to the fridge. He pulled out a bottle of beer, and then stiffened and put it back.

Jenna winced. He'd declared that if she couldn't drink during the pregnancy, then neither would he. Not that he ever drank that much, anyway.

'Everything okay?' she asked.

His shoulders dropped and he gave her a rueful smile. 'I really need to work on my poker face,' he said with a sigh. 'It's nothing much. Just a busy day at work and bloody parents pulling their kids out of school because they don't want to miss out on a trip to France. God, I hope I'm not that kind of father.'

'Impossible,' she said, and it was true. Paul was brilliant with children, from the students he taught through to the neighbourhood kids who usually cajoled him into a game of football every Sunday afternoon at the nearby park. 'You'll be amazing.'

'As will you. Speaking of which, I got you something to celebrate the three-month mark.' He rummaged round in his pocket and withdrew a small black velvet case. Jenna's mouth went dry. A jewellery box.

A ring-sized jewellery box.

'Paul.' She let out a soft gasp and stepped back. But he didn't drop down onto one knee; he simply handed her the box. Ice washed over her. It wasn't a proposal. It was silly of her to even think it.

'Go on, open it.' He grinned like an excited child who'd bought someone a present for the first time. She swallowed, pleased he hadn't realised her mistake.

Her hands shook from embarrassment as she flipped open the box to reveal a delicate gold chain with a tiny charm at the end of it.

A daisy. Her favourite flower.

'Oh, thank you. I love it.'

'Really?' he said, eyeing her uncertainly. Sometimes she forgot that underneath his affable, confident veneer there was a vulnerability to him. A fear of being rejected. She guessed it came from losing his parents at such a young age and growing up as an orphan, and she hated that it had left such a scar.

And so she swallowed back her own disappointment. Pushed down the image of another woman standing in the kitchen, receiving another small jewellery box. A tall, beautiful woman with long dark hair. And when that woman had opened the box, there *had* been a ring.

'It's perfect. Truly,' she assured him. 'My neck is probably the only part of my body that isn't swollen, so it might even fit.'

'You're beautiful,' he said in a fierce voice as the panic left his eyes. 'Here, let me put it on.' He took the box and nodded for her to turn round. He leaned into her, his breath hot against her skin as he gently slid the necklace round her throat and fiddled with the clasp. When he was done, he wrapped his arms round her stomach. She was usually self-conscious of the soft swell of extra flesh, but now she had a legitimate reason for her lack of washboard abs she didn't mind.

They stayed like that, gently rocking together, his warmth running through her skin and down her veins like a river. It wasn't until the timer pinged that she reluctantly untangled herself and pressed her mouth to his.

'Go and get changed. Dinner's nearly ready,' she said as the kitchen filled with the scent of buttery garlic bread. She swallowed back her own nausea.

'No idea what I did to deserve you, but I'm bloody glad it worked.' He headed to the door, picking up the post as he went.

She never received much mail. Just the occasional catalogue or the annual birthday card from her elderly grandparents. But Paul got a small collection of bank statements and doctor's reminders. She'd been trying to ease him into the digital world and stop receiving so much paper, but so far it hadn't been a success.

Still, considering they had a hybrid car and always recycled, they were ahead with their carbon footprint.

He returned five minutes later and, once they'd eaten, he shooed her into the lounge while he dealt with the dishes. The low buzz of Radio 2 kept him company as Jenna sat down on the sofa. It was a dull beige colour that reminded her of oatmeal, but was apparently Italian linen, and according to Paul it cost more than his car. Nicole had been the one to pick it.

Had it been his ex's revenge? To make sure that any woman who tried to take her place would feel uncomfortable in the room that had once been hers? If so, it had worked perfectly, and Jenna couldn't even bring herself to kick off her shoes and curl up her feet on the expensive piece of furniture.

She wriggled about, trying to get settled before firing up her laptop. Paul would probably scold her for working too hard, but she had a funding application to finish. They needed a grant to roll out the new school programme they'd spent the last six months developing. So far, the results had been astounding, and every life saved made the hard work worthwhile.

Paul reappeared in the doorway, his brow glistened from standing over a sink full of hot water. In his hands were two mugs and he passed her one and then slipped her phone out of his pocket.

'I brought this in. You've missed two calls from Lucy. Let me guess, now that your perfect sister knows about the baby, she wants to keep checking up on you.'

Jenna stiffened and then caught herself. They'd agreed that they wouldn't tell anyone until they'd hit the twelve-week mark, which meant Paul had assumed her family now knew the happy news. They would. Soon. It also filled her with annoyance that Lucy distrusted Paul merely because he hadn't proposed, yet Paul seemed to take her sister's constant needling with good humour and kindness.

'Must be.' She took the phone and studied the screen, as if seeing the messages for the first time. 'Probably wants to talk about vitamins.'

His eyes filled with concern. 'Don't commit to taking anything until we check them out properly first. There are so many out there that are filled with additives.'

'I promise,' she said, her fingers reaching up to touch the delicate necklace now round her throat. Most of the time she wasn't really sure why Paul had chosen her, but she had to remind herself that it didn't really matter any way. All that mattered was he had, and that they were about to have a baby. It might not have been enough for Nicole *or* Lucy, but it was enough for her.

4

There was always one. In this instance it was Jeremy Lewis. The twelve-year-old boy had decided to climb up onto the roof of the sports shed, via an apple tree, to retrieve his football. Unfortunately, he hadn't considered how he would get down, and the kid was now sitting there, his face almost as white as the ball he was hugging.

Paul turned to the ancient groundsman who was clutching at the ladder with arthritic fingers. He had to be at least eighty and had more chance of running a marathon than climbing up the rungs.

Sunshine had appeared and brought with it an audience of boys, all hollering with excitement. Paul gave them a quelling look, not for the first time wondering how kids could go so wild as soon as they were in the playground.

He sighed and rolled up his sleeves. Maybe the board would offer him a pay rise when they finally made his title official.

The groundsman tutted his tongue and held the bottom of the ladder as Paul climbed up and leaned over the guttering.

'I'm sure the views are nice up here, Jeremy, but it's probably time to come down.'

'I can't, sir. I feel sick. What if I puke?'

'Then we'll be both raiding lost property for something else to wear,' Paul said in a matter-of-fact voice as he swung himself onto the roof. It had a high rake, and the shingles were covered in lichen and moss. He held out his hand. 'Let's get rid of the ball and we'll go down together. Okay?'

Jeremy chewed on his lip but didn't protest as Paul plucked the ball from his hands and threw it down into the crowd of hovering students. They all hooted and one of them kicked it away. Several of the kids followed it and as the audience dispersed Jeremy's shoulders relaxed.

'See, that wasn't too hard. Now, I'll go first, and you follow. That way if you fall, at least you'll land on me.'

This drew a laugh and some of the colour returned to the lad's face. Then he pointed to Paul's outstretched arm. 'What's that?'

Paul's jaw flickered and he resisted the urge to look at the ten-inch burn scar that ran from his left wrist up to his elbow. In winter it often went an angry purple colour but in the milder weather it was a dull red. It was also why he usually preferred to keep his sleeves down.

'Nothing much. I had an argument with a barbed wire fence. As you can see, I lost,' he said in the same light voice he always used. Calm. Controlled. Nothing to see here, folks. 'Let's get you down.'

Jeremy swallowed, as if considering, then nodded. 'Don't let me fall.'

'I won't,' Paul promised as he swung his own legs back down onto the top rung. He climbed down two steps and held out a hand for Jeremy to cling onto. The scared boy shuffled along the roof until he reached the ladder. He then put a tentative foot onto the first rung, while Paul put an arm round him to keep him steady.

Rung by rung they went until they reached the ground. Jeremy turned to him.

'Am I in trouble, sir?'

'I'll need to tell your parents and will have to write up an incident report, but I'm sure it isn't something you'll be doing again in a hurry,' he said, making light of the fallout Jeremy's adventure would entail.

'No way,' Jeremy agreed before running over to where a group of boys were waiting for him. Paul yawned and pulled his phone out of his pocket to check the time. Twenty minutes before afternoon lessons started. He didn't have any classes to teach but there was the new health and safety policy that he was implementing, not including the incident report that he now had to do. But first coffee.

He'd spent the weekend marking assignments and sleeping badly, his mind replaying over and over the look of shock on Jenna's face when he'd presented her with the jewellery box.

The one that didn't contain an engagement ring.

How could he have been so stupid?

But he already knew the answer. The shock appearance of Nicole's post had thrown him into a panic, and he hadn't even considered his present might be misconstrued. Jenna's huge brown eyes burned into his mind as she'd valiantly tried to conceal her disappointment.

He was disappointed too. There was nothing he wanted more than to marry her, but each time he thought about it, he was overcome with guilt. He had blood on his hands, and if he married Jenna, he'd be tying her to any future fate that awaited him.

And then there was the question of Nicole's posts.

All weekend he'd checked for more updates, waiting to see a

message or email addressed to him, telling him how his life was about to be ruined forever. But nothing had happened. There hadn't been any more posts or replies to the comments. It should have been a relief, but it left him in a state of limbo.

Waiting for the axe to fall.

Something similar had happened last year when the patch of wooded land where he'd buried the body was sold to a property developer. For two months, he'd lived in terror that the bulldozers would move in, and she'd be discovered.

He'd even considered tying himself to a tree and joining the activists who always turned up every time builders threatened to break new ground. But in the end, he hadn't done anything except lie low and try to stay cool. And it had worked.

A month before excavating was due to start, one of the activists in question found a nest for some obscure owl, and before anyone could say 'I'd like the four-bedroom semi-detached with a spa pool,' the whole area had been reclassified The developers had slunk away to look at land in Bristol.

It was the same thing now.

I just need to ride it out.

He increased his pace, walking in through the sweeping red brick archway that led to the teachers' lounge. Alison and Doug were sitting at their usual table, and he swallowed. He should ditch the coffee and head back to his office, but before he could retreat, Alison looked up and waved him over.

Paul reluctantly headed over, stopping only to dump a teaspoon of instant coffee into a random mug and pour in some hot water. The stuff tasted like cardboard but at least it wouldn't keep him up half the night. He fumbled for some more painkillers and swallowed them down. Then, hot drink in hand, he wove his way across the room until he reached his friends.

'Ah, the hero returns,' Doug, the music master, sang out, and

Paul grimaced. The sports shed was clearly visible from the far window, and it was obvious that he'd had a bigger audience than he'd realised. 'Nice work.'

'It's not a big deal.' He slid into the spare seat. Doug was in his late forties and looked like he belonged in an inner city comprehensive, with his ratty beard and mismatched clothes that came straight out of a charity shop. But despite the indie rocker appearance, he was an exceptional teacher who'd led the Hepworth choir into first place in the Leicestershire inter-schools' choral competition.

'You're too modest,' Alison chided as she glanced round the lounge. 'Who else here would've done that?'

'I stand corrected. I'm fantastic,' Paul said with a mock smile. 'Now, can we please change the subject?'

'Sure.' Doug shrugged and recounted the *heated discussion* two parents had had on the journey to the mayor's concert the choir were appearing in. Paul and Alison both laughed, and the conversation moved onto the waning interest in the viral video. They were just standing up to go back to their respective afternoon classes when Alison's phone pinged with a notification.

She peered at the screen and then quickly crammed her handset into her pocket.

Doug's eyes widened with curiosity. 'Oh. A Not Safe for Work post. Let me guess, a dick pic.'

'Remind me again why we spend time with you?' Alison glared at him, not quite meeting Paul's gaze. A moment later, his own phone buzzed with a notification, and Alison's reaction suddenly made sense.

Nicole.

He rubbed his brow and excused himself. As he left, Alison gave him a concerned look. She was obviously worried about how he'd take the post.

Paul waited until he was safely in his office before daring to look at the screen.

A low buzz hummed in his ears as annoyance slithered up his veins, but he took a deep breath. And another. Losing control wasn't an option. His chest heaved in and out, and he reached for the bottom drawer. This time there was no coffee cup on his desk, so he held the bottle up to his mouth, careful to only take a sip. The burn helped push away the white noise and he let out a shuddering breath as he felt the building pressure disappear.

His shoulders dropped as he returned the bottle to its hiding place and dared to look at the post. The photo from their trip to Greece had been replaced with a newer one. One he'd never seen before.

Nicole was standing by a sweeping harbour and in the background were the famous white sails of the Sydney Opera House. Her dark hair was lighter and had been cut into a swinging bob that emphasised her cheekbones. She was laughing at something the person on the other end of the camera had probably said and her arm was raised, as if cradling the gigantic building in the palm of her hand.

Nausea rose in his throat, and he doubled over like he'd been punched.

This wasn't someone pretending to be his ex-fiancée. This was a photograph of her. In Australia. The place that he'd randomly chosen as her new home.

Except it hadn't been random. He really had discovered the letter congratulating her on her new position at KGI. But she hadn't taken the job, because she was dead.

Or so he thought.

His head spun as he flipped up the screen of his laptop and brought up the company's website. He clicked on the Sydney branch and scrolled through a list of employees.

A photo of Nicole flashed up. Another one he hadn't seen. Her hair was still long and pushed back behind her shoulders to reveal an expensive gold necklace and a silk blouse. She'd obviously been promoted from the first job because her title was now Head of Finance.

It was so like Nicole to climb the corporate ladder at the speed of light.

Paul put her name and company into a search engine and a series of links came up. There were several older ones that he recognised. Plus a photograph of her only wearing a bra. He'd told her not to post anything like that online. That it would last forever, but she'd laughed at him, saying he was old-fashioned. He stared at it now. The black lace was dotted with tiny red roses and Nicole's sultry expression was teasing and inviting.

It was all an act. Nicole had loved the attention but not the intimacy. But it had been enough for him. Until he'd met Jenna, and finally discovered what it was like to connect with someone.

He flicked back to his search, looking for newer entries, and there they were. A newspaper article in the Sydney Morning Herald and a LinkedIn profile that was littered with blog posts and updates. His stomach roiled and the taste of coffee rose up in his mouth while beads of sweat covered his forehead. His vision blurred and his skin tingled like it was being stabbed with a thousand needles.

Christ. He was going to be sick. He frantically reached for the rubbish bin and threw up, hot bile burning his throat. He threw up again as his forehead began to pound, like something was trying to cleave its way out.

It couldn't be true. She was dead. He'd killed her.

He raked through the fog of his memories, trying to step into the picture and relive what had happened.

There had been wine. Probably too much. And Nicole had

been standing in front of the stupid feature wall she'd insisted on, bright swirls of geometric colours, too loud against the wooden floorboards. Then she'd told him about the abortion. It had led to the argument, and then to her lying dead on the floor. Her body bent at a strange angle, and the tiny bruise on her forehead. Dead.

He looked down at his hands. They were covered in blood. It dripped down off his fingers and into thick sticky pools on the floor. So much blood. He dropped to his knees and scrubbed it. Over and over again, despite knowing it would never come out.

Wait. No. That wasn't right.

Paul abruptly dragged himself out of the memory, feeling weak and exhausted. There hadn't been any blood. Which proved that at least one part of the memory wasn't true.

What the hell did it all mean?

But he already knew the answer.

It was happening again.

5

'Has he experienced anything like this before?' a male baritone voice said from somewhere in the room. Paul forced his eyes to stay shut. Starchy hospital sheets rubbed against his bruised legs and he wanted to move, but didn't dare. He had to pretend to be asleep. It was best that way.

He'd woken up half an hour ago and had been trying to figure out what they were doing there. As far as he could tell, there were no broken bones though his hands throbbed, and his shoulders and neck felt like they were being crushed by an invisible weight. Unfortunately, when he tried to remember what had happened, the familiar wall of mist descended across his mind like winter snow, blanketing everything.

'Yes. Two months ago we said he couldn't go on a trip to London with the school. He punched a hole in the wall and then blacked out.'

The voice belonged to Elma Baros, which meant her husband, Yanni, was probably close by. As far as foster families went, they were okay. Strict, but lots of food and his own bedroom. There had even been talk of adoption, but that had fallen away recently. Paul's mouth went dry. He longed for some water but didn't dare move.

'And what about physical violence? Has he hit anyone?'

'No,' Yanni said. 'This is the first time.'

Hit someone? It explained why his hand was aching, but nothing else. He wasn't violent and had never even been in a fight before. At least not one he could remember. The wall of mist thickened, and his head began to pound.

Who had he hit? There were two other foster children living in the house. Lily, who was a kid, and Toby, who was thin as a reed and more interested in science than in talking, which meant they rarely interacted.

But who else? A neighbour? Someone from school?

There was silence and then a fumble of papers, as if the doctor was checking something. Finally, he spoke. 'Mrs and Mr Baros, it appears Paul's had a dissociative episode, where severe rage has caused him to blackout after the altercation with Toby.'

'Altercation?' Yanni's voice rose, the way it did when he was agitated. 'Toby has a broken nose and three fractured ribs.'

He sucked in a breath. So it had been Toby? But why? He tried to imagine what could have happened to make him so mad, but it was like grasping at straws.

'What I want to understand is what triggered the event. Was there a history of childhood trauma?' the doctor continued.

'I'm not sure about his early childhood and Paul never talks about the accident which left him an orphan,' Elma said in a soft voice.

With good reason.

Paul didn't remember anything about the accident except for head-lights. Burning bright, eclipsing everything else around him as they seared through his memories, leaving behind a blazing white light that he couldn't step behind.

Which meant all he knew had been pieced together by the stories he'd been told.

He was eight and had managed to walk away from the car accident that killed his parents with only minor injuries. Doctors had said that the trauma had given him fractured memories that might never come back. The police concluded that he wasn't wearing a seatbelt, which was how he'd been thrown from the car, his only injury the second-degree burns on his arm.

Everyone said it was a lucky escape, which was bullshit. If he was so lucky then why had he been sent to Arlington House?

Being fostered by Elma and Yanni had been his way out, but it looked like he'd messed that up, like he messed up everything else.

'There's a strong possibility that this isn't the first time he's experienced this kind of event,' the doctor continued.

It wasn't?

He knew there had been lost patches of time but had figured it was because he was tired, or hungry.

'Wait, so you're saying it might happen again?' It was a question but also a statement and he knew that any chance of staying with the foster family were now gone.

He was nobody. Nothing.

'It's entirely possible. But that's something we want to avoid. There's therapy and medication, though it's too early to say if either will work.'

Paul scrunched up his eyes, determined not to cry.

6

'Sir, can I ask you about the homework you set yesterday?'

'Not now, Giles, can't you see that I'm busy?' Paul snapped at the pupil as he headed towards the office. It had taken all his strength to actually teach his class without checking his phone or letting out a primal scream, and he certainly didn't want to spend any more time with them now.

'Okay. Sorry, sir.' The boy shuffled off in the opposite direction.

'Looks like someone woke up on the wrong side of the bed.' Paul looked up as Doug walked towards him, holding a snare drum. His eyebrow was arched in surprise. 'Can't say I've ever seen you lose it with a student before.'

Hell.

Paul winced, annoyed that he'd let his mask slip, but relieved it hadn't been someone like Tim Barnes. 'It's been a long day.'

'Hey, you don't need to explain it to me.' Doug let out a belly laugh. 'I'm pleased you're as mortal as the rest of us. Anyway, I've got a jazz band waiting for me, I'll catch you later.'

'Sure,' Paul said, relieved at how easily Doug had brushed

away his indiscretion. It was also a reminder that he needed to pull himself together.

He'd spent most of yesterday trying to sort through the tangle of images. But the more he pushed, the more messed up it all became. Sometimes it was just him and Nicole in the room, sometimes his boyhood dog Bucket was there, curled up in the corner, oblivious to the yelling. And then there was the fight itself. While he'd been washing up, he'd had a vivid image of Nicole pushing him, and he was the one lying on the ground. Yet an hour later, another jagged image had flooded his brain. One where he'd pushed her so hard she'd fallen, catching her head on the coffee table on the way down. There had been a sickening crunch of bones that was still with him.

But they couldn't *all* be true.

Even if Nicole wasn't dead, there was still the possibility that he'd tried to kill her.

Was that why she was back? To tell the world what he'd done? To ruin his life, the same way he'd ruined hers? But why wait until now? Was it because Jenna was pregnant?

Did Nicole regret the abortion, and now wanted some kind of sick revenge?

It was like a terrible movie that had far too many alternative timelines all tangling together, sending the characters into madness.

He checked his phone for messages. Last night, unsure what else to do, Paul had sent a message to Nicole's social media page. For someone who could clear his work inbox in under half an hour, it had taken a long time to construct, and even as he hit send, he wasn't sure he'd managed to get the wording right.

Long time since we've caught up. How are you?

Transit Slips

Transit to group: Full access to all libraries, LLC Libraries, Authority Tower Hamlets
Transit to: TH Cubitt Town Library (Tower Hamlets)
Transit reason: for a hold
Author: Rigby, Amanda,
Title: Remember me?

Item ID: M00767167
Transit date: 25/10/2022,13:20

There had been no answer, though a tiny tick had appeared next to the message at eleven-thirty last night. She'd read it. There was something about that tick that spurred him on and, before his first class, he'd called Sarah Jenkins, who would've been Nicole's chief bridesmaid at the wedding.

They'd vaguely kept in touch over the last two years, and while the call had gone through to voice mail, he was confident she'd ring him back.

Except she hadn't.

He finally reached his office and closed the door. There had to be something else he could do. He fired up his laptop and went back onto all of Nicole's social media feeds. No new posts or messages. He rubbed his chin. He could try calling more of her friends, but it was already risky enough leaving a message for Sarah. What if Nicole really was back, and had told other people what had happened?

He clicked onto her LinkedIn page and brought up her last employer in Australia. What about someone there? Could he ring up and at least confirm what day she finished, and when she'd left the country? It seemed less risky, so he clicked through to the company's contact page and carefully put in the international dialling code, along with the number.

His heart thundered as the call was answered.

'Hello—'

'You've called outside our normal office hours. If you know the extension you require, please go through and leave a message. If not, please try again tomorrow at nine a.m.'

How could he have forgotten about the time difference between the UK and Australia? He'd have to wait until later tonight before trying again.

He was about to compose yet another email to Nicole when

there was a knock on the door and Tim appeared in the doorway. 'Budget meeting in five minutes.'

Paul looked up, trying to hide his surprise. He'd forgotten all about it. This day really was going to the dogs. He forced himself to give Tim a calm smile as he got to his feet. At least he'd prepared everything for the meeting last week, before he'd received the message that was derailing his life.

* * *

Jenna shut the screen of the computer and tugged at the top button of her blouse. It had been a long day of video calls in order to put together a strategic plan for tackling Internet trolls. It wasn't helped by being unexpectedly saddled with organising a national forum that they were hosting next month.

The low-level nausea that had still refused to budge left her feeling giddy, like she'd stepped off a rocking boat. She took another sip of peppermint tea. She had no idea if it actually worked, but at least it distracted her body for a couple of minutes. The tea was lukewarm, but it still tasted good, and she contemplated getting a refill as Louisa appeared in the doorway of the meeting room Jenna had been using.

'I'm heading home but wanted to remind you to call your sister. She's left two messages.'

Jenna sighed. She was going to have to bite the bullet and do it soon. 'Thanks.'

'No problem,' said Louisa, who'd been working at reception for six months. She added, 'Someone came in to see you while you were on your video call.'

'Who was it?'

'They didn't leave their name but seemed anxious to meet up with you.'

She frowned. 'Sounds mysterious. I wonder if it was the caterers about the workshop we're hosting next week?'

'I've met Teri and it wasn't her. She had dark hair, tall, glamorous. Ring any bells?'

'No.' Jenna shook her head, not wanting to admit that the baby hormones were already playing mayhem with her memory so there was a good chance it was one of the many people she regularly networked with. 'But I guess if it's important she'll come back.'

'Yeah, I guess. Don't work too hard. You'll wear yourself out.'

Preaching to the choir.

Jenna plastered on a bright smile. 'I'm just packing up.' It was a lie. She still needed to go over the final details in the funding application. It had been a huge amount of work, but if they were successful, it would give them the much-needed money to expand the front line work they did. She was also hoping it would finally give her the promotion she'd been after.

Guilt chewed at her. She hadn't gone into the not-for-profit sector to make money, but after she'd met Paul she'd found herself up against the legacy of his ex-fiancée. His very successful ex-fiancée.

It was hard not to be jealous. The few times Paul talked about her, he made it sound like Nicole's career had been made up from a series of lucky breaks.

But Jenna knew the real reason. The Nicoles of this world, with their good looks, good education and charm, had the ability to open doors that stayed firmly shut to regular folk. Jenna included. She'd tried to explain it to Paul once, even pointing out that he led a similar charmed life, but he'd merely said that if she thought trying to fix timetable cock-ups and angry parents was charmed, then they needed to swap jobs.

So she'd left it alone. But while she knew she'd never earn as much money as Nicole, she still wanted to make a name for herself. Be the kind of woman that Paul would respect and admire. The kind of woman he'd propose to.

Two hours later, she was finally done, and by the time she pulled into Holloway Drive her back ached and her neck was sore. Still, it was nothing a long soak in the tub wouldn't fix. Paul was working late, which meant she'd have the place to herself.

She lifted out the shopping bag from the backseat and locked the car. The bush next to her rustled. The hairs on the back of her arms prickled and she spun round to see a woman standing in the shadows. She had short dark hair and a familiar smile.

Bridget Milton. Her neighbour.

'God, Bridge. You almost gave me a heart attack.' Jenna leaned against the side of the car and shook off the spurt of adrenaline that had started to fizz along her veins. Bridget and her husband Daniel had moved in at the same time as Paul and Nicole. They'd both been very welcoming to Jenna, especially Bridget, who shared her love of jogging.

'Sorry.' Bridget stepped through the gate that joined to the two properties and walked over to the car. She was followed by a small Jack Russell called Eddie. 'I heard you drive up and since we're meant to be leaving in ten minutes, I thought I'd pop over.'

'Leaving in ten minutes?' Jenna trawled her foggy mind but came up blank.

'To book club.' Bridget seemed to take in the dark circles under Jenna's eyes, and the ready meal poking out of the white canvas shopping bag. 'You forgot?'

'I did,' she admitted, thinking of the heavy hardcover book still sitting on the nightstand next to her bed. Guilt caught in her throat. Bridget had gone to great lengths to get Jenna invited to join the group. 'I haven't even started it yet.'

'I have and it's terrible,' Bridget confided as she gave her a smile. 'Tell you what, let's ditch it and have a glass of wine. You look exhausted.'

'You have no idea. I'd love to ditch book club but will have to pass on the wine—' Jenna broke off and winced.

Unlike with her own family, the reason she hadn't told Bridget about the baby yet was because her friend had spent the last twelve months going through several rounds of gruelling IVF treatment. The last thing Jenna wanted to do was rub her own happiness into Bridget's face.

'Since when do you pass up a glass of wine?' Bridget said before her eyes widened. 'Oh... you're pregnant?'

Jenna swallowed and nodded her head. 'We've only just passed the twelve-week mark. I was going to tell you, but—'

'You were worried how I would take it?' Bridget cut her off in a wry voice. She shut her eyes and when she opened them, tiny tears glistened in the corners. Bridget brushed them away and squeezed Jenna's hand. 'Congratulations. I'm so happy for you both. Or should I say for all three of you.'

'Your time will come.' Jenna returned the pressure, her own eyes pricking with tears. 'And don't get me started with the water-works. These days I seem to cry at the drop of a hat.'

'I've read that the first trimester can be a real bitch,' Bridget said, still holding Jenna's hand. Her friend's soft blossom perfume filled the air and Jenna felt the tension in her shoulders dissolve. She hadn't realised how exhausting it had been to not openly talk about her pregnancy.

'You have no idea,' Jenna said before catching her breath. 'So, you're really okay?'

'I'm thrilled. You and Paul will make amazing parents.'

The tightness in Jenna's throat lessened. 'Thank you. That means a lot.'

'Nonsense. It's the least I can do. Besides, now I can take notes for when it's my turn,' Bridget said before briskly taking her phone out of her pocket and sending a text message. 'Right. I've cancelled book club so that we can talk. I know Paul's out, and Daniel won't be home for hours. It will just be the two of us. My place or yours?'

'Mine,' Jenna said as she held up the shopping bags. 'I have ice cream. Is that an acceptable replacement for wine?'

'Yeah.' Bridget followed Jenna to the door and waited while she stabbed in the security code on the house alarm. 'By the way, Geraldine's coming to do my rugs tomorrow and said she could swing by to give you a quote. Can you get the morning off work?'

'No way,' Jenna said, the upcoming funding deadline looming in her mind. She rubbed her brow. Two weeks ago, she'd spilled coffee on the thick Persian rug in Paul's study. She'd meant to tell him, but he'd come home tired after a long day of dealing with badly behaved kids, and she suddenly felt like a young child again, waiting outside the school office. Instead, she'd turned the rug round and hidden the stain underneath one of the many potted plants she had dotted round the house.

But it was only a temporary solution, which was why when Bridget had mentioned she was getting her carpets cleaned, Jenna had peppered her with questions.

'Oh, that's a pity. I guess she could come back another day. Unless you want to leave your keys with me? I'd be happy to let her in.'

She brightened. If she could get a quote for the entire house, then the rug would get cleaned at the same time. 'That would be fantastic,' she said as they walked into the kitchen. 'I'll drop the keys off tomorrow morning on my way to work. Are you sure you don't mind?'

'Of course not. Don't forget to give me the code. I don't want to set the alarm off. Eddie goes crazy when he hears it.'

'He's not the only one,' Jenna said with a sigh. Personally, she could have done without it, but Paul refused to consider the idea of leaving the house without an extra layer of defence. And so, like learning to keep the house incredibly neat, she'd become used to the small blinking eyes that seemed to follow her from room to room.

An hour later, the pair of them had eaten a light supper and the ice cream and were sipping mugs of chamomile tea. Jenna had filled her in on everything, from the moment she'd stared at the pink line through to how her boobs had gone up two bra sizes. At the last part she let out a long groan.

'Sorry. That was too much information. I think it's the excitement of having someone to talk to besides Paul. Not that I'm complaining. He's a great listener.'

'Yes, but I can hardly imagine any man being sympathetic about the size of your boobs,' Bridget made a snorting noise then stiffened. 'Wait... does that mean you haven't told your family yet?'

'Not exactly.'

'Why not? I thought you were close.' Bridget leaned in, eyes curious.

'We are,' Jenna said then stared at her bare wedding finger. She sighed. 'When they find out about the baby, they'll start wanting to know why we're not getting married.'

Not to mention Lucy's acid comments about Paul himself. It wasn't something she was ready to hear.

Bridget raised an eyebrow. 'I didn't think you cared about that.'

'In principle I don't, and after everything that happened to him, I totally understand why Paul doesn't want to. But it's hard not to take it personally,' she admitted, her hands clasping together.

'What do you mean?'

'Nicole was a paragon. The gorgeous, successful career woman that Paul fell madly in love with. In love with enough to want to marry. Whereas I'm a slightly overweight charity worker with frizzy hair and chewed fingernails. What if I'm the rebound relationship who accidentally trapped him into fatherhood?' The truth of the words burned in her throat, like acid that was slowly dissolving her insides.

'Stop it. You're beautiful, and Paul's crazy about you. Trust me, he's much happier. When he was with Nicole, he always seemed to be on edge in case he upset her.' Bridget paused, and stared at her, as if weighing up whether to speak or not. 'I must admit, I wasn't sad when she upped and left.'

Jenna, who'd been toying with her mug of tea, pushed it to one side and looked up, trying to conceal her curiosity. Nicole was a puzzle. A conundrum. Her presence was still felt throughout the house, and she'd moulded Paul into the man he was now. Yet Jenna hardly knew anything about her. This curiosity had turned her into a silent collector, trying to weave together tiny threads of information, hoping the parts really were the sum of the whole. Hoping that one day she might better understand the woman who still cast such a long shadow over their lives.

'I thought you were friends?'

In fact, she was sure of it. There were several photographs of Bridget and Nicole enjoying boozy girls' nights out plastered onto Bridget's social media feeds, and from what little Paul had told her, the two couples had socialised often.

'Well...' Bridget bit down on her bottom lip.

'You don't have to tell me if you don't want to,' Jenna said. It was a lie. She was desperate to know more, especially since Bridget was usually tight-lipped when it came to Paul's ex.

'It's not that... I don't like bringing up the past. You have to promise not to tell anyone.'

'You have my word.' Jenna leaned in, the tiny fragments of information she already had arranging themselves in her mind like an incomplete jigsaw puzzle, waiting for the next piece to help everything make sense. 'What's going on?'

Bridget let out a long, steady breath and then straightened her spine. 'I suspected that Daniel and Nicole were having an affair.'

What?

Jenna's hand flew to her mouth. Was that why Nicole had called off the wedding? Had Paul known? Was that the reason he refused to talk about his ex-fiancée? Why he refused to propose to Jenna? Because he'd been betrayed before and didn't want to risk it happening again? Her mind raced through her precious collection of information. Had Paul ever implied Nicole had an affair? No. Definitely not.

'Are you sure?'

'No.' Bridget gave a brisk shake of her head. 'But whenever she was in the room, he couldn't keep his eyes off her. That in itself wasn't unusual because most people were drawn to her, but in the last six months before she left, it had taken on an extra intensity. Nicole could be very charming when she wanted to be.'

'Did you ever catch them together?'

'It was only fragments. A touch here, a half smile there. Looking back, perhaps I over-reacted.'

'Did she look at him in that same way, too?' Jenna asked. Annoyance filled her, along with a heady sense of voyeurism.

'I really don't know. Maybe it was one-sided? Even if they didn't have an affair, I'm sure he wanted one. If she'd have clicked her fingers, he would've gone running.' Bridget's voice broke, as if frustrated at how helpless she'd been in the situation.

'Oh, Bridge. That's terrible. How are things with you and Daniel now?'

Her friend brightened. 'So much better. After Nicole went to Australia it was like a fog had lifted. That's when we started seriously discussing IVF. So maybe she did me a favour? It wasn't so easy for Paul. When Nicole first left, he was devastated but then he met you, and I've never seen him happier.'

Jenna rubbed her brow, suddenly regretting her desire to know more. *Be careful what you wish for.* Because it was one thing for Nicole to leave him, but it was another for her to cheat on him. Did that mean his feelings for her hadn't gone away?

Was that why he hadn't proposed? Because she'd never be as good as the woman who'd broken his heart?

'I wish I could believe you, but it's hard.'

'Not helped by all those pregnancy hormones rushing through your body.' Bridget arched an eyebrow. 'Nicole was in his past, but you and the baby are his future. Promise me that you'll ring your mum and sister and tell them the good news.'

Jenna swallowed as Bridget got to her feet, signalling that their chat was over. She stood up as well, her hands lightly caressing the slight swell of her belly. The self-doubt faded. No matter what had happened between Paul and Nicole, it didn't change the fact Jenna was having his child. Her friend was right. She needed to focus on the future. One with Paul and the baby.

'I'll call them now. And thanks for the advice.'

'That's what friends are for,' Bridget said as she headed for the door. Once she was gone, Jenna walked to the kitchen, ignoring the sink full of dishes, and reached for her phone. It was time to call her sister.

7

Paul shifted in the red upholstery seat as a wave of noise surrounded him. The Rose and Crown was busy for a Wednesday, filled with local office workers, plus the village's darts team, who was celebrating a recent victory.

His head pounded and his eyes were gritty. For the last two years he'd been confident that what had happened with Nicole was the truth. But now it was like the picture in his mind had splintered into a thousand pieces, and no matter how hard he tried, he couldn't get them to shift back into place. He closed his eyes and was instantly transported to an icy road.

It was winter and the trees' branches were covered in a crystalline frost that turned the night into a glittering stage. Car headlights burst through the magical scene and pain exploded in the back of his neck, like a foot was crushing down on him. Smashing the bone.

His eyes flew open, and he leaned back in the booth panting.

He tried not to think about the accident. What was the point? He couldn't remember a bloody thing. A therapist had once said that the mind was always looking for meaning, which was why he'd developed his own version of events, where he was merely an observer. Apparently, that was meant to make him more comfortable.

It didn't.

God, he'd kill for a drink, but despite being in a pub, he didn't dare order anything other than an orange juice. He'd promised Jenna that he'd support her during the pregnancy. Guilt laced through him at the now empty gin bottle at the bottom of his desk. Instead, he felt in his jacket pocket for his pills. He'd finished the last of the amphetamines yesterday but he'd managed to find some of Nicole's old diazepam. Any port in a storm.

He shook two out and swallowed them, then glanced at his watch. It was almost five o'clock.

The Board of Governors had been meeting and, while Paul occasionally attended, his presence hadn't been required at this one. However, Tim had texted him earlier saying that they should catch up for a drink. No doubt so that the Head could fill him in on what was happening with Eric Chambers, and the ongoing interest in the school.

It was something he could do without. He rubbed his pounding head and leaned back in the chair as Tim appeared, holding a pint of bitter.

'Tired of me already?'

'Too bloody right,' Paul retorted as he lifted his glass and took a mouthful of orange juice, wishing he was at home. He'd hardly seen Jenna since his mistimed present.

Guilt swept through him, then annoyance that regardless of whether Nicole was alive or dead, he shouldn't be letting her interfere with his relationship. He loved Jenna. She was going to be the mother of his child and he needed to be with her to make sure she was okay.

'Well, tough luck. The board seems to have finally accepted that what happened with Eric Chambers was an isolated incident. Which is cause for celebration,' Tim said as he took a deep swallow.

'You do see the irony here, right?' Paul held up his orange juice and took another sip. It was disgusting. Full of sugar and God knew what else. Tim, obviously catching his grimace, burst out laughing.

'Having a drink after work is hardly the same as being tanked up before assembly,' Tim said as he put down his pint and stretched his long frame into the booth. Out of habit, Paul glanced at his phone, but there were no new messages or emails from Nicole.

'How did the rest of the meeting go? Were they happy with the health and safety report?' Paul had spent the better part of a term setting up a cloud-based system.

'A few were sceptical but, once they saw how much easier it was to comply with the guidelines, they came round,' Tim said, taking another long pull of his pint. Then he pressed his lips together. 'There was one thing that came up, and I'm afraid I couldn't convince them to change their minds.'

'Let me guess. They want to bring back boaters?' Paul said, since several of the governors were old-fashioned enough to still like the straw hats that once rested on every Hepworth student's head.

Tim didn't laugh. 'They've decided to advertise externally for the Deputy Head position.'

'What?' Orange juice caught in his throat, and Paul spluttered. 'But I've been acting in the position for eight months. I was told the job was mine.'

'And it will be,' Tim said quickly. 'What you've done is nothing short of miraculous, but in light of Eric, we can't afford to do any more internal hiring. Being an independent school means we're already under the spotlight enough, and we don't want enrolments to slip. Trust me, no one will be better qualified than you.'

God, he hoped not.

He'd spent the last eight months working his butt off and didn't want to go back to being full time in the classroom. He'd always said how much he loved teaching, but it was a lie. Most of the time it was like watching paint dry. Same kids, same problems. Occasionally it had been rewarding when he did manage to break through to someone, but most of the time it was like being pricked by thousands of tiny needles. Plus, not only did he find the new position more challenging, but he also liked the extra authority and respect that being Deputy Head gave him. He wasn't ready to relinquish it.

He rubbed his jaw and focused on his breathing. He did better when he had things under control. His house, his classroom, his life. Yet ever since he'd seen Nicole's post, it was like he was freefalling. He hated it. Hated the weightless sensation of being at the mercy of events. Of not getting any say in what happened to him.

The metallic taste of the pills filled his mouth.

'So, I'll need to apply for the position along with everyone else?' Paul gripped at the table, as a low buzz hummed in his ears. He sucked in a lungful of air. Breathe. Calm down. Find the centre.

'Like I said, it's a formality.' Tim took another sip of his beer, not seeming to notice how close Paul was to a meltdown. It was a small mercy. 'And while the decision isn't solely mine, I'll make sure the interview panel knows you're the best person for the job. Trust me. You've got this.'

His heart rate slowed and his breathing returned to normal.

Tim was right. He had this. Besides, with all the negative press the school had been receiving, there might not be many external applications of sufficient quality. And even then, his own record was exemplary.

'Are you sure you don't want a drink?' Tim asked.

Paul shook his head and tapped the glass. 'I promised Jenna,' he said, pleased his voice sounded casual.

He glanced up as Alison and Doug walked into the pub and headed in their direction.

'Well, here are two old soaks who might keep me company.' Tim got to his feet and walked towards the bar, signalling that he was buying them both a drink.

'I hope we're not interrupting anything.' Alison slid into the booth while Doug gestured he was going to the loo.

'Not exactly.' Paul ran a hand through his hair. 'Tim told me that the governors are asking for my job to be advertised externally.'

'They're *what*?' The words exploded out of Alison's mouth and her amber eyes glittered with annoyance. 'How insulting. When I think of the all the shit you've had to wade through to drag them into the twenty-first century, and now they're stabbing you in the back?'

Paul let out a reluctant laugh. The fact that Alison was so outraged managed to lessen his own anger. 'Apparently I'm still the preferred candidate. But considering what happened with Eric, they can't be seen to be running an old boys' club. It makes sense.'

'To you, maybe,' Alison retorted and then gave him a rueful smile. 'And that probably explains why I could never do your job. I'm much too fiery. The fact you're so calm about this proves what a great Deputy Head you are. But it's bullshit that they're making you jump through hoops.'

'Thanks for being on my side.'

'Always,' she said in a firm voice as she smoothed down her dress. Paul frowned. Since when did Alison wear dresses? He studied her. It was a black strappy affair and her blonde hair, which was usually scraped behind her ears, was hanging down her back. Like she was dressed for a date.

'Wait. Don't tell me that you and Doug are—'

'Christ, no.' She shuddered before self-consciously patting down her hair, as if she was unsure of it. 'I actually have a date and thought I'd come in here for some Dutch courage. Though, if I'd known half of Hepworth was going to be here, I might've picked a different place.'

So, she *was* going on a date?

'Anyone I know?' Paul leaned forward with interest.

Splotches of pink travelled up her neck and she pressed her lips together, as if uncertain. 'Actually, it's with Rob.'

Rob? He sat back, studying Alison's face. Her eyes were glittering like gold coins and her lips were slightly parted. He didn't need to be a rocket scientist to figure out if she was happy or not.

'I take it this is a good thing.'

'Very,' she said, colour staining her cheeks. 'I know it ended badly, but since he got back in touch we've been talking nearly every night, and he's in town for a week, so we thought we'd give it another go. You don't think I'm being naïve, do you?'

'No,' Paul automatically answered, then frowned. Part of the reason they'd broken up was because Alison had announced she was ready to have kids and Rob had run a mile. What a prick. 'Do you think he's changed his mind?'

A shy smile broke across her face. 'Yes. He's had a complete change of heart. Can you believe he went to therapy? He said it was the best thing he'd ever done because he finally got to understand himself.'

'And you think he's sincere?'

'I do,' she said simply. 'The change in him is incredible. I know you think it's a crock of shit, but I can't complain.'

Damn right he thought therapy was a crock of shit. After the accident, he'd been dragged to a grief counsellor who'd sat there and told him things like it wasn't his fault, that his parents would hate for him to be unhappy. That it was perfectly normal to feel guilty about surviving. That he would eventually remember what had happened.

It was lies. But the counsellor didn't care what he thought. She'd been too committed to her own narrative and had told the court that Paul's uncontrollable bursts of anger were his way of processing, and that they would pass. But they hadn't, and by the time he was twelve, his only foster family said they could no longer cope with his mood swings, and they'd handed him back.

That's when they'd first given him antidepressants. And he wasn't the only one. Most of the kids in Arlington had been drugged up to their eyeballs, in the hope of making them easier to deal with. The therapists had still continued to bleat in his ear about how they could help him, but in the end Paul had found his own way to control things. With booze and hash. It was amazing what they did to the antidepressants he was already taking.

Back then he'd been pretty reckless, but a night in a police cell was a wake-up call and he went to college and studied hard enough to get into university. He didn't stop with the booze and drugs, but he learned how to function while using.

It was why he'd gone to such great lengths to keep his past hidden, and to not raise any red flags. Because he knew that when people saw smoke, they also saw fire. There was only one place for kids from the wrong side of the tracks, and it wasn't Hepworth.

'I'm glad it's working out,' he said diplomatically, hoping by the glow on Alison's face that she believed him. 'If you're happy then I am too.'

'Thanks. You've been a great friend. Actually, would you and Jenna like to join us for brunch on Sunday? We're thinking of checking out that new place by the lake.'

'Sure,' he said, privately thinking that at least he could check out Rob for himself and see how sincere he was being. 'Sounds great. Though, Al, don't rush into anything.'

'Trust me, you're preaching to the choir.'

'Choir? Who mentioned choir?' Doug demanded as he returned to the table, closely followed by Tim who had in another round of drinks. Alison caught Paul's eye and gave a tiny shake of her head, as if letting him know it was a private conversation. He didn't blame her. Doug was one of the biggest gossips at school and could be guaranteed to spill a secret like a sixth grader could spill a cola down their white shirt, just before school photos.

'We were saying what a brilliant choirmaster you are,' Paul said. Doug shot him a suspicious look.

'Somehow I doubt it, but I'll take the compliment all the same,' he said, taking the glass Tim handed him. They all made a toast and Paul stayed for another half hour before finally slipping away.

* * *

It was a twenty-minute drive from Market Harborough back to the village if he took the A road, which he usually did. It used to drive Nicole nuts that he'd purposely go the longer way to enjoy the acres of green farmland that ran along the road, all dotted with a patchwork of fields. The sun was sinking down over the horizon, turning the sky into a canvas of smudgy pinks and purples.

He stopped at an off licence to buy a bottle of vodka, if only to get the bloody metallic taste out of his mouth. He knew it would go away soon, but right now it was driving him crazy. He splashed some alcohol into the reusable coffee cup that Jenna had bought him last year. The booze had helped slow down his racing mind.

Tim and Alison were right. It was a formality, and there was no way he wouldn't get the job. It was his. He was about to start the engine again when his phone rang, and 'Sarah Jenkins' flashed up on the screen.

He snatched up his phone.

'Hey, Sarah. Great to hear from you.'

'You, too,' she said, in her clipped-vowel, home-counties accent. In the background was the sound of splashing water. 'Sorry it's taken me so long, the kids have been a handful. How are you?'

You mean apart from trying to remember if I killed someone or not? Just great.

'I'm okay. School is always chaotic, this time of year.' He eyed the vodka bottle, wondering if he should have one more drink for courage. But thought better of it. He still had to drive. 'I was wondering if you've spoken to Nicole. I heard she'd come back, and we still have some loose ends to tie up regarding the house.'

Which was technically true, since even though the house was in his name, Nicole had contributed to it while living there. His lawyer had advised him at the time that she might be able to claim some of the property despite not being married. At the time he hadn't been worried since the possibilities of that happening were zero.

Or so he'd thought.

'I saw that post too and was soooo excited. She landed last

week, and we've had a few messages, but she's stuck up your way. She promised to come down to London soon. She hasn't seen her goddaughter in over two years, though she sent her the most gorgeous kangaroo last week.'

Paul sucked in a breath. 'Messages. Have you spoken to her on the phone?'

'No, up until recently she was living on the other side of the world. Trying to figure out the time difference made my head hurt, and since she's back, I've been flat out with the kids. But we will make up for it when she gets here.'

His head pounded. She hadn't spoken to Nicole. Which meant he still couldn't be sure if the social media messages were really her or not.

He couldn't go on not knowing.

'I don't suppose you could ask her to call me, could you?'

There was a pause from down the other end, as if Sarah was considering it. Then she let out a soft sigh. 'I know things ended badly between the pair of you, but I really don't want to get involved.'

He rubbed his jaw, swallowing down his frustration. He wasn't really surprised. Sarah and Nicole had always been tight, but he'd been hoping to somehow sneak through the wall of female solidarity. Obviously not today.

'Okay, but if you—'

He was cut off by a long wail and the sound of a bath draining.

'Shit,' Sarah muttered with a weary sigh. 'Look, I've got to go. But if you want my advice, wait until she comes to you.' Without another word, she finished the call. Paul rolled his shoulders and forced himself to ignore the vodka bottle.

He started the engine and drove home, trying to think about what his next move would be, but all the threads of his mind started scrambling together, and he ended up flicking on a radio station to create some white noise.

By the time he pulled into the garage he was almost calm. He turned off the engine, stopping only to chew on a breath mint. As usual, he carefully locked the car, shut the garage door then stepped into the house. Some of the tension left his tight shoulder muscles as he walked down the hallway. Unlike Daniel and Bridget's house next door, which was always full of stacked newspapers, kicked off shoes and various jackets, here there was nothing out of place. Jackets hung neatly on the hooks behind the door and there was a spot for shoes in the garage.

When Jenna had first moved in, she'd laughingly called him fastidious, and perhaps she was right, but all Paul knew was it was easier to relax if things were neat and tidy. And so she'd kissed him, teased him, and always made sure that she kept her possessions in the same order he did.

Not that he was totally controlling. She'd moved the rug in his study to hide a coffee stain and he hadn't moved it back or asked her about it. He'd smiled, loving that she'd been so concerned about his feelings. Plus they were getting the carpets cleaned in a few weeks and then the rug could go back to its regular spot.

It was almost eight and the kitchen light was off, but the soft sound of classical music told him that Jenna was in the lounge. He dropped his keys on the hallstand, ignoring the stack of letters that were sitting there. He'd deal with them tomorrow.

He had half expected her to be asleep, but she was sitting on the sofa, with a throw covering her legs as she tapped away on her laptop.

'Sorry I'm late. Trying to get away from Tim and Doug once they've had a beer is like trying to get kids to put away their phones. I hope you weren't waiting up.' He kissed her on the forehead, before resting his chin on her hair.

She shut her laptop and leaned into him. 'No, I've been talking to Lucy.'

His skin prickled. He knew that Jenna's older sister didn't like him, and the feeling was mutual. It wasn't enough to rule her husband and daughter's life, but she also thought she had the right to rule Jenna's as well. So far he'd managed to keep his feelings to himself, mainly for Jenna's sake, but he wasn't sure how long he could last.

'How is your perfect sister?' He dropped down next to her on the sofa, then winced as the stiff cushion jolted his back. They really must get a new one soon.

'Perfect as always,' Jenna said with a laugh. 'Ever since I told her about the baby she's moved into protective big sister mode. How did it go tonight?'

He stiffened as annoyance threatened to spill over once again. He pushed it back down, toying with whether or not to tell Jenna about his job being advertised externally. But she had enough going on with her pregnancy without worrying about him. She was so different from Nicole, who'd been driven and was competitive with everyone, even him. Jenna was smart and worked hard but she knew how to leave the office at the end of the day. It was one of the things he loved best about her.

'Good, and don't worry, I only had orange juice. Doug and Alison joined us, though she was off on a date,' he said, more to stop her probing too much. 'You'll never guess who with.'

'Not Rob,' Jenna said with a gasp.

He blinked. 'How did you know? I thought he was the last guy she'd ever date after what happened.'

'Since when did the course of true love run straight?' Jenna said. 'The few times I've met Alison I had the feeling she was still hung up on him. I mean she's gorgeous, but she never seems to date anyone. Was she happy about it?'

'Extremely,' Paul agreed as he slipped Jenna's shoes off and put her legs onto his lap so he could massage her feet, the way she liked. 'He's down for the weekend. I agreed we'd meet them for brunch on Sunday. I hope that's okay?'

'Sunday?' Jenna pulled her legs away and sat up, her nose wrinkled. 'But that's my parents' anniversary party.'

It is? Paul's mouth went dry as Jenna stared at him, searching to see if he'd been joking. He rubbed his brow, trying to recall any mention of the party, but he drew a blank. 'Did you tell me about it?'

'Numerous times.' Jenna leaned forward, her eyes now filled with concern. 'Remember we were at Lucy's, and you promised to man the barbecue?'

His stomach went tight. He could recall going round to Jenna's sister's house several times during the last few weeks, but he couldn't say when, and he certainly couldn't remember any mention of a party. Was this another memory blackout, or had he been blanking out Lucy's shrill voice?

'Christ, I'm so sorry. I totally forgot. I'll cancel Alison.'

'Thanks,' she said, still studying him. 'Are you still okay to go? I can't really get out of it. It's a big deal for my parents, and you know what Lucy's like. She'd flip if we didn't play the part of the perfect family. D-does it bother you?' she asked in a cautious voice, as if she had to walk over eggshells to get the words out.

'No. I love your folks,' he said truthfully, since he really did like Jenna's parents. It was only her sister who was hard work. And even if he hated them all, he'd still want to go to the party, because it was important to Jenna.

He swallowed hard, as the uncomfortable sofa dug into his legs, acting like a metaphor for his situation with Nicole. He wasn't sure what any of it meant, but he got the feeling that none of it was a good thing.

8

'You still want a lift to the station? I'm leaving in ten minutes,' Paul called from the doorway.

'I'm almost ready,' Jenna said from her dressing table. Truth was she was running late thanks to another bout of morning sickness. It had become a lot less regular, but she couldn't help but wish it hadn't happened right before an important meeting. Her phone beeped as a text message came in. She glanced at the screen. It was from Lucy, checking she'd taken her magnesium tablet, followed up with the doctor about an appointment, and finished reading the article on breast-feeding. Yes, yes and no. She sent a quick reply then glanced in the mirror.

Her pale face was in need of make-up but she didn't have any time, so she turned away and slid open her jewellery box in search of the daisy necklace. She put her hand into the small drawer, but it wasn't there.

That was odd.

She lifted the tray and looked underneath in case she'd put it back in the wrong place the other day.

'Is everything okay?'

'I can't find the necklace you gave me.'

'Let me take a look for you.'

He walked over to the dressing table and peered into her cream leather, two-tiered jewellery box.

'I always keep them in here,' she said, pointing to the drawer in the middle. 'But it's definitely not there.'

He lifted up the tray as she had done and rummaged through the jewellery.

'It's not in here, either,' he said.

'Where is it?' Her voice caught in the back of her throat. It was the only piece of jewellery Paul had ever given her, and while it wasn't the engagement ring she'd been hoping for, it was still precious.

'Let's think back,' Paul said, calmly, guiding her to the bed where they both sat on the edge. 'Are you sure you didn't take it off in the bathroom?'

'I don't think so,' she said, though there was a hint of uncertainty. The pregnancy hormones had been messing with her head and last night she'd put the milk in the cupboard and not the fridge. But she couldn't see herself being careless with it.

'Could it have slipped off somewhere? Maybe you left it on the side, and you accidentally brushed it off onto the floor.' He got on his hands and knees and looked under the dressing table. He emerged a moment later. 'Or what about in the vacuum?'

'No. I'd have heard it go up the pipe,' she said, walking over to her dresser and pulling out all of her tops. What if it had snagged on one of them? But it wasn't there. She did the same thing with her underwear drawer and even her shoes. Her throat tightened again. 'I can't believe I lost it.'

'Hey, it's okay.' Paul gathered her up in his arms and pulled her head against his chest. 'It's just a trinket. Easily replaced.'

But that wasn't the point.

What if Paul *had* given her an engagement ring? How would he feel if she'd managed to lose that? 'All the same, I'm so sorry. I don't want you to think I didn't love it.'

'Jenna, it's fine. Besides, it will probably turn up somewhere in the next week or so. Try not to worry about it.'

'Thank you. Sorry for being so emotional,' she said, dabbing her eyes.

'Don't apologise. It'll turn up. I know it will. Now, come on, we need to get you to work.'

* * *

'You made it.' Jenna's boss, Nancy looked up from the table in the meeting room. She was in her late forties but had a trim figure and was wearing an expensive linen dress and spiked heels. She'd joined the charity two years ago, and when Jenna's old boss had left, so had most of the staff. Jenna was one of the few who'd stayed because she'd been halfway through an educational programme helping teenagers who'd tried to commit suicide, and hadn't wanted to let her students down. Since then she'd worked hard to impress Nancy, but with only minimal success.

Securing such significant funding would hopefully change that.

'Sorry I'm late,' Jenna said, struggling to catch her breath. One of the earliest pregnancy symptoms she'd had was losing her breath, especially when she was climbing stairs, and with the lifts out again, she hadn't been given much choice. She walked into the meeting room and put down her files and laptop, trying not to notice the patches of sweat gathering under her armpits.

'Sit down and get set up,' Nancy said in a brisk voice as Louisa poked her head in, balancing a coffee pot and two cups in her hands.

'Jenna, you're here. Let me go and get an extra cup.'

'It's okay,' she quickly said, the rich scent of the coffee making her stomach churn again. Then she blinked as Louisa pulled up another chair and delicately slid into it.

'Did I forget to tell you that I've asked Louisa to sit in?' Nancy said, seeming to catch Jenna's surprise. She didn't wait for an answer. 'I think she'll have some valuable insight for us, and since you'll be off on maternity leave soon I thought it might be good to get her up to speed.'

What?

Louisa had only been working for the charity for six months, as a receptionist, whereas Jenna had a social work degree and years of industry experience. Yet she was about to stroll in and take what Jenna had worked so hard to achieve. She peered at Louisa, who was gorgeous with long blonde hair and a full face of make-up. Louisa, who caught the look, gave her an apologetic smile.

Jenna swallowed. The young receptionist was lovely and was great at her job. She'd also turned out to be a comms wizard and had taken over all of their platforms for them. It wasn't her fault that Nancy had dragged her into it.

'Sounds great,' she forced the words out before opening up her laptop. 'So, should I take you through what I've done so far?'

Nancy gave her a little nod and Jenna brought up the application. She took a breath and touched her collarbone where the necklace should have been.

The meeting took an hour and, after it was finished, Nancy pushed back her chair.

'Excellent. I think we have everything we need,' she said before casting an eye at Jenna's sweat-stained armpits. Then she gave a little sniff and walked out.

Louisa gathered up the coffee cups. 'I'm so sorry she sprung that on you. I thought you knew. I'm not even sure why she's bringing me in. You've done a brilliant job and, when we get the funding, I'm sure they'll only want to deal with you.'

Jenna sighed and leaned back in her chair. 'Nancy's right. It's better that they have another contact person while I'm on maternity leave. But we have to get the funding first.'

'We will,' Louisa said in a loyal voice that made Jenna feel even guiltier for being upset. Besides, even if she didn't get the promotion she wanted, she really didn't have anything to complain about. Her job made a difference to people's lives, and she had Paul and the baby. It was everything she'd ever wanted, and it was enough.

9

The cool air prickled his skin and night insects darted in and out of his vision as Paul crawled along the rough ground. Stones jabbed at his knees and hard soil broke his fingernails. He needed to go faster. If he stopped it would be over. But he was so tired. Suddenly the night sky shimmered, and the blazing hot sun appeared, beating down on his pale skin. Sweat poured from his brow and the heat bounced off the ground, burning his palms. Don't stop. Don't stop. He chanted the words over and over again, but his aching muscles began to scream.

He dragged himself into a clearing and over to where a pile of sun-dried soil had been heaped. Next to it was a shallow hole. Just large enough for a body. Just large enough to sleep. A worm slithered over his hand, but he hardly noticed. So tired. He half fell, half rolled into the shallow recess and the stabbing sensation behind his eyes retreated as his aching limbs settled against the dirt bed.

'You poor lamb,' a voice crooned, soft and low like a lullaby. He forced one eye open. Bright lights jabbed at his retinas, and he blinked. It was headlights and they were coming towards him, brighter. Faster.

No. He tried to scream but the words were drowned by the soil filling his throat.

'Hush,' the voice said again, and this time when he opened his eyes the headlights were gone, and a woman was standing over him. Her long hair was pulled to one side, and her beautiful face covered by a tiny widow's veil. Next to her was a man with a long nose and eyes identical to his own. It was his parents.

'Mum? Dad? What do you want?' he croaked.

'To say goodbye, you silly boy. That's what happens at funerals.'

Funeral? But Paul wasn't dead. He opened his mouth to protest but his throat was filled with soil. He coughed, trying to stop it from choking him. The woman ignored him and shovelled more dirt onto his face. It went up his nose, down his oesophagus. Everywhere. The body that was Paul thrashed, trying to stop it from going on, but it was like the earth was holding him prisoner. Taking him back to where he belonged. Taking him back to who he really was.

Nobody. Nothing.

Then the dream was over and he was sitting in a room.

'How many times have you had the dream?' the woman across from him asked.

Paul said nothing. What was the point? He didn't even know if it was a dream. What if life was a dream, and the grave he woke up in everyday was real? The clock on the wall ticked. It was the third time he'd seen the woman. She hid her annoyance better than the last one, but he could still see it. The twitch, twitch, twitch of her little finger. Did she know she was doing it? He wanted to laugh. She might have been the therapist, but she didn't have a clue what was going on.

Anger fizzed along his veins like a train hurtling to its destination. It sped up, going faster and faster. Drowning out her words. He didn't need to hear them. They were all lies anyway. She might say it wasn't his fault, but that wasn't true. He was being punished. That's why no one wanted him. That's why he was stuck in Arlington House with the pills and the punches. And that's why his parents visited him at night. To taunt him. At least during the day he could hide from the dream.

There was a cage in his mind that lived beyond the mist. That's where he kept it. It was only at night that it slithered out into his mind.

'Mrs Ember said she found you sleep-walking up on the roof. Was that part of the dream?' she persisted, but Paul just sat there. If he spoke he might get mad, and bad things happened when he was mad. Besides, it was his tenth birthday today. They might give him extra gravy on his dinner.

10

The sky was a swirl of pinks and purples as Jenna jogged past the duck pond and turned right down a narrow lane that led to one of the more private tracks on the reserve. The damp smell of onion weeds filled the air, accompanied by the low buzz of insects. Her nausea was fading, along with the bone aching heaviness that had left her feeling so inert.

It was only six in the morning and Paul had still been sound asleep when she'd left the house. He'd had another one of his bad nights where he'd tossed and turned, flipping around like a salmon trying to make its way upstream.

She'd asked him once if he suffered from nightmares. She wouldn't have been surprised, considering the car accident that had killed his parents and scarred his arm. But he'd been so quick to shut it down that she hadn't dared to ask again. She'd learned to let him catch up on his sleep whenever he could.

A fellow jogger came along the path in the opposite direction, nodding as they ran past. Jenna returned the greeting and increased her speed, relishing the burn in her lungs. Damp leaves muffled her footfall, helped along by the classical playlist pounding in her ears.

The music pumping through her headphones was suddenly cut off by an incoming call, the ring tone far too loud in her ears. She came to an abrupt halt and studied the screen. Private number. Jenna immediately answered it. She was no longer on the hotlines, trying to help people down from the ledge of the suicidal thoughts, but old habits die hard. Plus, after the meeting with Nancy, she didn't want to risk making any mistakes.

'Hello?' she said. There was no answer, just a sharp scratching sound, like a knife edge running down steel. She tightened her grip on the phone. 'Hello? Is someone there? If you need to talk, I'm here.'

Still no answer. The scratching was accompanied by a burst of shallow breaths. Jenna's skin prickled as she looked round. The other jogger had disappeared, and it might be an hour before the reserve started to fill up with Saturday morning families, out trying to make the most of the day.

Then with a click, the call disconnected.

The endorphin buzz from her jog was gone and her skin was cool. She shook her arms as she walked, trying to release the mounting adrenaline trapped under her skin. She yanked off her headphones, ignoring the dappled light rippling through the overhanging trees.

There had been several dropped calls lately. And twice now a woman with dark hair had come into the office asking for Jenna and refusing to leave a name. It was unnerving and not something she was used to. At school and university she'd been the invisible girl. The one people forgot to ask to parties, the one who was called only when everyone else was busy. Even then she didn't take up much space in the world.

Certainly not enough to be at the receiving end of nuisance phone calls and mysterious visitors. Then there was the missing necklace. But none of it added up to anything, and so she'd decided to ignore it. Whoever it was would realise their mistake and move on.

Her phone rang again, and she jumped before studying the screen.

Lucy.

'Hey, did you call me before from another number?' Jenna said by way of greeting.

'No, why would I?' Lucy demanded in her ever-practical way. Her sister was a lawyer who didn't tend to waste her words. Instead she went into any conversation with a ruthless efficiency that sometimes made Jenna's head spin.

She let out a breath as she stepped back out into the main part of the park. A couple of dog walkers were at the far end and the shadows of the narrow lane were gone. She walked over to a nearby bench and sat down.

'No reason. My phone rang and there was no one there.'

'Must've been a butt dial,' Lucy said. Jenna didn't feel up to explaining the low breathing. Besides, there were plenty of reasons why someone could be out of breath. She had been herself only a few minutes earlier. 'Where are you?'

'I'm at the park. Jogging.'

'Good. It's important not to let yourself go just because you're pregnant.'

'Let myself go?' Jenna said before she could stop herself. 'What does that mean? I've always jogged and eaten well.'

'You also go to work without make-up, and I can't think of the last time you went shopping for clothes.'

'I work in the not-for-profit sector. The people we help deal with suicidal thoughts probably don't care if I'm wearing the latest piece of fast fashion that was made in a sweatshop,' she was stung into retorting.

'That shouldn't be an excuse for not taking care of your appearance,' Lucy said in a quelling voice. Jenna winced, hating that she'd been dragged into an ongoing argument. It was one that neither of them were ever going to concede. Besides, it wasn't like Jenna went out looking like a tramp. She preferred plain, simple clothing that was neat and comfortable. As for make-up, most days she didn't wear more than a dab of lipstick when she remembered, unlike Lucy, who was perfectly groomed at all times.

She rolled her shoulders and decided a subject change was necessary.

'Why are you up so early?'

'I had a few last-minute things to go over before tomorrow,' her sister said. 'One of which was checking that Paul is still happy to man the barbecue.'

'Why wouldn't he be?'

'No reason,' Lucy answered a little too quickly. Jenna cringed, hating the way her sister had tiny little digs at Paul. Sometimes she wondered if Lucy was actually jealous. It seemed ludicrous since her sister had always been the prettier, smarter, more successful one. But lately Lucy had started complaining about Gareth's lack of ambition. Did she look at Paul, who was gorgeous, smart and about to be made Deputy Head of an exclusive school, and wish he was hers?

'I know how busy he gets at work, and since he's not technically family he might not consider an anniversary party a priority,' she said in an off-hand voice.

'Of course he does.' Jenna bristled at her sister's comment. Just because they weren't married, it didn't mean Paul wasn't part of the family. After all, he was about to be the father of her child.

'Okay. No need to jump down my throat,' Lucy said in a calm voice, as if she hadn't been the one trying to stir the pot. 'The other thing I need is the photographs of mum and dad when they took that trip to America before we were born. I want to use them tonight as part of a memory wall, and I distinctly remember you took the whole album.'

Jenna winced at the veiled accusation. The irony was that when her parents downsized into a smaller house, they'd let them take what they wanted. Jenna had only been interested in the photos, but her sister had walked away with their parents' best dinner service and a collection of oil paintings that now graced her walls. Yet somehow she made Jenna feel like she'd been caught shaking the change from her parents' empty purse.

More teeth gritting. 'Do you want me to drop them off?'

'That won't be necessary. Scan and email them over before five,' Lucy said in an efficient voice. 'Now, if that's everything, I need to go.'

The phone clicked before Jenna could even say goodbye.

She rolled her shoulders, feeling wrung out as she slowly jogged back to the house.

There was no sign of Paul when she returned, which wasn't unusual. He liked to head out to the markets early and would reappear at some stage with a bagful of organic fruit and vegetables, along with the newspaper and a coffee for himself and a hot chocolate for her. Another one of his rituals that she adored.

He'd never told her much about his life as a child at Arlington House, but it was obvious he revelled in building up a new version of what a family should be, including gold daisy pendants and organic produce. Soon he really would have a family of his own. *With me.* A bubble of warmth filled her, sweeping away her insecurities as she walked upstairs and unhooked the drop-down stairs leading to the attic.

Usually she'd get a shower straight after her jog, but considering how dusty the attic would be, it would be better to get the photos for Lucy first. Plus, it was probably better that she did it while Paul was out, since she doubted he'd want her climbing up the narrow tread while pregnant.

Again, the warmth infused her as she flicked on the lights and navigated the stairs. She'd only been up there twice before. Once when storing the extra boxes when she'd first moved in, and once when looking for a recipe book that had the walnut and balsamic vinegar salad she thought Paul would like. Both times she'd been in a hurry, not stopping to look round, but as she poked her head through the ceiling space she blinked.

It was larger than she'd remembered, and there were rows of boxes all neatly marked with Paul's meticulous handwriting. *Guest towels. Crockery. Computer hardware.* She climbed up into the room and walked past them until she found her own boxes that she'd merely labelled *miscellaneous.* Helpful.

She used the small knife she'd carried upstairs to split the tape. The first box was stuffed with old bras, some textbooks and a pair of red boots that she'd paid too much money for and had never worn.

She closed the box and moved onto the next one. A familiar burgundy and gold photo album lay on top. That hadn't been too hard. She lifted it out. It wasn't worth trying to separate the photos up here, so she'd take the whole thing downstairs so she could select the best of them to scan.

She stood up, her shoulder brushing the sloping rafter. Pain shot down her arm as dust motes filled the air. Jenna coughed and lurched to one side, this time managing to knock over three of Paul's neatly stacked boxes. Talk about a bull in a china shop. Still, it was better she'd knocked the boxes over rather than falling herself. Maybe it hadn't been a good idea to come up on her own?

More dust tickled her throat as she put down the photo album and restacked the boxes. *Books. Stationery. NW.* Jenna frowned. What was NW? Curiosity curled in her stomach and before she could question it, she slit open the packing tape and looked inside.

She was hit by a heady scent of cedarwood and lemon. A dark sultry perfume that caused her to once again cough. Inside was a pale pink soft cashmere sweater that must have cost a fortune. Her fingers, by their own volition, trailed over the sinfully soft fibres. Whoever owned this must've had expensive tastes.

Like an expensive linen sofa.

Horror filled her as she whipped her hand back like she'd been stung.

NW was a person.

Nicole Williams.

At the same moment, there was the buzz and whizz of the garage door winding open. Guilt slithered through her as she hastily folded the lid back over and replaced the box onto the stack. She had no right to be touching Nicole's things. What if Paul had caught her? Would he think she'd been snooping? Invading his privacy? Violating his trust?

She pushed back down the jealous green tendrils that were threading through her veins and carefully descended the attic stairs and pressed the button to raise them up, before depositing the photo album in the drawer beside her bed. She slammed it shut as the click, click, click of Paul's shoes fell across the hallway.

Usually she would wait for him to come and say hello before stepping into the shower, but right now she needed some space to figure out why Paul still had a box of Nicole's scent-drenched clothes hidden away in the attic.

11

Lucy, Gareth and their young daughter, Saffie, lived in a large Victorian semi-detached house on an older estate with established trees and a snooty air. According to Jenna, they'd picked it for the school zones, despite the fact they hadn't even tried to have a baby until five years later.

It had been some end game.

Jenna's arm brushed his as they walked up the path, and she flinched, before giving him an apologetic smile. He frowned.

'Everything okay? You seem jumpy.'

Guilt laced her eyes, and she didn't quite return his gaze. 'I'm a bit tired. I didn't sleep well last night.'

Now it was his turn to feel guilty. He knew that sometimes he thrashed around in his sleep while caught in a nightmare of the past. He hated the idea he might have kept her awake. It didn't help that he'd stayed up half the night on the pretence of marking papers, but like a fisherman throwing out his nets, he'd been sending out messages and emails to anyone who might have seen Nicole recently.

'I could start sleeping on the sofa. You and the baby need to get your eight hours.'

Some colour returned to her pale face, and she gave him a grateful smile. 'Don't you dare. Besides, as I get bigger, the baby will start kicking. I don't want you to miss out because you're on the sofa.'

The idea of feeling his child move for the first time swamped him and he put an arm round her shoulder and buried his nose in her hair. Her scent was floral and innocent and longing rose up in him. 'I'd hate that, too.'

'Good. So no more sofa talk,' she said as they walked up the path. Then she turned to him. 'Thank you for coming along.'

'You kidding? Your sister's cakes are legendary. Plus, it means I get to spend more time with you,' he said, stopping to kiss her. Her mouth was warm and tasted of toothpaste, and the vice-like tension in his chest began to dissolve. God, he was a lucky bastard. He'd endure a hundred of her stuck-up sister's parties if he could be with Jenna.

It was Jenna who pulled away first, her cheeks pink. 'I heard voices coming from inside the house and remembered that sixty of my parents nearest and dearest will be turning up here. Probably best not to let them see us all over each other.'

'I think they know what we do,' Paul said as his hands cradled the small swell of her stomach. The colour in her cheeks heightened and she gave him another quick kiss before leading him toward the door.

Whatever had been bothering her was obviously gone.

There was already a crowd of people when they walked through the house and out into the back garden, and Jenna was immediately engulfed by several women all vying to touch her belly. Paul's spine stiffened as a territorial feeling ran through him.

'I suspect that's the last you'll see of her for quite some time,' a voice said, and he spun round to face Gareth. Lucy's husband was a mild-mannered surveyor who seemed happy to blend into the background at most family events, but today he was wearing a colourful button-up shirt and was clutching a can of lager. 'By the way, congratulations.'

'Thanks,' Paul said as he swivelled around, searching for the barbecue. It was set up in the far corner of the patio and he and Gareth automatically beelined for it. 'We're thrilled.'

'I bet,' he said as a blur of pigtails streaked past him. Gareth and Lucy only had the one daughter, thanks to an emergency hysterectomy, which put paid to their dreams of having more kids. 'Between you, me, and the wall, if you guys have a baby boy to carry on the rugby tradition, I'm sure all will be forgiven.'

'Forgiven?' Paul, who had started inspecting the grill plate, looked up. 'What do you mean?'

Gareth swallowed. 'Hell. I shouldn't have said anything. It's not important.'

'Clearly it is.' Paul swallowed as he glanced over to a well-dressed couple holding hands, looking comfortable being the centre of attention. Jenna's father was long limbed with a wide mouth and the same eyes as his daughter, while her mother wouldn't have been out of place playing a Victorian matriarch, with a stark grey bob to show off her cheekbones. They were a traditional family with traditional values.

He thought of Jenna's flushed face when he'd given her the necklace. She obviously wasn't the only one who'd been expecting the ring. He swore under his breath at what a cock-up he'd made.

'They're crazy about you. Hell, it took me years to win them over, but you have them wrapped around your finger. The fact that you can operate a power drill puts you right at the front of the line,' Gareth said, nodding to the garden shed that Paul had spent the better part of a weekend helping Jenna's father build last summer. Gareth hadn't been exaggerating at his lack of building skills, and by the end of the first hour he'd been relegated to making the tea and carting away the off cuts. 'Don't feel pressured just because they're old-fashioned. You and Jenna seem happy, and that's what counts.'

'We are,' Paul said, not wanting to go into detail about *why* he hadn't proposed yet. He rubbed his jaw as he looked across the lawn to find Lucy staring at him, her glacial gaze freezing the air between them. Their eyes locked and he forced a smile onto his lips, pretending that he was too stupid to sense her disapproval.

The moment was interrupted as Saffie rushed over and threw her arms round her father's legs before letting out a flood of laughter. Gareth scooped her up and threw her into the air. The laughter increased.

Most of the party stopped what they were saying to look over and smile at the little girl clutching Gareth round the neck. Soon Paul would have a child of his own, doing the same things to him, while surrounded by the family he'd never had. But first he needed to tell Jenna that he loved her, and that the reason he hadn't proposed was... well... it wasn't because of her. He'd make her understand that she was the best thing that had ever happened to him.

* * *

Five hours later, Paul held open the door leading from the garage back into the house. The party had finished but there had still been some close family friends gathered in the lounge. However, Jenna had caught his eye, letting him know that it was the perfect time to escape.

And so they had.

'I need a long hot bath,' Jenna declared as they walked into the house.

'You must be exhausted. I think you got more attention than your parents,' Paul said.

Her mouth lifted in one corner, in the shy smile that he found irresistible. 'Most of them have known me since I was a little girl. They're just excited.'

'That makes two of us.' He wrapped her up in his arms, the gentle swell of their unborn child warm against him. Her hair smelt of apple blossoms and he breathed it in. 'Have your family been giving you a hard time because we're not married?'

She stiffened against him and then relaxed. 'What did Gareth say?'

'Nothing. Not really. He implied it. Why didn't you tell me it was a problem?'

'Because it's not,' she said in a firm voice before twisting in his arms so she could look up at him. Her irises flickered with tiny golden lines. 'All I care about is you and the baby.'

'Jen—' he started to say but she cut him off, voice fierce.

'I mean it, Paul. What we have is enough.'

Relief drenched him. 'I'm the luckiest guy in the world.'

'Yes, and you're about to get luckier,' she said in a low voice. 'Because I'm going to take a bath, and you can join me if you want.'

Did he ever.

'Now that sounds like a great offer.'

'It definitely is. But first you need to put out the recycling for tomorrow.' She stood up on her toes and pressed her mouth to his. The heat raced up his spine but before he could deepen the kiss she slipped from his arms and winked.

'Torment,' he groaned.

'It will be worth the wait,' she teased before heading up the stairs. Eager to join her, he jogged to the garage where the recycling was kept. He picked it up as a sharp beeping sound filled the air. The tiny red eye of the security monitor in the corner, flickered to life. Paul cursed himself for forgetting that he'd set it. It was Jenna's fault for kissing him like that.

Beep. Beep.

The sound got louder, and he stalked to the keypad to disable it before it went through for a callout.

He flipped open the cover and stabbed in the code. The beeping faded and his shoulders relaxed. He'd beaten the alarm and Jenna was hopefully naked and waiting in the bath for him.

Definitely a victory.

He unlocked the garage door and jogged over to the footpath, recycling bin in his arms. The daylight had faded away, but the night hadn't quite taken over, and long shadows fell across the garden. He put it down next to the gutter and returned to the house. He could hear Jenna humming upstairs and heat spread through him as he walked down the hallway. He reached the stairs when a pile of letters caught his eye.

He paused. Jenna always teased him for receiving snail mail, but he refused to be put off. He still kept in touch with a couple of friends from college and the host family he'd stayed with while touring France in his gap year. Not to mention the handful of ex-students who liked to send letters and postcards. It made him feel connected to the world in a way that social media couldn't replace. He kicked off his shoes and flipped through the pile as he took the stairs two at a time.

Steam was coming from the bathroom and Jenna came out wrapped only in a towel. Desire coursed through him, and he dropped the letters to the side. Several slid to the floor, revealing one with Jenna's name typed on the front.

'This one's for you,' he said, passing it over. Curiosity widened her eyes as she examined the heavy envelope made from thick linen. The kind that one needed to make a special trip to Harrods to buy.

'It doesn't look like a bill, and there's no stamp on it,' she said in a hopeful voice as she ripped at the paper. Part of him flinched. He preferred to use the sharp knife he kept in his study, but Jenna was more impatient. Her eyes glittered with excitement as she pulled out a single card, but as he watched her scan it, her expression dropped.

'Everything okay?' he said, not liking the way the colour had drained from her face. His mind whirled trying to figure out what the bad news was. It couldn't be from the hospital because their scan was still a week away. Unless it was a follow up from the last appointment. 'Is it the baby?'

'No. It's from your ex-fiancée.' With one hand she tightened her grip round the towel and with the other she thrust the elegant card at him. It stunk of the rich, spicy scent Nicole always wore, and there on the page in her familiar cursive was a note.

I hope your pregnancy goes better than mine.
Now I'm back we should catch up and exchange notes.
Nicole xoxo

The room began to spin, and the floor buckled. No, not the floor, it was his knees. Blood pounded in his temples, and he dropped down on the bed. His neck was stiff and forced him to bow forwards to try and relieve the terrible pressure building up.

It was her handwriting. The same looping cursive that he knew so well. He'd never mentioned the abortion to anyone, and to his knowledge Nicole hadn't either. And there was no stamp...

Which meant she'd walked up to their doorstep and pushed it

through the mail slot. It must have happened while they were both at work. What else had she done? Walked around the house and peered through the windows? He wouldn't put it past her.

Oh, hell. Jenna's missing necklace.

Had Nicole been in their house?

But that was impossible. The alarm system was always set, so if someone had tried to break in, he would've been notified. But the fact she'd visited the house was bad enough.

Silence bounced between them before Jenna finally walked over to the oversized reading chair in the corner of the room and sat down. Keeping her distance from him.

'Why didn't you tell me that you and Nicole had lost a baby?' she said in a hoarse voice. 'We're meant to be having a child together and you kept something like this from me?'

'I didn't know how to tell you,' he said, the words raw in his throat. Some of the pain on her face disappeared and her mouth softened.

'I thought this was your first child. That's what you said to me,' she whispered.

'It wasn't a lie. Nicole terminated before I even knew she was pregnant. She didn't want it to interfere with her career.' He looked up, but he wasn't in the bedroom, and he wasn't looking at Jenna. He was in the lounge and Nicole was standing in front of him. Her hands were on her hips, and she brushed her hair from her shoulders in that definite way of hers.

Daring him to argue with her.

'Oh.' Jenna let out a soft gasp and once again he was in the bedroom. The frigid wall between them was gone and Jenna's eyes brimmed with compassion. Compassion he didn't deserve.

'I didn't get to know what it was like to think about being a father. To imagine painting the nursery and reading bedtime stories. So this *is* the first time for me. But I should've told you.'

'Yes, you should.' Jenna stood up and finally joined him on the bed. 'We're meant to be a team. You can't keep blocking me out. How long have you known she was back from Australia?'

He swallowed hard. 'Since last Friday.' Shards of his memory battled together, trying to smash their way out of his mind. He forced them back into the cage and waited for his breathing to slow down.

A single tear rolled down her cheek and she stayed statue still. Eternity passed before she spoke. 'You hid it from me this entire time?'

'I'm sorry, I was wrong about it. I thought it was best not to say anything. Jenna, I love you. The fact Nicole's come home doesn't mean anything. I doubt she'll even stay here long. She always hated it. Probably why she left,' he said, so quickly that it almost felt true. 'You believe me, right?'

'I wish you'd told me,' she said as she stepped back towards the bathroom, the wafts of steam wrapping round her. 'I need some time to think. Okay?'

He moved off the bed as if to follow her but stopped. 'Whatever you want.' It was a lie. He wanted to step into the bathroom with her. Plunder her mouth with his. Breathe in her scent. Let her inherent goodness cleanse him. But he'd messed up and needed to give her the space she'd asked for.

The door shut and he slumped against the wall.

The euphoria of the day had disappeared, as if prison bars had clanged down in front of him, preventing him from the life he wanted. The one with Jenna and their baby at his side. He tightened his fingers round the letter in his hand, as if trying to bend the bars that were trapping him.

Memories twisted and snaked in his mind, evaporating every time he tried to focus. Paul clenched his hands. He couldn't keep living like this. The uncertainty of not knowing what he'd done was unbearable. It was a sword hanging over his neck. Had he killed Nicole, or was she still alive?

What was it that Alison had said? *We all need to face our demons.*

There was only one way for him to do that.

He needed to visit the grave.

12

Paul ran down the stairs after cleaning his teeth and grabbed his coat from where he'd thrown it over the banister the night before. Jenna had already left for her job, citing a breakfast meeting as the reason she was out of the house so early. He usually hated it when she worked too hard. Worried it might not be good for her and the baby. But after last night, he knew better than to stop her.

At least she'd kissed him goodbye.

They hadn't mentioned Nicole's name again, and he hoped it was a sign she believed him.

He climbed into his car and headed south, past the crumbling housing estate that was the only blemish on Market Harborough's otherwise middle-class appeal. He took a right turn past the quarry that made the place even more of an eyesore and followed the winding road up to a secluded wooded area.

He'd first gone there four years ago when he'd been roped into taking the orienteering club. There were no proper footpaths going through it, or any benches for people to sit, which made it so popular for orienteering and ramblers. But the thing that made it stand out was the abandoned farmland that ran alongside it. It was acres of overgrown trees and rocky gullies that had been left to rot and ruin. A large fence had once ringed it, declaring it to be private property, but the fence had fallen into disrepair over the years, and it was easy to cross over.

That's why he'd chosen it.

Adrenaline spiked through him as he navigated the dirt road that led to a small car park. This was the first time he'd been back since he'd buried Nicole or was it? The palms of his hands were moist against the steering wheel. He took a deep breath and climbed out.

There were no other cars or people around and he retrieved the spade. He'd taken it from the garden shed and had stashed it in the car the previous night after Jenna had gone to bed. He reached for the metal detector and slipped off the gold signet ring and put it in his pocket. It wasn't an heirloom. Far from it, since his parents left him nothing when they'd died. He'd bought the ring for himself before his first interview at Hepworth.

If he encountered anyone, he would simply say that he was looking for a lost ring.

He swallowed and stepped into the woods.

A blurred vision formed in his mind of another time. The sky had been gunmetal grey, the kind that usually came out in February, the air laced with frost. He blinked and the vision dissolved like sugar in a cup of tea. This time when he looked around he was greeted with birdsong and insect chitter as the morning sun pushed through the canopy, while the path was covered with buttercups and bluebells. Paul stepped round them as his breath became shallow.

I need to remember.

He stepped forward, and concentrated. But his only reward was a stab of pain that exploded in the back of his neck, jagged and sharp, and in his mind, where there had only been one path, now there were many. They snaked out from between the bars of the cage in his mind, all criss-crossing over each other, vying for his attention. Pick me. Pick me.

It was Paul, dragging a wrapped-up corpse along the trail.

Another Paul was sweating profusely as he carried Nicole's blood-soaked body over his shoulder.

A solemn Paul with tear-stained skin clutching a box of ashes that hardly weighed more than the air itself.

Nicole was laughing as the pair of them walked along the path together, holding hands, a picnic basket slung over Paul's shoulder, and the promise of wine and sex in the lazy afternoon sun ahead of them both.

No. He squeezed his eyes shut, trying to force out the truth to appear from amidst the intruders, but it was like popping a balloon and the many images evaporated, leaving him panting and back in the present moment.

He sucked in a breath of air and tried again. This time he only saw one Paul, a blur of frantic movement as he pushed his way through the undergrowth, branches scratching at his face like angry hands.

Then there had been digging. That part he remembered. Or at least the callouses on his soft palms had let him assume he remembered, which meant it was the logical conclusion.

He quickened his pace until he reached the old fence line. Evidence of the property developers still lay there. Staked pieces of wood, the kind used by surveyors jutted out of the dirt, while various trees had been marked with spray cans.

To the right was an old walnut tree, which shaded a stretch of land. *And hidden away behind it lay an abandoned cottage, the outline of a vegetable patch barely visible below the weeds.*

His breath now caught in his throat.

How did he know about the cottage unless he'd been there before?

He stepped onto the abandoned farmland, arms aching from the weight of the shovel and metal detector.

The sooner it's done, the sooner I know.

A bird flew out of the walnut tree as he walked past, the swish of its wing slicing the air like a razor. Paul jumped at the sharp sound, then chided himself. *Get a grip.* He finally reached the edge of the paddock, and sure enough, there was the dilapidated cottage. Unlike the random paint marks left behind on the trees, the cottage had been tagged with crude drawings and expletives.

Julies a dum bitch.
Max can sux my dick.

Usually, he longed to correct the appalling grammar and spelling, but now he was too busy switching the metal detector on. At the time he'd bought it on a whim, but he wondered if it was because he subconsciously knew his fractured memories couldn't be trusted. Was it also why he'd decided at the last minute to drop the gold crucifix in with Nicole's body? Not because he was religious, but because it might help him find her again if he needed to.

Unsure he wanted to know the answer, he turned on the detector and waved it across the weeds by his feet. It let out a faint beep that became erratic when he swept it past the same spot. He methodically moved forward. Silence and then another erratic beep. Still faint and sharp, which meant whatever it was wasn't what he was looking for.

He got to the border of the garden and moved to the right, repeating the whole exercise. Still nothing. He stepped left and started again. Another sharp beep. He swore and was about to stop when an unfamiliar honking sound rang out from the machine.

It was the same noise it made when it found gold.

He slowly swept it across the same patch of tangled weeds.

Honk. Honk. Honk.

He carefully put the metal detector down and hurried back to retrieve his shovel. The dew-laden weeds came up to his knees, leaving smudges of pollen and droplets of water down his jeans. He barely noticed as he used the shovel to break into the ground. His body was stiff, bracing for the pain of trying to dig into the hard compacted earth, but instead the shovel sliced through it like butter.

Paul swallowed and lifted up a shovelful of freshly turned rich loam. He used his foot to kick at the surrounding weeds, the force lifted them into the air before they fluttered back down. This time he tossed the soil away and used the shovel like a broom, sweeping away the weeds, horror catching in his throat.

They weren't growing. Someone had just placed them there to conceal the newly turned dirt. It was in the shape of a grave, but it was like it had only been dug a few days ago, not almost two years. His head began to pound as he pushed the shovel back down into the soil and piled it to one side. He worked carefully, in case he hit bone. But there was nothing. He frowned and reached for the metal detector. Not wanting to step into the trench for fear of what he might find, he leaned over it, waving the metal detector.

Honk.

Sweat broke out of his forehead as he dropped to his knees, using his hands to push away the soil. Something cool hit his skin and a flash of gold caught his eye. He carefully brushed more dirt to reveal a slim golden chain with a familiar crucifix attached to the end.

The same one he'd buried with Nicole.

He leaned further over, using his hands to paddle away more soil. If the necklace was here, then Nicole should be as well. Soil filled his nails as he worked faster, but there was still no body. Sweat beaded his brow and he leaned back on his knees staring at the empty grave that had once held a body.

His gaze swept over it again and he stiffened as he finally noticed a mottled envelope poking out from the dirt, and he leaned down and brushed it off. The paper gave way in his hands as he opened it up. A single sheaf of paper was in there and, in the same familiar hand that had written the note to Jenna, it said:

We need to talk. Call me.

13

Nicole was back.

Jenna clutched at the menu as the waitress pointed her to a table at the back of the small café. Her mind was still whirling from the letter, and from Nicole's intrusion back into their lives.

I hope your pregnancy goes better than mine.
    Now I'm back we should catch up and exchange notes.

Notes about what? That Jenna was having a baby? That she and Paul were happy? Or something else?

Did Nicole want a second chance at having a marriage and child? How could Jenna compete with that? She was nothing like Nicole. In fact she sometimes wondered if Paul had picked her because of how ordinary she was. Because she wouldn't remind him of what he'd lost.

Because I can't hurt him.

She'd told Paul that she had a breakfast meeting, but it had been a lie. She needed to get some space. *And* some answers, which was why she'd texted Bridget and arranged to meet at the coffee shop near their house.

She slipped off her coat and sat down, clasping her hands firmly in her lap to stop herself from fidgeting. Maybe she should stick them in her mouth to stop the hysterical laughter from bubbling up.

Paul assured her that he was over his ex, but the fact he hadn't told her about the pregnancy, and the way his face had drained of colour when he saw the letter, told Jenna all she needed to know. That Nicole might have betrayed him and broken his heart, but he wasn't over her.

What was she meant to do with that?

'Sorry I'm late,' Bridget called from halfway across the café. Her neighbour was wearing her gym gear and her cheeks were tinged pink with exercise. 'I had to take Eddie home after my run, or he would've barked the place down.'

'That's okay. Thanks for coming. I really need someone to talk to.'

'That's my job.' Bridget poured herself a glass of water from the jug on the table. 'What's up?'

'Nicole's back in town,' Jenna said, the words like acid on her tongue. Part of her wanted to mention the termination, but she couldn't bring herself to say it out loud.

'Oh.' Bridget carefully put down the jug and pressed her lips together, a crimson flush spreading across her face.

'You knew?' Jenna wasn't sure if it was a question or an accusation.

'I've always followed her on social media, but she hasn't posted in ages, then suddenly she was back.' Bridget flashed her an apologetic smile. 'I was going to tell you, but then I found out you were pregnant... and, well... I know it's lousy timing. How did you find out?'

'She sent me a letter.'

'She contacted you directly? What did she say?' Bridget leaned forward.

'She hoped that my pregnancy went better than hers,' Jenna said, this time unable to hide the ache from escaping. The one thing that she and Paul had together was the pregnancy. The hope of a baby. And now to find that it was something he'd shared with Nicole was like losing her mooring. She was drifting in the same sea of invisibility and ordinariness that she'd come from.

And then there was the darker question. That one that had stabbed at her skull all night. Why had Nicole *really* had an abortion? Was it because of her career, like Paul said, or was it something else? If Daniel and Nicole *did* have an affair, was it possible he was the father? It would explain why Nicole hadn't told Paul about the pregnancy until after she'd had an abortion.

Across from her Bridget was perfectly still, her face drained of colour. 'Nicole was pregnant?'

She didn't know? Jenna winced at her own insensitivity.

'I'm sorry. I shouldn't have said anything. Are you worried about Daniel?'

'No, we're in a great place right now,' she said in a tight voice, though Jenna couldn't tell who her friend was trying to convince.

'And you really didn't know she was pregnant?'

'She never said a word. She certainly didn't look pregnant. Then again, Nicole was a great one for only telling half the story.' Bridget gave a sharp shake of her head, a flash of pain skittering across her face. 'I wish she'd never contacted you.'

'That makes two of us,' Jenna said, hating the desperation that spilled out. 'Have you seen her?'

'No. And can we change the subject? There are better things to talk about than Nicole.'

Jenna widened her eyes. Bridget had never been that forth-coming about Nicole, but she'd never been so abrupt before either. Part of her longed to dig deeper. To find out what Bridget thought Nicole might do now that she was back, but Bridget's lips were pressed together, and she looked dangerously close to tears.

Jenna swallowed down her questions and took a sip of her tea. 'You're right. Life's too short, and all that.'

'Exactly.' Bridget brightened as she reached in her bag and pulled out a present. It was book shaped and wrapped in ridiculously expensive paper.

'What's this?'

'Don't be mad. I know you don't want presents, but I couldn't resist,' Bridget said, colour returning to her face, as if relieved they really had changed the subject. 'Go on, open it.'

Jenna carefully used her thumb to cut under the tape, careful not to damage the paper, and folded it back to reveal a linen-covered book. *Waiting for You* was written along the front in heavy gold font. Then she widened her eyes as she turned the pages. It was a baby journal. There was a place to put all of her scans and appointments as well as places to write letters to her unborn baby. And at the back was a place for family trees and history, right down to blood types.

'I love it.'

'You do?' Her friend broke into a smile. 'I'm so pleased. I mean it's the sort of thing I'd want but I wasn't sure how you would feel.'

'It's perfect.' Jenna's hands trailed over the thick pages. Between her morning sickness and then Nicole's shock reappear-ance, she hadn't really given enough thought to what she wanted her pregnancy to be like, but this was the perfect reminder. 'Thank you so much. It's really sweet.'

'You're welcome,' Bridget said as Jenna's phone alarm beeped. She switched it off and gave her friend an apologetic smile.

'I need to go. I have a funding meeting at eleven.'

'Oh.' Bridget's gaze swept over Jenna's hastily put together outfit. 'I thought you were working from home today.'

She looked down at the old black cardigan she'd thrown on over a random floral blouse and the only pair of trousers that still fitted her. Lucy's words filled her mind.

That shouldn't be an excuse for not taking care of your appearance.

Jenna was suddenly filled with loathing. It was so easy for her sister, and for Nancy and Louisa. They seemed to have been born with endless confidence that never let them fall victim to the dark shadows of indecision and panic that walked with Jenna wherever she went. Then she swallowed it back. It wasn't their fault. And how many times had Lucy tried to warn her not to take her job for granted? Not to take Paul for granted.

Jenna forced herself to give a light-hearted laugh. 'I'm going home to change first. I didn't want to spill coffee on my outfit. You know what a klutz I can be.'

The frown between Bridget's brow disappeared. 'You had me worried for a moment. Anyway, good luck with the funding.'

'Thanks.' Jenna made a quick goodbye and hurried back to the car. She'd planned to drive into work, but first made a detour back to the house and took the stairs two at a time, hating how out of breath it made her.

She was still panting as she stepped in front of the mirror. No wonder Bridget had looked horrified. The black seemed to highlight the lack of colour in her face and the formless shape of the cardigan made her growing figure look even bigger than the baby in her stomach. Worse, she looked dowdy.

Was this what Paul saw when he looked at her?

She flung open her small wardrobe. Boring prints and

sensible skirts and trousers. Lucy had often tried to take her shopping, but Jenna had never wanted to stand next to her size eight sister in a changing room. Besides, spending too much money on herself felt like a wicked waste when there were so many people suffering in the world.

For the first time, she wondered if that had all been an excuse to let herself go?

She checked her phone. There was no way she had time to drive down to the local shopping centre and buy something a bit more appropriate. There must be something at the back of the wardrobe. But after pulling out two suitcases, all she found was an old ski suit and a moth-eaten winter coat that she'd owned since she was eighteen.

Why didn't she have anything that wasn't ten years old or looked like it had been owned by a grandmother? This would never happen to Nicole, who, from what Jenna had heard, was always meticulously groomed. Had she stood there at the same mirror, inspecting her gym-honed body while shrugging on wildly expensive clothing? Patting the tiny swell of a human life that lay underneath a taut stomach?

Jealousy twisted in Jenna's throat as she imagined racks of expensive clothes all hanging in the wardrobe. They were all long gone, replaced by Jenna's own tatty collection.

Except they weren't.

The heady scent of Opium seemed to flood the room as she recalled the soft-as-air cardigan in the packing boxes up in the attic. It had been pale pink and looked like it had cost a thousand pounds. For all she knew, it had. What if she wore it? Just for one day. Then she could go out on the weekend and buy herself a better wardrobe.

No. It was a terrible idea, but somehow she found herself walking into the hallway and lowering the stairs to the attic.

The cardigan was still there, and as Jenna lifted it out of the box, the price tag dangled from the label. Did that mean Nicole hadn't worn it before? Somehow it made her feel better.

Her fingers brushed along the fibres, so soft it almost felt sinful, and then, before she could stop herself, she tugged at the tag and slipped the cardigan on. It was designed for someone taller and leaner, but it had long ties to wrap around the waist. She carefully tied it up, relieved that it somehow fitted her. A wave of sensual energy rushed over her, and she shook as she carefully climbed back down the attic stairs and examined herself in the mirror.

The delicate shade put some much-needed colour into her cheeks, and the wraparound style once again gave her a figure. Jenna marvelled as she turned from side to side. It was ridiculous that one simple piece of clothing could change how she looked, but there was no denying. Besides, it was only for one day. No one would be any the wiser.

She smoothed down her hair and reached for the tube of lipstick she hadn't used in ages before she finally headed out to the car, feeling better than she'd done in weeks.

The day dragged. Paul rolled his shoulders and looked out over the sea of dipped heads. He'd thrown an impromptu test for his last class of the day. Despite the groans, most of the kids had settled down into it, with only a few restless ones glancing out the window, clearly bored. He made a mental note to work on some activities for them next week, to re-engage them.

But, right now, he was happy to let them go.

He peered down at his cell phone, discreetly nestled in his lap. A few of his colleagues openly used their devices in front of the classroom, Paul wasn't one of them. That was until Nicole had left him a message in the empty grave.

We need to talk. Call me.

He'd composed several emails before deleting each one. After all, what was he meant to say?

Glad you're not dead. Relieved I'm not a murderer. But, while we're chatting, could you fill me in on what did really happen? Oh, and don't even think of contacting Jenna again.

Besides, he knew her well enough to know there was only one reason Nicole wanted to talk to him. To cause trouble. But why had she waited two years before coming back? It couldn't be because Jenna was pregnant. The Nicole he knew might have had a vicious streak, but she was also impatient. She didn't have the mindset for the long game. She preferred action. Fast and brutal.

And yet here she was. Telling Jenna about the termination. As if it had been his fault. As if he hadn't wanted the baby.

Was that her plan? To make him look like a terrible father?

It was definitely a possibility.

Nicole was malicious like that.

His gut cramped.

Until he knew what had really happened between them, he could never be fully honest with Jenna. He hated that part the most.

The other thing he hated was the strange detachment that had taken over his body. For the last two years he'd taught himself to accept what he'd done. To stare at his hands and think: *killer.* To be the person who would grow old and gnarled as his secret dragged him down to the ground, seeping through his veins like a cancer. All the time believing the cruel words his mind told him. *Evil. Bad. Nobody. Nothing.*

But, if Nicole was alive, that meant he was none of those things. He was no longer held down by an anchor of dead bones buried behind an old farmhouse. There was now a huge gaping hole where the Paul he thought he was had once resided. And he had no idea how to fill it.

Who was he without Nicole's blood on his hands?

He put down his phone as the final bell rang out. Most of the heads looked up, expectantly hoping to be dismissed. He waved his hand at them.

'Pens down, class. Please bring your test to the desk on your way out.' His students silently obeyed, as if able to read the tension he was still feeling. Once they were gone, he gathered up the papers, then swore. The problem with an on-the-spot test was that he now had more marking to do. Not to mention finish writing his job application.

For the job he was already doing.

His mood soured as he stalked back to his office, not bothering to stop and chat to the several students who tried to catch his attention. Once inside, he yanked open the bottom drawer. He'd replaced the empty gin bottle with vodka, and it beckoned him, but he forced himself to look away. He couldn't risk being caught, and he'd finished the last of the diazepam yesterday. He closed the drawer and then opened the filing cabinet by the bookcase, to where a crumpled packet of cigarettes lay hidden. He'd given up years ago. It was a filthy habit, and one he knew Jenna hated. Yet every now and again he was hit with the overwhelming need for nicotine. And not bloody vaping, with the sickly-sweet scents and long trails of smoke.

He pulled one out and pocketed it, along with a lighter. Then he headed across the playing fields and over to the small clump of trees that bordered the school. Feeling like a criminal, he turned his back to the building and put the cigarette in his mouth. He held up the lighter and inhaled deeply.

It was stale and the smoke burned his throat, causing his head to feel like it was spinning. But oh, how it pushed away the growing frustration. He took another drag and his shoulders loosened.

'There you are,' a voice said, and he turned to see Alison walking towards him. Her bag was bulging and she had a laptop in her arms. Her eyes widened at the sight of the cigarette in his hand. 'Christ. You must have had a rough night.'

'What?' He stiffened.

She blinked. 'Um, the anniversary party for Jenna's parents. It was the reason you couldn't come to brunch yesterday.'

Oh, right.

The party felt a lifetime ago.

'Yeah, it did run late,' he said, not quite returning her curious gaze.

'Don't worry, your dirty little secret is safe with me,' she said, holding out her hand and gesturing for him to pass it over.

'You smoke?' Paul widened his eyes. They'd been friends a long time, and he'd never known.

'Not often,' she said, taking a long drag and then releasing the smoke in a long trail. 'And not in front of Rob. His father died of lung disease, so it wouldn't go down well. I take it Jenna doesn't know?'

She handed the cigarette back and he took another drag. 'God, no. Even before she was pregnant, she found the smell nauseating.' He leaned against the tree and studied the ash. 'But it is bloody good for clearing my mind.'

Just a pity that it didn't help fill his mind with what had really happened.

'Hell. Does this mean you found out about Penny?' she said, taking the cigarette from him.

'Penny?'

'You didn't know?' She blew out a column of smoke and then dropped it to the ground, before elegantly grinding it out with the heel of her shoe, like it was a bug. 'I had a phone call from Penny Rivers. I've known her for years. She's Deputy Head at Littleton Prep school, down south. They have a roll of seven hundred and last year were nominated for "Best use of technology" at the Independent School Awards. Technology is her remit.'

'Sounds like a paragon. What's it got to do with me?'

Alison didn't return his gaze. 'Her husband's an anaesthetist at Kettering General and has been commuting each week. They're trying for a family and Penny's sick of never seeing her husband, so she's been looking to relocate. She wanted to find out more about the school and the board before she applied.'

'Oh.' Paul swallowed. His throat was raw from the unfamiliar nicotine. It was one thing to beat off local teachers, but it never occurred to him that he'd be competing against high calibre applicants. Especially considering the recent scandal with Eric Chambers.

'Don't worry. I told her it was a shithole, and that Tim was a prick to work for,' Alison said, though judging by the tiny frown lines round her mouth, she didn't think her attempt to put the woman off had been successful. 'I should never have told you. I'm sorry.'

He gave her an apologetic smile. 'Don't look so guilty. You haven't done anything. And it's not just the job, I've got a lot going on right now.'

'Is it the baby? I hope everything's okay.'

'Jenna and the baby are fine,' he said and then let out a sigh. 'Nicole sent Jenna a note.'

Silence settled between them before Alison reached for the crumpled packet of cigarettes still in his hand. She plucked one out and put it in her mouth. Without words, Paul held up the lighter. Once she'd taken a deep drag, she passed it to him and leaned against the tree, looking concerned.

'I take it that Jenna didn't know she was back.'

Paul shook his head. 'I didn't see the point. You know how badly our relationship ended. I have zero interest in seeing her, and Jenna was struggling with her morning sickness. I didn't want to upset her.'

Alison quirked an eyebrow. 'How did she take the news?'

'It upset her. Guess I'm damned if I do, and damned if I don't. Any suggestions on how to make it right?'

'Flowers always work, and lots of grovelling. But it's not like you asked Nicole to come back to England, or for her to send the note. I'm sure Jenna understands that.'

The nausea crept up his throat, as if willing it to open up, but he gritted his teeth and pushed it back down. Would Jenna understand that his memory was so blurred he hadn't been able to remember if he'd killed someone or not? Or that the fits of anger he'd had as a child had stopped him from even having a foster family, let alone being adopted? And that without the booze and pills he couldn't say for certain it wouldn't happen again.

'Thanks for the advice. Now, enough about my problems, did you and Rob have a nice time?'

Alison beamed. 'We did. I'm still pinching myself. He's applied for his old position back.'

Paul raised an eyebrow. Rob had been working as a painter and decorator for a local firm. If he got the job, it meant he'd be moving back to Market Harborough. 'Wow, things are moving fast.'

'That's what I said,' Alison admitted. 'But it feels right. We'll have to do brunch some other time.'

'Sounds good, though I'll remember to check with Jenna first,' he said diplomatically. 'That is if she's still speaking to me.'

'She loves you, you idiot. She's hardly going to call it quits because your ex is in town,' Alison said as her phone beeped. She glanced at the screen. 'Go make peace with Jenna, and I'll see you tomorrow. You're a good guy, Paul. Don't you forget it.'

He gave her a weak smile. For the first time in two years, there was a small chance he actually *was* a good guy. It was a lot to get his head round.

* * *

'Are you sure these are the only ones you have?'

'Yeah.' The girl behind the counter didn't bother looking up from her phone. Paul dubiously studied the wilted lilies. It was either that or a car air freshener.

'Fine. I'll take them,' he said.

'Ten quid.'

Paul blinked. Ten quid was daylight robbery, but since beggars couldn't be choosers, he pulled out some notes and passed them over. Then, suddenly remembering the illicit cigarette he'd had earlier, he grabbed a packet of mints, and gave the girl some coins.

Outside, the sun was still bright and he shaded his eyes as he walked past a dilapidated pub. The King's Head was notorious for bar fights and bad company, and Paul was about to cross the road when a figure stumbled out of the doorway.

'Paul?' A voice slurred. He turned to see a tall man, stooped at the shoulders with thinning hair and a nose that had sprouted a highway of fine red broken capillaries.

Eric? It had been less than a month since the science teacher had been stood down, but he'd aged ten years.

'How have you been?' Paul asked before kicking himself. It was quite obvious that things hadn't been going well.

'Top of the world,' Eric said before burping. 'Hey, you should come and have a drink with me.'

'It's five in the afternoon,' Paul said before wincing. He was the last person who should be making judgements. But still, how could Eric have let himself go? It was one thing to lean into the alcohol, but it was another thing to let it control you. It was like managing a classroom. You always needed to be in charge. 'Sorry, I shouldn't have said that.'

Eric sighed and ran a shaky hand through his thin hair. 'I know. I'm a mess.'

'You're going through a hard time. Do you want me to take you home? I'm sure Chloe's worried about you.'

'I doubt it. She's kicked me out, said I was a waste of space.' Eric's voice went bitter as he swayed from side to side.

'I'm sorry to hear that,' Paul said truthfully. It was never good when a marriage fell apart, especially when there were kids involved. 'Do you have somewhere to stay?'

'My sister's putting me up until I get myself together. Do you think Tim would consider letting me come back to work once I'm better?'

Paul blinked. Eric really was delusional if he thought he still had a chance of a job at Hepworth. Or anywhere.

'Probably best to take it one step at a time,' he said in a neutral voice before fake glancing at the screen of his phone. 'I've got to go, but it's been good to see you,' Paul lied.

'Yeah, you too. Though, I don't suppose you could spare a fiver?'

Paul flinched, and any sympathy he'd felt for his old colleague vanished. If Eric really cared about his family he'd be doing everything he could to make things better. Not drowning his feelings into a bottle. Suddenly he wanted to get as far away as he could from Eric, so he fumbled round for some notes and thrust thirty quid in his direction. Eric glanced at it with longing before finally shuffling off in the direction of the bus stop. Poor bastard.

They weren't exactly friends, but it wasn't nice to see someone self-destruct like that. Still, he had his own problems to deal with. Without looking back, Paul opened the car and deposited the sad lilies on the passenger seat, praying they would survive the short trip.

Jenna was curled up, asleep on the sofa when he finally arrived home and the half-drawn curtains let thin shafts of light dance round her face. There was an open book on the floor along with her laptop, and the coffee table was covered with a spread of files. Careful not to wake her, he moved into the kitchen to find a vase for the flowers. There was a half-drunk cup of tea on the counter and a smattering of crumbs on the marble bench, while a stack of dishes were waiting to be loaded into the dishwasher.

He put down the flowers and picked up a plate.

It was irrational to be angry, since he knew Jenna wasn't as neat as he was. But lately she'd been so exhausted from work and the pregnancy that things had been slipping. And she suddenly seemed a lot more interested in her career. Leaving early in the morning. Getting home late.

A dark thought slid between the cracks of his mind.

The timing is all wrong. I'm trying to get my career back on track, and I can't do that in a bloody maternity dress.

What if Jenna decided she no longer wanted the baby?

No. He pushed it away. Jenna was nothing like Nicole. She wanted a family as much as he did. She was tired. The doctor had said that. But soon she'd be feeling better, and things would go back to normal.

He finished loading the dishwasher and was wiping down the bench when the kitchen door pushed open.

'Oh, you're home.' Jenna appeared in the doorframe, her face groggy from sleep. 'I wasn't expecting you for another hour. I would have tidied up.'

'I bailed on a meeting.' Paul picked up the wilted corner shop lilies and walked toward her. Guilt from realising how badly he'd judged her swam through him. Her body was soft and warm from napping, and her lips were still stained with a rose-coloured lipstick. She looked sweet and sexy all at the same time. He wanted to kiss her so badly but considering how they'd left things last night he wasn't sure of the reaction he'd get. 'How did the pitch go?'

She reached for the flowers and gave them a tentative sniff. 'It was great. I think I really impressed them. And Nancy.'

'It's about time she got on board with your brilliance,' he said, and let out a sigh of relief. 'I'm pleased it went so well. I was worried that after what happened last night—'

'That I would turn into a blithering mess, and screw it up?' Jenna said with a twitch of her lips.

'A justifiable mess,' he said, the guilt he'd been feeling all day finally finding a voice. 'I should never have tried to hide the truth from you. About the baby, or about Nicole being back.'

'Agreed,' she said, eyes once again filling with worry. 'So why do you think she sent me the note?'

The million-pound question.

'I honestly don't know,' he finally answered. 'Maybe she's jealous? She made a decision and now she has to live with it. But I promise she won't come between us. You and the baby are the two most important people in my life.'

Silence settled between them before Jenna finally let out a wistful sigh before raising his hand to her mouth and pressing her lips against his skin. Hope flared.

'Does that mean you forgive me?' he said.

'I can forgive you for not wanting to hurt me, but we're in a relationship, which means you need to trust me with the truth.'

'That's what Alison said,' he admitted.

'Really, did she also tell you to buy me flowers?'

'Is it that obvious?' Paul wrinkled his nose as he pulled her closer. 'For what it's worth, the reason I didn't tell you is because Nicole is a master manipulator and I know if we let her into our lives in *any* way, it will end badly. I don't want anything to spoil what we have.'

'I don't want that either,' Jenna said, her voice husky. A shudder ran through him, and he reached for her chin to guide his mouth to hers. The kiss lasted quite some time and it wasn't until the timer on Jenna's phone beeped that they broke apart.

'So, are we good?'

'As long as you're honest with me, that won't happen. But no more secrets.'

Paul swallowed as he thought of the half-finished job application sitting on his hard drive. Nicole was trying to drive a wedge between them, which meant if he didn't tell Jenna the truth, he didn't doubt Nicole would. And there was no way he was going to let his ex ruin his life.

'There's something else I need to tell you. It's about my job...'

14

'Looks like someone is celebrating,' the woman with the perfect blonde hair said as she handed over the box of ridiculously expensive handmade chocolates.

'You could say that.' Jenna swiped her debit card and tried not to look at the eye-watering price. It was the sort of the upmarket gift store that she never usually went into, preferring to buy a box of Quality Street if she wanted a treat. But today was different. She carefully placed the box into her shopping bag, along with the fresh salmon and bunch of asparagus that she'd bought for supper.

It was only a quick walk to the station, and then she was on the way home, still grinning at how her day had gone. The funding application had been approved. They'd also made it clear that as soon as her maternity leave was over, Jenna was the person they wanted to deal with. Her sister had been right about taking the time to dress up.

Her happiness was compounded by the frank talk she'd had with Paul last night. There had always been a layer of reserve round him, thanks to his shitty childhood and the fact he'd been dumped so close to his wedding, but last night he'd really made himself vulnerable, and he'd told her about his job. A slither of annoyance had gone through her.

How dare Hepworth treat him like that? After all the late nights he'd worked, all the students he'd helped. But at the same time, it made her feel good that she could finally support him. Give him the comfort and reassurance he'd always given her.

It was like they were now on an equal footing.

Then he'd spent the rest of the evening helping her fill in the baby journal.

They'd added in the appointments they'd already had, and also some research notes on which midwife they'd be going with, as well as the start of a birth plan.

'Sorry, love,' someone said as they jostled her arm while trying to get to the train doors. Usually she hated that people were so impatient that they couldn't even wait their turn, but she smiled and followed the crowd of commuters as they spilled out onto the platform.

The train station was only a ten-minute walk from the house and the late afternoon breeze danced round her as she walked. Paul wouldn't be home for another hour, which would give her plenty of time to follow the YouTube tutorial on how to cook the salmon.

She walked up to the front door and put down the shopping bags to retrieve her keys when a sharp sound came from the side of the house. Jenna stiffened and the hair on her arms prickled. There it was again. Scrape, scrape, scrape. Last year one of the trees that dotted the fence line had grown too big and the branches had brushed against the window, making a similar noise. But Paul had cut them down.

Fumbling for her phone, she walked over to the side fence that blocked the garden off. Should she call Paul? But that was silly. He was still at work. No, if it was an intruder she would dial 999 and run out onto the street, where there were still plenty of people making their way home from work.

The scraping was louder now, and she took a shuddering breath as she reached the side fence. It was almost as high as her head and she stood on her toes to peer over, as a sharp bark sounded out.

Jenna jumped back. Eddie?

There was a second bark and this time a little nose appeared from under the gate.

'Eddie, how on earth did you get in here?' she said, pocketing her phone so she could unlock the gate. The moment she opened it, the little dog shot out and ran through the shrubbery back to Bridget's house. Jenna followed the dog, who was now sitting on the front door mat, barking.

There was no sign of Bridget, so Jenna rang the bell. Eddie barked some more until the door finally opened and Bridget appeared. Her cheeks were flushed, and her hair was crammed under a baseball cap, the way that suggested it needed a wash.

'Oh, God. Eddie, there you are. I've been looking everywhere for you,' Bridget said, her voice breathy as she scooped the little dog up. She then gave Jenna a questioning glance. 'Where did you find him?'

'He was in our garden trying to get out through the side gate,' she explained. Bridget's eyes widened before her brow knitted together, as if confused.

'In your garden? That doesn't make any—' she broke off and let out an annoyed sigh. 'I've been telling Daniel for weeks that Eddie's been digging up the garden. He must have found a way through. Still, I'm relieved you found him. I've been worried sick.'

'It's no problem.' Jenna studied Bridget, trying to place what was wrong, but she couldn't place her finger on it. 'Are you okay?'

'Yes.' Bridget's arms snaked tighter round the little dog, who was now trying to wriggle free. 'I was worried, that's all. Do you want to come in for a cup of tea?'

For a moment Jenna was tempted, to try to find out what was going on, but then she remembered the salmon that still needed to be cooked.

'Sorry, I can't, I've got to start dinner,' she said and slipped back through the shrubbery and let herself into the house.

Stopping only to dump her laptop and workbag in the hall-way, she put the food into the fridge, and then went upstairs. Once in the bedroom, she carefully slipped out of the navy silk dress she'd been wearing, and into the more familiar tracksuit with the bleach stain on the knee and the frayed neckline. She really needed to go shopping this weekend. Not just for work clothes, but for some loungewear as well.

A tinge of guilt stung her as she lowered the attic stairs, the dress in hand.

She'd hadn't meant to borrow anything else of Nicole's, but when she'd been returning the cardigan she'd discovered the wrap-around dress and had realised that it might fit her. It had, and so she'd waited until Paul left for work before putting it on.

She stepped back into the attic and flipped the cardboard lid back so she could return the dress. She'd been in a hurry yesterday but now she had more time, she pushed her hand deeper into the box, not wanting to question why she was looking.

There were several more pieces of clothing. A black pencil skirt, a silk blouse with blood red roses all over it and a handful of skimpy camisoles, all size 8. Okay, so maybe it wasn't such a great idea. She lifted the last one up, in the vain hope it was different. It wasn't. It was a pair of black suspenders made from delicate puffs of lace.

Jenna swallowed. Were these the kind of things Paul liked? God, what did he think of her sensible Marks and Spencers bras and knickers?

She folded the clothes back up and lowered them into the box before noticing that was something sticking out from what she thought was the base of the box. Jenna put the top down and reached in. She lifted up a separate piece of cardboard at the base and underneath it was a plain black diary with the year 2019 embossed on it. Two years ago.

Jenna's hand shook. Nicole's diary.

Did Paul even know it was here?

She reached in and pulled it out. The cover was real leather and a musty scent rose into the air as she opened the first page. The writing was identical to the note she'd received the other day. No wonder Paul's face had gone so pale when he'd seen it. He'd known who it was from before he'd even read it.

Jenna swallowed. This was private. She shouldn't be reading it. And yet, she couldn't look away. Besides, trying to get information about Nicole from Paul and Bridget was virtually impossible. And here was her chance, straight from the horse's mouth, so to speak.

I know. Lame, right? I always thought that diaries were for thirteen-year-old girls who want to write about their dreams of tonguing the science teacher, or about how many lip-glosses they stole from Boots. But here I am. I blame Gwendolyn. She says that the more I can dig into my thoughts and beliefs, the more successful our sessions will be. That I can overcome the trauma of my childhood if I dare to face up to the shadows and find the truth. So... here goes nothing...

Jenna shut the book with a snap. It was one thing to borrow

Nicole's cardigan, but it was another thing entirely to read her diary.

No matter how much I want to.

Her phone pinged. It was a text message from Paul saying that he would be home in thirty minutes. Jenna tapped on the cover. In the book contained the clues to what kind of woman Nicole really was. What she'd done to get Paul to propose to her. *What she might be planning now she was back.* Something swirled in her belly. She knew it was too soon for the baby to be kicking, but it was something. A reminder that she was starting a family with Paul, and that the woman who might be a threat to her future was back in the country.

She thought of what Nancy had said about needing a competitive advantage. That's what Nicole's words were giving her. Before she could change her mind, she opened up the first page of the diary and took a photo of it with her phone. She did the same for the second and third. She put the photos into a cloud folder with a password on them. Paul had never been the kind to check her phone, but she hated the idea he might accidentally stumble onto them.

She quickly put the diary back where she'd found it and piled the clothes carefully on top before going downstairs to start dinner. Maybe Nicole's reappearance had been what Jenna needed to get her own life back under control?

'Look at this, isn't this rocking chair gorgeous?' Jenna said, eyes bright as she walked into the baby section of the department store. Two weeks ago, Paul would have explained that he'd already researched the best kind of chair to use while nursing and that while it cost a bit more, it would be worth it since Jenna wanted to breastfeed the baby. But right now he was so tired he could hardly think straight.

School was at that time of the year when stressed out kids, concerned parents and tired teachers all competed for his attention on a minute-by-minute basis. And while it had been almost a week since Paul had gone to Nicole's grave, the dreams had become more vivid. Of him lying in an empty grave as a woman smothered him with dirt.

He'd had the dream for as long as he could remember. Headlights so bright that he couldn't see. Then there was a face. It changed over the years, but it was always a woman. His mother. Mrs Ember. And, more recently, Nicole. But the dream was always the same. It always ended up with him dying in an unmarked grave. Forgotten, as if he never existed. *I'm nobody. Nothing.*

'It's lovely.' He nodded in agreement.

'It would look fantastic in the nursery. I'm thinking that three of the walls should be white with a signature wall in pale yellow and some ducks in a pond painted on there. That would be so cute. I love ducks,' Jenna said excitedly.

She did? Was that something he'd known and then forgotten? He wrinkled his brow. It was a strange thing to forget, but he didn't want to risk another bout of nausea by trying to remember.

'We can have whatever you like,' he said.

'Oh, look over there.' Jenna marched off in the direction of the pushchairs without even acknowledging his comment. He hurried to keep up with her. 'I've read about this pushchair. It's easy to manoeuvre and folds up small so you can put it into the back of the car. This is absolutely perfect for what we want.'

'It is?' he said, rubbing his brow.

'Yes. And we'll also need a high-chair and baby walker. And we mustn't forget the car seat. It's best we buy that before I have the baby so we're able to transport it home after I've delivered.

Oh, look—' Jenna broke off and pointed in the direction of a rail of baby clothes that said fifty percent off. She darted away before Paul could answer.

He blinked. Where was all this stuff going to go? There was clearly too much to fit in the nursery, which meant it would spill out into the rest of the house. And the garage. His head pounded in response. The house was already getting messy, with the small piles of dishes in the kitchen, the shoes lying around in the hallway and baskets of laundry lying by the machine.

Don't think about it, he commanded and headed in the direction Jenna had gone, when he caught a movement out of the side of his eye.

He looked over as a tall figure with long dark hair walked past a display of mannequins. Nicole.

She was dressed in a flowing black dress and her face was partly shielded by an oversized hat.

Like she was going to a funeral.

Paul's head began to pound and the carpet beneath his feet faded away, replaced by icy concrete and sodden leaves. The winter his parents both died in the accident. Their funeral hadn't been like the ones in the movies. No graveyard. No priest. Only a social worker, dragging him along to a crematorium.

'There are a few anger issues,' the social worker said on the phone as she'd pushed Paul toward the wall plaques where his parents now lived. Was it possible for people to live in a thin sheet of metal? Paul didn't think so, which meant there was no reason for him to be there—

Crash.

Something hit his ankle and a jolt of pain ran up his leg. He snapped open his eyes to see a young mother snatching control of a motorised toy car from a young boy. The boy immediately started to cry.

'I'm so sorry,' the woman said as she hauled the boy to his feet and carried him away. Paul swallowed down his snarling retort as his heart hammered in his chest. Let it go. Let it go. Let it go. He reached into his jacket pocket for the vial of pills, but it was empty. He swore. He needed to go to the doctor to get a new prescription, but he'd been putting it off because it wasn't the kind of thing he wanted on his record.

The alternative was buying something online, or from one of the many dealers that clung to the shadows of every town in the country.

He turned back to where Nicole had been, but she was gone. Then he looked over to the sales rack, but there was no sign of Jenna either. Panic tore at his chest that had nothing to do with his sore ankle.

What had he been thinking? How had he let himself be sucked into a memory when Jenna and Nicole were in the same shopping centre?

'Jenna?' he called out, not caring that he sounded like a worried mother looking for her child. 'Jenna, where are you?'

'Can I help you?' A woman with too much make-up and a nametag hurried over, but he shook his head and ran back in the direction of the rocking chair.

'Jenna,' he called out, this time using his Deputy Head voice. Several people turned round and suddenly from between the crowd, Jenna emerged, a worried look on her face.

'I'm here. Is everything okay? Did something happen?'

Paul wrapped his arms round her, breathing in the fresh jasmine and vanilla of her shampoo. The slight swell of her belly pressed against his hip and the panic in his chest faded away. He finally released her then blinked.

She was no longer wearing jeans and the soft sweatshirt with a tiny smudge down one arm. Now, she had on a figure-hugging red dress that clung to her waist and highlighted her growing breasts. It was nothing like what she usually wore. In fact, it was... almost identical to the one Nicole had been wearing the night of the argument.

'Where the hell did this come from?' His mouth was dry, voice sharper than he intended. Jenna's face drained of colour, and she stepped back, as if she'd been hit.

'I-I just bought it. You don't like it?'

He ignored the question, panic making his pulse thump. 'Yes, but *where* did you find it? Did someone give it to you?'

Jenna's brows pushed together in confusion. 'What do you mean? I bought it here. Over in the clothing department. I was trying on maternity jeans, and someone had left this hanging up in the fitting room. I-I thought you'd like it.'

Like it.

Like it?

There was no way this was a coincidence. Nicole must have left it in there, hoping Jenna would try it on. *Mocking me. Threatening me.* Rage tore through him, red as blood, and thick as treacle. How dare she come back and try to taunt him? His knuckles tightened as the need to explode raced through him.

He scanned the store but there was no sign of her. His jaw flickered, and Jenna let out a tiny whimper.

'Paul, what's going on? Are you okay?'

It was like she was speaking to him from a very long way away, and the floor started to buckle. Too late, he realised what was happening. *Where* Nicole was trying to take him. She was trying to push him. Prod him. Taunt him. To make him lose his temper with Jenna.

Did she know he'd run out of pills?

He took a wobbly step back and sucked in a shuddering breath. Then another.

Ruthlessly he dug his nails into his flesh, trying to ground himself. It wasn't Jenna's fault. Nicole was playing with her, the same way she was playing with him. Again he took a slow breath in and then released it until his racing heart began to slow down. He swallowed, finally trusting himself to speak.

'It's not that I don't like it... but is it a maternity dress?' he said, not quite sure how it would accommodate her growing bump. She shook her head.

'Not exactly. I figure it will fit for a couple more months and it's not like I'm going to be pregnant for the rest of my life. Once the baby's born it will be perfect for when I go back to work.'

'But that won't be for at least another year. Shouldn't you wait?' Paul said, the lingering after-effects of the rage still pouring through his veins. They'd discussed it several times, and even though she loved her job, she'd never been particularly career focused.

'Yes, but that might change now we have the funding,' Jenna said as she lovingly touched the dress. 'It's such a good opportunity that I don't want to waste it.'

Good opportunity? He blinked. They were having a baby, and he wanted to support her career, but he'd seen first-hand how lonely the latchkey kids at school were. How haggard some of the parents looked as they tried to balance work and home life.

His pulse quickened and he took a deep breath.

'You think having a baby is a waste?'

Colour spread across her face. 'No, of course not. But let's face it, having one parent stay at home full time isn't a luxury many people can afford any more. Besides, we don't know what's going to happen with your promotion.'

Paul flinched. Was she suggesting he couldn't take care of his family? His skin prickled. Nicole had often teased him that her corporate salary was a lot higher than his teaching wage, but

Jenna wasn't like that. And he was no longer a newly minted teacher. He was a Deputy Head. Albeit an acting one. Was Jenna using that against him?

Then he let out his breath.

No.

Jenna was nothing like Nicole. She wasn't trying to manipulate him. She was excited about having success at work. He could relate to that. He dug his nails deeper into his skin so that underneath his shirt he could feel the surface break, releasing the blood.

Releasing the rage.

'You're right,' he said in a controlled voice. 'And the dress looks great on you.'

Jenna opened her mouth as if to protest, then she simply shrugged.

'Thanks. And sorry for being snippy. I'm actually starving. Now that I'm not sick all the time, I really do feel like I'm eating for two.'

Relief flooded him. He should've known she was hungry. After all, he'd spent enough time in the classroom to see the difference it made when kids were working on a full stomach.

'You have nothing to apologise for,' he said, realising how on edge he was. As they walked past the mannequins he searched for Nicole again, but there was no sign of her.

Had he imagined it?

She'd been on his mind so much recently and the mind could play tricks on a person. That's what it was. How would she know they were there? Unless she'd followed them.

We should talk. Call me.

He put his arm round Jenna's shoulders, ignoring the pumping in his heart, and they left the department store.

* * *

'Do you remember what year Grandad Joe was born?' Jenna leaned over the baby journal as Lucy scooped up a selection of books and carried them over to the play mat where Saffie had spread out her toys. She'd come round to her sister's house to get help with the journal, and because Lucy had insisted on taking her to a spa to celebrate the funding application. It had been luxurious, and Jenna had felt all the tension leave her shoulders.

'In 1925,' Lucy automatically answered as she planted a kiss on her daughter's head and joined Jenna in the bay window where the sun was streaming in. 'And Grandma Mary was born in 1931.'

'My granddaddy isn't called Joe,' Saffie shouted in disagreement and launched herself at Jenna, demanding a hug. Jenna obliged and swept the little girl up into her arms, breathing in the sweet, soft scent of her niece. As she moved, the journal that had been in her lap fell to the ground.

'You're right. Your granddad is Mathew,' she explained as Saffie nestled into Jenna's lap, her large eyes starting to droop. A jab of maternal longing went through her. Soon she'd be doing this with her own child.

'We're talking about Granddad Mathew's father.' Lucy gave her daughter a loving smile before she sat back down and opened up the journal. She frowned as she flicked through the pages. 'You don't have much here for Paul's side of the family.'

'Don't start,' Jenna said, her hand automatically stroking Saffie's silken hair. The little girl shifted again, then rubbed her eyes and snuggled further into Jenna's lap.

'I'm not starting anything,' Lucy said in a low voice, so as not to wake her daughter. 'Just making an observation. You don't even have his parents' names written down.'

Jenna gritted her teeth. 'He's an orphan. His family memories aren't like ours. I can hardly ask him to write about how it felt to be the only survivor in a fatal car accident, or what it was like to grow up in care.' Jenna had never told her sister about the dreams that kept Paul tossing and turning so many nights. Or about the burns that ran down one arm. The ones he always tried to keep hidden.

She swallowed. And then there was the incident at the store yesterday. His face had gone from mild concern to... something else. His eyes had become blank and distant, as if a switch had been turned off, making him almost unrecognisable.

Although she'd done her best to hide it, Jenna had been scared.

Not something she could admit to Lucy.

'I get that they're painful memories, but he must have told you something about them. Like what their names are, where they were born. Where he went to school,' Lucy continued to press.

'And he will,' she said, hating that her sister always made her feel so defensive. Especially since it wasn't until she'd started filling in his section last night that she realised how little she actually knew about Paul. 'He's busy.'

'So are you,' Lucy pointed out and then held up her hands. 'No, don't bite my head off. I'm playing devil's advocate. Now, do you want to come along to watch Saffie have her swimming lesson this afternoon?'

Jenna pressed her chin against Saffie's warm head. 'I wish I could, but I need to go shopping.'

'For the baby?' Lucy arched an eyebrow and Jenna gave a vague nod. Truth was she was going to spruce up her wardrobe. And after the disaster of trying to buy anything when Paul was around, she realised it would need to be a solo mission. Besides, she wasn't buying clothes for him. It was to help with her job. And to make herself feel better.

'Are you going to buy a baby?' Saffie said in a sleepy voice as she blinked her eyes open. Jenna grinned and planted a kiss on her niece's cheek. 'Can I see it?'

'No, munchkin. It will be a few more months before you can see the baby, but I promise you will be the first.'

'Good,' Saffie murmured and then fell back to sleep. Lucy's mouth twitched.

'You're going to make a great mother, Jen.'

'Thanks,' she said as she tightened her arms round Saffie's tiny body. 'I really can't wait.'

15

I got a promotion today. Stuart Barclay looked like he'd swallowed a spider. He'd been walking round for weeks with that irritating sense of smug superiority some men get for no other reason than the fact they have a penis. Like one appendage justifies a pay rise. Maybe if he'd spent more time working rather than on the golf course or in the pub, he might have done better. Then again, it wouldn't have made any difference. If he'd chosen to treat me as a real competitor, he would've realised I was simply a better candidate. I was the alpha he never saw coming. Gwendolyn hates it when I talk in absolutes, but what's wrong with knowing your strengths?

It also explains why Stuart kept trying to float the policies he'd implemented even when the data showed they were dead in the water. Because he was trying to keep the ego happy at the expense of the balance sheet. The law of diminishing returns should have told him to cut his losses, and if he'd actually listened, it might have been a different story.

Still, Stuart isn't my problem. I need to finish organising the *wedding and put in the extra hours the new job will require. But it's so worth it. And you know what? I bloody well deserve it.*

After everything I went through when I was a kid, this is my pay off.

It shows that some people do get a happy ending.

Even if you are born in the mud, it doesn't mean you need to stay there.

Christ. That got dark fast. Still, I suppose it's good to put everything out on the page.

Oh, Gwendolyn also wanted to start questioning what it is that I love best about Paul. Well, if he's reading this then I'd have to say it's his great dance moves and the way he kisses me. But if he's not reading it, it's because he's the only one who doesn't make me feel apologetic for who I am. ~~He loves that I'm successful and powerful.~~

Jenna's gaze lingered over a scratched-out line. The text was in black and the crossed-out line was red. It was the last sentence on the page and Jenna scowled that she hadn't photographed more of the diary.

Had something happened to make Nicole go back and cross out a single line?

She frowned as she thought of the shopping trip with Paul the other day. He'd looked visibly shocked when she mentioned going back to work early. In every conversation they'd had, he'd always supported equal rights for women, but for the first time, Jenna wondered if he really did.

Is that what Nicole had found out?

'Sorry I'm late. I hope you haven't been waiting too long.'

'Not at all.' Jenna quickly turned off her phone and placed it face down on the table for good measure. As usual, Bridget was wearing her running gear and her hair was tucked back in a sports cap. She looked out of place compared to the rest of the lunchtime crowd who had all spilled out from the surrounding offices and were attired in suits and neat dresses. Bridget didn't seem to notice.

She'd hardly seen her neighbour since discovering Eddie in the back garden, though she had walked along the fence line, searching for a hole between the properties, but hadn't been able to find anything. Which meant she still had no idea how Eddie had managed to be there.

'Good. Daniel's had me darting all over town for him. It's like he wants to fill up my day with silly errands. Still, it keeps me fit,' she said as she sat down and rolled her shoulders. 'By the way, have you had your hair coloured?'

'A few highlights,' Jenna said, her hand self-consciously going up to her fringe. After her weekend shopping trip, where she'd bought three new dresses, new underwear and two new pairs of boots, she'd realised that a new hairstyle was in order. Gone was the dull auburn colour and in its place was a rich burgundy that felt like silk to touch. 'Do you like it?'

'Sure,' Bridget said as the waiter came to get their order. They both ordered a salad, but it wasn't until he'd gone that her friend frowned. 'Is it safe to use chemicals when you're pregnant?'

Jenna flinched, not expecting that reaction. 'Yes, I checked with the hairdresser first.'

Bridget seemed to sense the shift in mood, held up her hands. 'Sorry. I sound like an old-fashioned grandmother. It looks great,' she said and lowered her voice. 'Have you heard from Nicole again?'

'No.' Jenna shook her head, though it wasn't technically true.

Since while she hadn't had another letter, she *had* been back to the attic three more times, each time photographing a few more pages of the diary, and deleting the other pages from her phone's memory. She knew she shouldn't. What if Paul found out? Would he think it was a betrayal? Maybe, but there was something so compelling about getting to know Nicole through her writing.

Before, she was the gorgeous ex-fiancée whose shadow Jenna couldn't escape from. But now she was a real person, wildly arrogant, but also charmingly vulnerable, and for the first time Jenna understood why Paul *had* fallen in love with his ex. Why Daniel had been so obsessed with her, and why she broke hearts everywhere she went.

It was helping her fill in the composite in her mind. Turning Nicole from a thumbnail sketch into a real human being.

Jenna might even find out why she'd decided to terminate Paul's child and leave him at the altar.

Bridget took off her cap and fiddled with her ponytail. 'Well, that's good. If you do hear from her, you should let me know. Definitely don't try and meet her on your own. Nicole's brilliant and beautiful but underneath it all she was deeply troubled.'

Jenna looked up sharply. There was the barbed comment again, making it impossible to know if Bridget liked Nicole or despised her.

'What do you mean? Did something happen to her?'

'She never talked about her past, but I got the feeling that there was a reason she acted the way she did. And I think it was pretty dark. Which is why you need to be careful. She's got a talent for making people lose control of their common sense.'

A streak of irritation ran through her. She was hardly Nicole's number one fan but both Paul and Bridget seemed happy to throw her under the bus. And for what? Wanting a career? Taking care of her appearance? Suddenly Jenna felt ashamed of her own beliefs about Nicole. She'd always been so convinced that beautiful people had it easy, but it seemed like Nicole had as many challenges as the rest of them.

But she'd risen above them and succeeded.

So what was it about her that got under everyone's skin so much?

Besides, why should she believe Bridget, when it was obvious her neighbour was hiding something.

She considered probing further, but Bridget's face was guarded.

'I promise I won't go near her. Though I don't think it's going to be a problem. Paul hasn't heard from her either,' Jenna said as their salads arrived. They didn't talk much over their meal, and Jenna's phone rang as the waiter was clearing away the plates.

Louisa's name flashed across the screen.

'I have to get this,' she mouthed to Bridget and then answered the call.

'Jenna, so sorry to interrupt your lunch break but Nancy's out of the office and things are getting a little crazy here. Cameron Wright is on the line and he's furious. He refuses to leave a message. I'm not sure what to do.'

Cameron's IT company had been building their online platform but the software they'd tried to integrate simply wasn't working. Nancy had already written to them terminating the contract.

'Transfer the call to me. If he'd actually listened to our feedback and used different software rather than being driven by his ego, it might have been a different outcome. But we can't afford to stick with something that clearly isn't working. It's time to cut our losses.'

'Are you sure? I mean, they're owned by one of the board members.'

'Then they should know better than anyone that if you can't compete in a fair marketplace then you need to reassess your product.'

'Wow,' Bridget said from across the table once Jenna had finished the call. 'I'm impressed with how you handled that. No wonder you're doing so well at work these days.'

Jenna's cheeks heated up, not wanting to admit that her newfound confidence had actually come from reading Nicole's diary. Besides, she would have figured it out for herself eventually, this was just like taking a shortcut.

* * *

Paul stifled a yawn and jogged down the street. He usually left the jogging to Jenna and preferred to go to the gym, but lately he'd been skipping workouts. Jenna had headed into office early again, keen to move forward with her new programme now that the funding had been secured. Seeing her finally get some recognition for all of her hard work was the tonic he'd needed, and last night they'd gone out for an impromptu celebration.

It was the first time he'd managed to forget about Nicole since she'd announced her return to the country. He hoped it was a sign of things to come.

He'd managed to buy some Valium online and the red pulsing rage that had surged up during their shopping trip had finally dissolved.

The alarm on his phone beeped, reminding him that he had a meeting with Tim in forty minutes, so he turned round and jogged back through the neighbourhood. His brow was covered in sweat by the time he reached the doorstep, and his breath was coming in laboured gasps. Note to self, don't leave it so long between workouts.

It took ten minutes to shower and change and he was reversing out of the garage when Bridget appeared through the gate that separated the houses.

'Paul, hold up a minute.' She waved her hand in the air as she ran over to him. She was wearing her own running gear and was holding a plastic courier bag while Eddie danced round her ankles, excitedly yapping.

'Everything okay?' He wound down the window, while also glancing at the clock on his dashboard. He liked Bridget but she did tend to talk a lot, which was why he usually let Jenna entertain her whenever they all socialised.

'Yes,' she said in a bright voice, though her mouth was drawn into a tight line. 'The courier delivered it to our house by mistake.'

She passed over a slim bag that didn't weigh much more than a feather. His name was printed onto the bag along with the tracking code.

'Thanks,' he said with a frown, trying to recall if he'd ordered anything online.

'Sure,' Bridget said, her eyes drifting to the bag like it was an unknown Christmas present. But even if he wanted to open it in front of her, he didn't have time. On cue his alarm beeped again, and he gave her an apologetic smile.

'Sorry, I've got to fly. Staff meeting in fifteen minutes and if I don't leave now, I'll hit the traffic. But say hi to Daniel for me.'

'Will do,' Bridget said, her eyes still tracking the courier bag in his lap. He ignored her and reversed the rest of the way out the drive. Then he waited until she started running in the opposite direction before finally opening up the courier bag.

A small bubble-wrapped item fell into his lap with the all-too familiar spicy scent of the Orient. Nicole. Paul sucked in a breath as he peeled back the bubble wrap. There in the middle was a delicate gold necklace with a daisy charm on it, along with a note.

She can't even take care of a gift, how will she take care of a baby.

16

We were at a party tonight and as usual Paul got drunk. Not even sure why I'm surprised. At university he always drank too much. We all did. But we're older now. Not to mention that I'm trying the whole sober thing. We'll see if it sticks.

I had to literally drag him away before he threw up on Janice's new carpet. Don't think he won't be paying for that later, because he will. I managed to get him out of the house, but as we were crossing the road, some lunatic in an oversized SUV barrelled towards us. It was going at three times the speed limit, and what did Paul do?

Just. Bloody. Stood. There.

He was like a deer caught in the headlights, staring at them as if he'd lost his mind. There's drunk and there's drunk. And I swear that for a half a second I thought about leaving him to get flattened. If he wants to play chicken, then far be it from me to stop him. But I couldn't. Like I always tell people, my bark is so much worse than my bite. So I dragged him out of the path. Just in time too since the moron didn't slow down.

And you know what the worst thing was? In the morning he didn't remember a bloody thing about it.

So he says. For all I know he's faking it because he doesn't want to talk about the past. Not that I can judge. We all have our secrets, and it's not like I'll ever tell him mine. But all the same, sometimes he scares me.

Jenna put down her phone and tightened the throw rug round her knees. It was Saturday afternoon, and she was meant to be out shopping with Lucy but had decided to stay home. Paul had opted to go into Hepworth for a couple of hours, which meant she had the place to herself. Which was just as well.

Sometimes he scares me.

Jenna let out a breath as she once again remembered their shopping trip. Something had changed when she'd walked out of the changing room in the red dress. His whole face had drained of colour and his jaw was as tight as a guitar string. And if she didn't know better, she would have thought—

No. She cut the thought off. Paul loved her. Whatever it was, he was having a bad day. Plus she knew he was worrying about the upcoming interview, even if he didn't say anything. He was fine. Just tired.

All the same. What did Nicole mean? Part of her was tempted to go back up to the attic and take photos of the rest of the diary, but before she could, the garage door beeped open. She waited for the tap, shuffle, scuff followed by the sound of the electric door closing behind him, but it didn't happen.

She frowned. Paul never left the garage door open because he hated the idea of neighbours looking inside. Curiosity got the better of her and she walked out there. The engine was still warm and Paul's leather briefcase was sitting on the floor by the light switch. There was a low murmur of voices coming from the side of the house, and Jenna stepped closer to the garage door.

The sun was hanging low in the sky and Paul was silhouetted against it, while next to him was Bridget. Her hair was brushed behind her ears, and she was wearing her running gear, but her usual smile was gone. Her arms were gesticulating in the air, as Paul glared at her, a stony expression on his face.

Jenna leaned forward, but their voices were low and muffled, and it was impossible to hear what they were saying unless she left the cavernous shadow of the garage.

Now it was Paul's turn to raise his arms. The muscles in his jaw flickered and his eyes were narrowed into two angry slits. Jenna rubbed her brow. What on earth could they be fighting about? Even though Paul had known Bridget a long time, he'd never seemed very close to her. Whenever they got together, Paul and Daniel would talk about football, and Jenna and Bridget would have their own conversations. As far as she knew, it had been the same with Nicole.

Unless that's who they were talking about.

She sucked in her breath, unsure what to do. There was no way she could join them, because she wouldn't be able to hide her confusion. But if she stayed where she was, she ran the risk of them turning round and seeing her. Hell. Reluctantly she stepped back into the house.

Moments later, there was the familiar tap, shuffle, scuff as Paul walked across the concrete floor, past the neatly stored gardening tools, the emergency chest freezer and her own little car.

Click, click as he shut the garage door, turned off the lights and simultaneously locked his car, and then he was in the doorway, an eyebrow quirked.

'Hey, I wasn't expecting you to be home.' His voice was a little higher than normal. Was it from guilt? 'Everything okay?'

'Fine,' she said, tucking her phone into her pocket, despite the fact the photos of Nicole's diary were hidden away in a password protected cloud account. 'I thought I heard the car come in, but then you didn't appear.'

For a moment he stiffened before waving his hand. 'Oh, the damn newspaper was halfway down the block again. Anyway, I've got a bit more work to catch up, if you don't mind.'

'Of course not,' she managed to reply as he gave her a friendly smile and disappeared back down the hallway. She sat down and massaged her temples, trying to figure out why he'd lied.

* * *

'What are you doing?' Jenna said the following morning. Paul looked up from his workbench, where the window latch he'd bought at the hardware shop yesterday was spread out.

He still had no idea what Nicole wanted, but the fact she'd somehow managed to get Jenna's necklace made him feel sick. Had Jenna left it in it a public place and Nicole somehow found it, or had she managed to get into the house and steal it?

Both scenarios were a concern.

He'd even quizzed Bridget but she'd been next to useless. Claiming the parcel had been wrongly delivered to her house. He'd tried to probe her further and she'd acted like he was attacking her. He'd never liked her much and the fact she and Nicole had once been friends did raise alarm bells.

'I'm making the place baby proof,' he said in a casual voice. It was a warm morning and he'd rolled his sleeves up, but now he tugged them down. He knew it was silly, since Jenna had long ago seen his scars, but old habits die hard.

'Baby proof?' She picked up a second window latch and stared at it 'I'm pretty sure the baby won't be able to open a window for at least two years.'

'All the books say it's better to do things sooner rather than later,' he reminded her and then took in her tied back hair and the running gear she was wearing. He swallowed, visions of Nicole trailing after Jenna filling his mind. 'Are you sure you should be jogging?'

She immediately put down the window latch and frowned. 'We talked about this, and the doctor agreed that staying fit was important. You can't wrap me in cotton wool.'

'That's not what I'm doing. I'm trying to look out for you. Besides, there's plenty to do around the house,' he said, thinking of the scattering of new clothes that had littered the carpet by her side of the bed. Not to mention the collection of hair products on the bathroom bench and the laundry that was waiting to be folded.

Her back stiffened and she took a step back. Too late, Paul realised his mistake.

He let out a groan. 'Shit. That came out all wrong.'

'Did it?' she said in a chilly voice, for the first time sounding like her bitch of a sister.

'Yes. I meant that you've been working late this week. I don't want you burning the candle at both ends. It seems like you haven't had any time to slow down and relax.'

Some of the tightness left her jaw and she relented. 'I did plan to tidy up when I got back. But you know that when we have a baby, things aren't always going to get done straight away. You can't control everything like you do a classroom.'

He gave a rueful smile and held up his hands. 'Guilty. I'll work on it. Promise.'

The silence stretched out between them. God, he hated this.

He wanted to go back to how things had been before Nicole had turned up.

He wanted to press himself into the warmth of her skin and get lost in her scent. He wanted her to look at him as if he was the most important person in her world. As if reading his thoughts, Jenna let out a soft sigh and stepped into his arms.

'Thank you,' she breathed, her mouth finding his.

Her kiss was hot and demanding and his insides coiled with desire but as she tugged at his shirt, he remembered the necklace that he'd dumped on the workbench yesterday. Hell. He stiffened and gave her a tiny push, trying his best to stand in front of it.

A hurt look flashed across her face, before her gaze slid past him, and she let out a squeal and reached forward. 'My necklace! You found it.'

Damn. Paul's throat tightened and he dredged up a calm smile.

'I know, isn't it great? It was in the car. Here, let me put it on for you.'

He winced, hating that he was lying to her, but at the same time he couldn't tell her the truth. He nudged his hip so that instructions for the window locks covered the small courier bag with his name and address on it, and the warning note that was still nestled inside it.

'I can't believe it. Now I can wear it to the scan, which I know is silly and sentimental, but I really wanted to have it on.'

'It's not silly.'

'Liar. But thank you. Though you should've told me straight away,' Jenna chided as she leaned her head forward and carefully dragged her hair to one side, leaving her neck exposed. 'I've been driving myself crazy trying to think where it was. I thought I was losing my mind.'

Paul gritted his teeth, hating that Nicole was dragging Jenna into her games.

It was even more annoying that no matter what he did, he couldn't seem to keep her out of their lives. He fiddled with the tiny latch on the necklace and clasped it back together before planting a kiss on Jenna's neck.

'It's my fault. When I found it the clasp was broken,' he lied. 'So I took it to the jewellers' to get it mended. You shouldn't have any more problems now.'

As he spoke, he rolled his shoulders. So far his attempts at keeping Nicole out of their lives had backfired spectacularly. And it wasn't like he could go to the police. Which meant he was going to do the one thing he'd been avoiding. He was going to have to play by Nicole's rules, and that never went well.

But he couldn't let this go on any longer. He knew how Nicole's mind worked. The necklace was a taunt.

She wanted him to think of her every time he looked at Jenna.

He waited until Jenna had put on her headphones and jogged away down the street before retrieving his phone and going into Nicole's social media account. Then he sent her a message.

Fine. You want to talk? Let's talk.

He hit send before he could change his mind, then he smoothed down his shirt and began to tidy up. He needed to get things back under control.

17

They were talking. He could hear them. Little whispers that slithered under the door, down the hallway and into his ears. It was about him. It was always about him. You're nobody. Nothing. Something bubbled under his skin, like a tiny ball of fire that was searching for a way out. More whispers. They shouldn't talk about him. Teacher said it was bad manners. The fire under his skin grew bigger, redder. It made his head hurt. He clutched at his ears, trying to make it stop. The fire. The whispers.

They didn't like it when he got mad.

He clenched his fists and climbed out of bed. If he wanted to hit something, it was better to do it outside. He silently made his way downstairs. The door was locked but he knew where the key was. It was quiet in the garden. No more whispers, only the chirp, chirp, chirp of insects. The stars were gone, covered by murky grey clouds that cast dark shadows everywhere. But that was okay. He knew the way. He carefully walked along the grass. It was crisp against his feet, making the fire in his veins cool down.

They would come looking for him. They always did. And then they would stop whispering and say nice things. Like he was theirs, and that they loved him.

At least for a little while.

He went to the usual spot. It was by the old tree. He sat down and pressed his spine against the bark. He could see the house and waited until the lights turned on in the bedroom. First his parents', then his. He always thought it made the house look like it had eyes. Then the door opened, and he could see them. His parents both racing out of the house and into the car. He smiled. Soon they would find him, and it would all be okay. The car reversed out of the drive and then disappeared behind a bend before it reappeared, coming towards him on the road. The lights were still far away. Two bright dots, shimmering against the night as they came to take him home.

He stood up and hurried down to the middle of the road.

Pale white frost licked the bitumen, turning it white, and the cold burned up through the soles of his feet. But he didn't move.

It was the best way to make sure they loved him. He needed to stand perfectly still and wait for them to stop. The lights turned into two giant halos hurtling towards him. His eyes burned but he didn't look away. He needed to stay there. Make sure they knew they'd made a mistake.

The roar of the engine filled his ears, and the smell of petrol made his head pound, but he still didn't move. Then, a moment before it reached him, the car swerved. Through the bright lights he could see their faces. His father looked like he was swearing, and his mother was clutching the dashboard.

The wind blew through his hair as the car swung past him. But it didn't stop. The frosty road glittered like a mirror and the tyres squealed as the car rammed into a tree. It made a thumping noise as metal crunched together and glass shattered. A hiss of steam came up from the engine like an old-fashioned train. Then a burst of flame ran *along the hood of the car, encasing the doors, bright against the grey night.*

No. That wasn't right. This wasn't how it was meant to happen.

His brow pounded and a low hum sounded in his ears as he began to run. The night seemed to spin and whirl around him, filling with white mist that surrounded him like a blanket of snow. It was so thick. Like pushing through treacle. He reached for the door, but flames reached up into the night and sparks landed on his arm, burning the flesh. Pain seared through him. The same red-hot pain as his anger. The fire from the car matched how he felt inside, and he took a step back as the stench of charred flesh filled the night.

Was this what he'd meant to happen all along?

* * *

Jenna toyed with the tiny flower that was once more round her neck as an email pinged into her inbox. It was from Nancy, letting her know the schedule had changed and she needed to finish the blog post she'd been working on by the end of the day.

She flipped back to her screen, but the words blurred in front of her as her grip tightened on the necklace. She still wasn't sure how it had turned up in the car, or why Paul hadn't told her he'd found it? He'd seen how upset she'd been. Yet despite that he'd kept it a secret.

And she had no idea what it meant.

Lie. It meant she didn't know Paul as well as she thought she did. Especially lately. It was like he'd morphed from being the perfect boyfriend to a remote stranger.

She thought about the baby journal and the blank pages where his family history should be. She'd tried to talk to him earlier about it, but he'd excused himself and disappeared into his study, his shoulders bowed, like he was carrying heavy pails of water in each hand. *Besides,* he'd said, *the past isn't important. It's the future that counts. We can make more memories together.*

Which was his way of saying she needed to back off.

So why can't I?

But she already knew the answer. Because the Paul who starred in Nicole's diary was one Jenna hardly recognised. Her sister's tight jaw flashed into her mind, as Lucy asked her how much she really knew about Paul. Turns out it wasn't as much as she'd thought.

She turned back to her computer and brought up a search engine before stabbing in his name along with car accident. Several articles came up, but none of them were about an accident that happened twenty-two years ago. She tried again and this time she took out the accident. This time she got more hits. Several articles of Paul, all wearing his Hepworth cap in some capacity or other. And one time when he was interviewed by local media because he was first on the scene when a pedestrian had suffered a heart attack. But that was it.

Even her mother had more of an online presence.

She tried a few more times before bringing up her work. It lasted all of ten seconds before she once again returned to the search engine. But this time she typed in Nicole Williams. It wasn't the first time she'd searched for Nicole on social media, but it was the first time she'd found much, mainly because Nicole's pages were private, and she could hardly send her a friend request. But she'd suddenly realised that Bridget had been tagged in some of the photos and other times Bridget had her own copy of the image tucked away in her history.

She studied the photographs. One was of Nicole in the foreground, proudly standing in front of the Sydney Opera House. The sky was impossibly blue, and the sun glinted off the white sails. It was a long way from Market Harborough, that was for sure.

'Whoa. Photoshop fail,' Louisa said as she walked into the office balancing a stack of folders.

'What?' Jenna blinked, hating that she'd been caught looking at a photo of Nicole. What would Paul say if he found out?

'Whoever put this together had wildly average skills.' Louisa stepped closer and pointed to the screen. 'See those warped lines? And considering how far away she is from the Opera House, we shouldn't be able to see the details so clearly.'

'Are you sure?'

'Um, yeah,' Louisa said in a voice that suggested Jenna had been living under a rock. 'Why? Is it a friend trying to make you jealous with their overseas jaunts?'

'Not exactly,' Jenna said and quickly shut down the screen as her mind raced. Yet another anomaly that didn't make sense. Why would Nicole have doctored herself in front of the Opera House?

But there was only one reason she could think of. Nicole wanted Paul to believe she lived in Australia, even if she didn't.

Sometimes he scares me.

Her skin prickled and the room began to spin.

'Everything okay?' Louisa said, her mouth turned into a frown.

Jenna realised she must've been pulling a face. 'Yes, it's fine. Nancy moved forward the deadline on that post.'

'That's actually what I'm coming to talk to you about. I've found a gorgeous stock photo and made a headline, so I'm ready to go when you are.'

'I still need to give it a final edit, which means I'll never make the early train.'

Louisa frowned. 'Anything I can help with? I'd be happy to go over it.'

Jenna chewed her lip. Usually she'd never agree, but she'd been feeling more and more stretched lately and she really did need to get home. 'Are you sure?'

'Yes,' Louisa assured her. 'Give me permission to edit the draft. Then when it's ready I'll load it up. You can always double check it on your way into work tomorrow. It's not like Nancy will see it until after her meeting tomorrow.'

Jenna let out her breath and quickly gave Louisa editing permission and shut the document. 'Thanks. You're a lifesaver.'

'You're welcome.' Louisa gave her a wide smile. 'Now go home to that gorgeous guy of yours.'

Paul opened the front door when he arrived home from school and the smell of spices invaded his nostrils. His stomach rumbled.

'Hello?'

'I'm in the kitchen,' Jenna called. Out of habit he checked his phone again, but there was still no message from Nicole, only a barrage of happy photographs displayed on her main feed. It had been almost twenty-four hours since he'd sent her his message.

He dropped his keys on the hallway table and scooped up the mail. This time he checked it carefully. There were none from Nicole. Thankfully there were only a couple of bills. He put them back down and walked into the kitchen.

Jenna was standing in front of the stove. Steam sizzled from the wok and her cheeks were flushed, but there was a sparkle in her eyes and her hair hung down her back in smooth waves. The necklace he had given her was once again round her neck, and he swallowed.

She'd been so pleased to get it back, but to him it represented how easily things could be taken away from him.

No. *She's mine.* His gaze racked over her exposed collarbone and the dip at the base of her neck, and primal longing flooded him. He needed to have her. Claim her. He stepped up behind her and wrapped his arms round her waist. Her scent trailed up his skin. 'You smell good enough to eat. How about we have first course upstairs?'

'Bridget and Daniel are coming round tonight for dinner.'

'Screw them,' he murmured as he pushed back the top of her blouse to reveal a tiny scrap of lacy fabric. It was the same kind of stuff Nicole used to wear. Designed to titillate. Control. Dominate. Nicole hadn't loved him or their child. She'd put herself first. Put her job before him.

Paul whipped his hands away and stepped back, as if he'd been stung.

His parents' whispered conversations about Paul's habit of pulling wings from butterflies filled his mind. They hadn't loved him either. Said he was bad. They'd made him do it.

His vision blurred, as bright light seemed to fill the room. His fingers twitched, wanting to rip it from her skin and replace it with the plain white bras she usually wore. To put her back in the spot she'd always had in his mind. Pure, sweet, kind. Not this person dressed in lace.

Heat pounded in his brow as he took a step closer.

'What's wrong?' Jenna turned to him, her shoulder still exposed from where he'd pushed back the blouse, eyes full of confusion. Her words broke the madness that had been coursing through him, and he staggered back, sucking in some much-needed air.

He needed to breathe. And again. And again. Stay centred. Stay calm. His hammering heart finally slowed down, and he forced a smile onto his face.

Jenna wouldn't betray him.

And he wouldn't hurt her.

He loved her.

'Nothing,' he finally said, proud of how relaxed he sounded. 'I realised you were right. We have visitors about to descend on us. So, what can I do to help?'

Jenna studied him, as if unsure how to respond. Then the oven timer beeped, and it broke the tension.

'You could make sure there's enough beer and wine in the fridge. They should be here soon. By the way, have you arranged to leave work early tomorrow?' she asked.

'I have,' he said. It was the scan and he'd booked out the date weeks ago. The last of the tension left her shoulders and she pressed her mouth against his.

'Good,' she murmured, but before they could deepen the kiss the doorbell rang.

This time he reluctantly untangled himself. 'I'll get it.'

Bridget and Daniel were waiting on the doorstep, all smiles, holding a bottle of wine and a carefully wrapped present. Paul flinched. Since his fight with Bridget, when he'd accused her of knowing about the necklace, she'd kept her distance from him.

'I told her it was too early to buy baby things, but would she listen?' Daniel said, by way of greeting.

'And I said that it's never too early to buy romper suits,' Bridget retorted before disappearing into the kitchen to where Jenna was.

'Sorry about that. Lately all she does is go shopping,' Daniel said as they walked into the dining.

'It's not a problem.' Paul passed him a beer before pouring himself a mineral water, trying not to notice his hand was shaking.

'Thanks,' Daniel took the drink and then eyed Paul. 'Still not drinking, I'm impressed.'

'Least I can do to support Jenna. She's the one doing all the heavy lifting. Missing out on a few beers won't kill me,' he said in a smooth voice, not wanting to think about the half empty bottle of vodka out in the garage. God, how he could use it now. Adrenaline was still flaring through him, lighting him up from the inside out, burning away the layers of reason and control that he'd fought so long to establish.

'Better you than me.' Daniel took a long gulp of beer and walked across the room. Paul shoved his hand in his pocket and extracted a couple of tablets, hastily swallowing them down before the other man noticed. The heat in his veins cooled down and he managed to follow Daniel across the room.

'How's your week been?' he asked. Daniel was a heart surgeon at the nearby hospital.

'What?' Daniel blinked before seeming to realise he'd drifted off. He sighed. 'Sorry, I was miles away. Work's been a bitch, but it's not anything I can talk about. How goes the pregnancy? Any idea of sex yet?'

Paul shook his head, wondering what the fascination with sex was. 'Scan is tomorrow. Until then I'm none the wiser.'

Daniel seemed to take it as a sign to change the subject and they talked about football until Bridget walked in holding a large serving dish of glistening strips of beef and broccoli.

'Hope you're hungry.'

'Ravenous,' Daniel agreed, draining his beer. Paul was about to get him another one when his phone beeped with a notification. He excused himself and slipped into the bathroom. Once the door was firmly closed, he unlocked his phone.

It was a message from Nicole.

Finally. Unexpected nerves stabbed at his belly. Facing her, after all this time, would finally put an end to the nightmare he'd been living in his head. His fingers slid across the screen and the message opened up.

4pm tomorrow at the Olive Tree.

The air was dragged from his lungs. Four o'clock. The same time as Jenna's scan. *And* in what had become their favourite café. Did Nicole know about the scan? He wouldn't put it past her. She was a master manipulator, and while most of the time he considered what she did harmless enough, he now realised what it was like to be on the receiving end.

Can we make it Thursday instead?

Her reply was instant.

We meet then or not at all.

He winced and sent a reply. Now he needed to figure out how to tell Jenna.

19

Jenna walked through the hospital car park while self-consciously smoothing down the soft fabric of one of her new dresses. The floral fabric clung to the swell of her belly, her hips and breasts, but rather than making her feel like a beached whale, she felt sexy.

As she reached the entrance, she was greeted by a collection of people in white hospital gowns who were smoking and vaping. Nearby taxis snaked along the side of the road, waiting for their next fare. She walked into the lobby to search for Paul. They both worked in different directions, which was why they'd agree to meet there half an hour before the scan. There was no sign of him.

Wafts of antiseptic hung in the air and the low hum of nurses and doctors seemed to flood all the spaces. When Jenna said she didn't like hospitals, what she actually meant was that they filled her with an unnamed sense of dread. It wasn't something she'd ever been able to account for since she hadn't lost anyone close to her and had never been ill herself. All she knew was that from the time she'd done a field trip to the local rest home while in fourth form, a leaden weight had settled in her belly and taken over her limbs, not releasing her until she was safely back in her bedroom.

Where was Paul?

She took out her phone and was about to call him, when his name flashed up on the screen.

'Speak of the devil,' she said by way of answering. 'I've just arrived, are you far away?'

'Um...' He hesitated.

'What is it?' She tensed, sensing that he was going to say something she didn't want to hear.

'I'm really sorry, but I'm not going to be able to make it to the scan.'

'B-but we've planned this, and you've arranged to have time off work. Why can't you come with me?' she said, hating how desperate she sounded. Her head began to spin. He'd said her and the baby were the most important things in his world, but already he was letting them down. Was this what had happened to Nicole? Was this why she'd—

'There's been an issue with a staff member. It's not anything I can talk about.'

'But...' her words faded away.

'I'll tell you all about it when we get home. Is there time to call Lucy or Bridget?'

She chewed her lower lip. 'I guess I can try.'

'I'm so sorry I'm leaving you alone. Please tell me you don't hate me.'

'I don't hate you,' she said. 'I'm disappointed. It's our first scan.'

'I know. Remember that I love you, and I'll make it up to you as soon as you get home.'

She swallowed back the tears, her mind busy tallying up all

the ways he'd let her down in the last few weeks. The missing necklace. Lying about his fight with Bridget. And now this.

'I'd better go.'

Paul was silent at the other end, as if he wanted to say something else. Then he murmured goodbye and finished the call. Jenna stood there, unsure what to do. For so long this scan had been all Paul could talk about, but now he'd ditched her. So much of his behaviour didn't make sense any more. *He* didn't make sense.

What was she meant to think?

She rolled her neck as she called her sister, but it went straight through to voice message. She toyed with calling her mother but thought better of it. They didn't have that kind of relationship. She scrolled through her address book and called Bridget.

'Jenna?' Bridget answered, sounding out of breath and distant. 'I wasn't expecting you.'

'Have I caught you at a bad time?'

There was the sound of something shattering, and then little Eddie let out a series of yaps. 'Hush,' Bridget said, presumably to the dog. 'Sorry about that. What's up?'

'Um, well, I'm actually at the hospital waiting for my scan. Paul called and he can't make it.'

'He stood you up?' Bridget said in a sharp voice, before there was another crashing sound. Eddie barked again, and her friend swore. 'Sorry. Eddie's going crazy here. I can't believe Paul cancelled on you.'

Neither could she.

'You know what his job's like,' Jenna forced herself to say, not sure why she was defending him. 'I was wondering if you could come down here. I know it's stupid, but the idea of going in alone is freaking me out.'

Eddie finally stopped barking and the line went silent.

'Bridge, are you still there?'

'Yes,' Bridget said. 'And hell, I wish I could be with you, but I'm right in the middle of something. Have you tried Lucy?'

'She's not answering,' Jenna said as she glanced at the large clock on the wall. Fifteen minutes to go. Bridget swore again.

'Christ. I'm so sorry. Will you be okay?'

'Yes. Anyway, I'd better go. I'll come over later and tell you how it went.'

'You better,' Bridget said before ending the call.

Jenna swallowed hard and took a step forward, trying to push down her rising panic. Her mouth was dry, and beads of perspiration sprung up on her forehead as the large room began to spin. Oh, no—

'Jenna?' A hand slid round her waist, helping to steady her. Jenna looked up into a pair of amber eyes.

'Alison? What are you doing here?'

'Rescuing you, apparently,' Alison said in a light voice as she gently led her to a bank of nearby seats. 'You are as white as a ghost. Is it the baby? Should I get someone?'

'No,' Jenna said as the wave of dizziness passed. She gratefully lowered herself down. 'I'm fine... well... I will be. I'm here for my scan, but I have a thing about hospitals.'

'Yes, they're definitely not my favourite place in the world,' she said in a soothing voice before frowning. 'I guess it was lucky I came along. My aunt broke her hip last week and I'm on visiting duties.'

'Oh, I'm sorry to hear that.'

'She's fine, and I had a free period last thing, so it wasn't too bad. Is everything okay with you?'

'I've got my scan today, that's where I'm heading.'

'That's right. Paul mentioned it,' she said before looking

around. 'Is he parking the car? Finding a space can be a nightmare.'

'No. He couldn't make it. There's a staff emergency.' Jenna forced her voice to stay calm. Paul and Alison were close and the last thing she wanted to do was let him know how upset she felt.

'Hell. That's all the school needs. I better check what's going on in case I can help,' Alison said as she brought out her phone and opened up an app. Her smile faltered.

'What's wrong?' Jenna said in alarm. 'Did you find what it is?'

'Actually, it's not something I can speak about,' Alison said in a quick voice as she pocketed her phone, though a guilty flush had stolen across her cheeks. She was doing a bad job of covering up the truth.

Jenna sucked in a breath. Was Alison trying to hide the fact that there wasn't a staff emergency? But if Paul wasn't at school, where the hell—

Nicole.

Her gut tightened. Was she somehow behind this? Ever since she'd come back, Paul had been tense, and on edge. And Jenna had read enough of her diary to get a clearer picture about the other woman. Nicole was used to getting what she wanted. Looks did that to a person. They opened doors, gave opportunities, and raised their sense of entitlement.

All making it impossible for the likes of Jenna to compete. What did she have that Nicole didn't? Nothing. Only a slightly improved wardrobe, a job that paid below the living wage, and a belly that was already covered in stretch marks.

Was that why he'd been so turned off yesterday? It wasn't the bra, it was her.

The unfairness of it cleaved at her chest. Nicole could have anyone she wanted, so why did she still—

'Oh, no you don't,' Alison broke in, her gaze sweeping over

Jenna. 'I know that look. It's the one students get right before they hand in an assignment, or think that their best friend hates them, or that they'll never master grammar. I will tell you the same thing I tell them. Try using that amazing mind of yours to think of the good things that could happen, rather than the bad things. For instance, you might find out that your baby is perfectly healthy and is sitting in the exactly right position. Or that you're having twins.'

'Twins?' Jenna yelped and Alison grinned.

'Okay, so maybe not twins. But it's so easy for our minds to go to the worst-case scenario and not the best one.' Alison patted her hand and gave her a smile. Jenna let out a breath and the heavy dread dissipated.

'Thank you. That really helped. Paul has always said what an amazing teacher you are. I can see he wasn't lying.'

'I don't know about that,' Alison said before glancing at the clock on the wall. 'Why don't I go with you, to keep you company?'

'I couldn't ask you to do that. Besides, won't Rob be waiting for you? Paul told me you're back together,' she said. 'I was really happy to hear it.'

Alison broke out into a smile that took over her whole face. 'Me too. It's hard keeping it to myself. But he's had to go back to work out his notice and pack up his flat, so the only thing I'm missing out on is leftovers and a pile of marking. I'm not in any rush. Being in a hospital can be daunting and sometimes it's nice to have someone there to hold your hand. Besides, I know Paul wouldn't want you to be alone.'

Jenna sucked in a breath. She should say no. Alison had done enough, and she knew far too well how busy teachers were at this time of year, but there was something so soothing about her presence. And it would stop her from obsessing about Nicole.

'If you're sure you don't mind,' Jenna said.

'It's my pleasure,' Alison said. 'Where are you heading?'

'I've got to go to radiology but I'm not sure exactly where that is.'

'There's a notice board by the lifts, we'll go and take a look. You must be really excited. Are you going to find out whether it's a boy or girl?'

'I'm not sure. I'll decide when I'm in there, because it's not always accurate so early in the pregnancy. Imagine how terrible it would be to spend six months buying the right clothes and painting the nursery, only to discover there had been a mistake?'

'Goodness, yes,' Alison said as they both stood up. 'It's always disappointing when things don't go the way you plan.'

* * *

'Anything else?' The girl behind the counter didn't bother to look up as she slide the packet of cigarettes towards him. *Yes, something to ease my guilty conscience.*

'No, thanks,' he said and then glanced at the breath mints on the counter. 'Actually, I'll take those as well.'

'Ten pounds fifty,' the girl said. He pulled out twenty quid and passed it over before gathering up his purchases.

As soon as he stepped out of the store, he tore open the box, quickly pulling a cigarette out. He pressed it up to his mouth and exhaled deeply once it was lit. The heady combination of exhaust fumes and nicotine competed for his attention as he leaned against the brick wall. He took another drag and then stumped it out against the side of the rubbish bin.

Then he walked back to his car and turned on the engine.

It was time to go face Nicole.

The afternoon traffic was busy, full of commuters and cyclists, and Paul was forced to wait at the lights. Shit. He shouldn't have stopped at the shop. It was two minutes past four, and while Nicole wasn't known for her timekeeping, he'd originally planned to get there early. The car in front finally moved and he reached the coffee shop five minutes later.

He glanced in the rear-view mirror.

Not good. His face looked like he'd been dipped in grey paint and there were tight lines round his mouth. He didn't know how much longer he could go on. Hurting Jenna was destroying him. Missing the scan, too. His first chance to see his unborn child.

The sooner this was sorted out, the better. He needed to make sure Nicole stayed in his past, not his future. No more notes to Jenna. No more stealing necklaces. And he could find out what really happened that night.

Do I really want to know?

He pushed down the small voice. One social worker had told him that the gaps in his memory were because his mind couldn't cope, so it had simply blocked them out. But he'd been a child then and unable to deal with his life. It was different now he was older. Going to be a father. Going to have the life he never thought could be his.

All he had to do was talk to Nicole and clear the air.

He climbed out of the car and walked towards the café.

The décor was Mediterranean, and there was a low hum of conversation and the hiss of the espresso machine at work. Paul scanned the room but there was no sign of his ex-fiancée.

He swallowed and took a seat by the far wall.

The waiter came over with a jug of water and Paul ordered a cup of coffee and a muffin, his eyes never leaving the door. It was quarter past four, and still no sign of her. He checked his phone, again. No new posts from Nicole.

Jenna would be having her scan now. Was she going to find

out whether it was a boy or girl? They hadn't made a final decision, as they were planning to wait and see on the day. She'd have to decide on her own. He hated not being there with her.

The waiter brought back his coffee and food, and Paul thanked him, absently picking up his knife and toying with the butter, knowing he wasn't going to eat or drink a thing. His heart thumped in his chest, and he tapped the table, unable to hide his nerves.

'Excuse me, sir. This is for you.' A young waitress appeared at his side. Her hair was purple, and she barely looked old enough to be in high school, let alone working in a café. Not seeming to notice his scrutiny, she handed him a large envelope.

Ice went down his spine and he caught his breath.

'Who gave you this?' he said, his voice sharper than he'd intended.

'It was delivered by a woman with the instructions that we were to give it to you at four-thirty on the dot.'

Four-thirty. Long enough to ensure that he couldn't get across town to the hospital.

'What did she look like?' he said, already knowing the answer.

'She was tall with long, dark hair,' the girl said. He'd always known that by agreeing to see Nicole he would be dragged into whatever game it was she wanted to play. But if he hadn't agreed, then she would've kept escalating it.

It was something she'd done enough times with her work colleagues. But back then it never occurred to him she would do it on a personal level.

'Thank you.' Paul waited until she walked over to a nearby table and started to stack up the empty coffee cups onto her tray. His pulse beat out a rhythmic warning, reminding him that whatever was in the envelope probably wasn't good news.

He used the knife from his muffin and slit open the envelope.

A single black and white photograph slid out once he upended it. It was of the two of them at their engagement party. He remembered it being taken. Nicole had insisted on wearing a diamond necklace that she'd hired from one of those places that rent things out to the stars. It had seemed over the top, but she'd been so happy that it had been hard not to be charmed by it.

It seemed a very long time ago.

He studied the photo, trying to recognise the two people in it, but they were both strangers. He'd been so naïve. So oblivious to what the woman next to him was really like, and Nicole obviously hadn't known him either. If she had, she never would have killed their baby.

He turned the photo over and then dropped it, letting it fall to the table.

Written on the back in Nicole's very distinctive scrawl were the words:

You weren't at my scan. Why should you be at hers?

Paul was statue still. How dare she? Nicole hadn't even given him the option to be at the scan. He didn't even know she'd gone for one. Was it before she decided to get rid of their child or after?

Fire thundered in his temples and his hands shook as he sent her a message.

What the hell do you want?

Her reply was instantaneous. She'd obviously been waiting for him to open the letter and contact her.

I thought that was obvious, lover. I want you to leave her. And I won't take no for an answer.

20

CELLAR OF HORRORS
by Aaron Richards

An unnamed eleven-year-old child has been found in a cellar, locked in a cupboard, not much bigger than a coffin. She had multiple wounds on her chest and head. It's unclear how long she was in there for, but she was also suffering from malnutrition and dehydration. The child, who was in the care system, was first discovered missing when a concerned neighbour hadn't seen her for around for several weeks.

The seventy-eight-year-old woman, who'd lived next door to the house for over twenty years, said, 'She was a quiet child, but every Wednesday she would walk down my path and sort out my recycling. Never asked for a penny, either. It was strange when she didn't show up, but I figured she had a cold. Then there was the fact those people had stopped yelling at the poor little mite. It didn't add up.'

A second neighbour told police that twenty-eight-year-old Stefan Taylor and his girlfriend, Sharon Willis, had only moved

into the house several months earlier and kept to themselves.
Stefan, who has a history of assault and domestic violence,
hadn't been named on the foster agreement. It's not known
how the child managed to be placed in the couple's care. So
far the government have refused to comment on the situation
because it's part of an ongoing investigation.

21

Jenna clutched the photo as she walked out into the waiting room. She wasn't sure the blurry image really did justice to what she'd seen on the screen. The pounding of the tiny heart that filled the room and caused her eyes to prickle with tears. The radiologist had pointed out the baby's head and body, finally announcing everything was perfect.

Her relief was tempered by the fact that Paul wasn't there to share the moment.

Was that something she would need to get used to?

She swallowed down the thought and joined the throng of people in the lift.

A bag jabbed her in the ribs, and the stench of body odour filled the small steel cage. The irrational desire to blame Paul for all of it sung out in her mind. If he'd been here the lift wouldn't be full. People wouldn't bump into her like she was invisible. With Paul she was someone.

Except she wasn't with him because he'd let her down.

The lift doors opened, and everyone spilled out into the main reception area, Jenna trailing behind them. She slowed down, as the leaden weight once again claimed her legs, leaving her feeling heavy and off kilter. She suddenly wondered if she should have let Alison stay. There were some seats nearby and she headed toward them when there was a commotion from over by the door.

'Let me through,' a voice commanded. There was a desperate edge to it, but she still recognised the deep alto tones. Paul? She craned her neck and managed to spot him desperately pushing his way through the throng of people. 'Jenna. Jenna.'

'Paul,' she called out, but her voice was lost, and he continued to frantically search the sea of faces. In the end she raised her hand and his eyes locked on hers. Relief replaced the haunted set of his brows as he navigated his way over and wrapped his arms round her.

'You're okay,' he said, nuzzling his face into her hair. She let herself sink into his embrace. His whole body trembled. Jenna reluctantly wriggled out of his arms. Up close, he looked terrible. His hair was in disarray, like he'd run his hands through it one too many times, and his jaw was clenched.

Some of her anger dissipated.

After all, it was hard to be mad at him when he'd run through the hospital foyer, like something out of a movie.

'What's going on? I thought we were meeting at home.'

'I know, but I couldn't bear it,' he said, his hands cupping her chin, as if inspecting her for an injury. 'I think I ran every orange light I hit.'

'You did?' she gulped. Technically she knew she should tell him off for taking such a risk, but there was something exhilarating about the fact he had been so determined to get to the hospital. Treating her like she was the most important woman in the world.

'I did,' he agreed. 'I'm so sorry I wasn't here earlier. I kept imagining that something had happened—' he broke off and coughed. 'Because you hate hospitals so much. Where's Lucy and Bridget?'

'They couldn't make it,' she said and the guilty flush that ran up his neck almost made her feel sorry for him. 'I ran into Alison, and she was wonderful. She calmed me down and took me to the radiologist.'

'Alison?' he said in surprise. 'What was she even doing in the hospital?'

'Her aunt has a broken hip, which is bad for her, but lucky for me. She was so calm and supportive,' Jenna said, enjoying the swirling heat still running along her skin as he continued to cradle her face in his hands. She should ask him where he was. What he was really doing, but there was something so perfect about this moment that she didn't want to ruin it. Didn't want to see the guard coming up in his eyes. Besides, it was ludicrous of her to jump to conclusions about Nicole.

'I'm so pleased she was there to help you.' He leaned forward and kissed her. Jenna melted into his embrace, her bump pressed against him. The three of them together. Then she stepped back, laughter catching in her throat.

'What's so funny?' Paul blinked, as if he'd been woken from a dream.

'I realised I forgot to introduce you to your son.'

'It's a boy?' Paul's eyes were filled with awe.

'Yes, it's a perfect, healthy baby boy,' she said as his arms slid round her waist, and he lifted her into the air. His excitement was contagious and the smell of antiseptic, the hushed tones over everyone round them all fell away, leaving the two of them.

'I promise that from now on I don't care *what* comes up. I'll be at your side every step of the away.'

'I'd like that,' she said and the haunted look in his eyes disappeared. He kissed her again and this time her stomach rumbled. She stifled a laugh.

'Your son seems to have quite an appetite and the last thing I feel like doing is cooking.'

'Then let's go out and celebrate. How about that Mexican restaurant we tried last month?'

'Perfect,' Jenna said as Paul snaked his arm round her waist and they both walked back to the car park. She still had no idea where he'd been.

22

'Right everyone, listen up,' Tim said from the middle of the teachers' lounge. Paul was behind to the left, along with the heads of each department and the support staff, while all the teachers were fanned out round them, clutching coffee cups and grumbling about having to come in at seven o'clock. 'We've appointed a new science teacher, who will start next week. Her name is Ingrid Wilson and she specialises in marine biology.'

'Mustn't be a very good one if she wants to teach in a county that's landlocked,' Doug muttered under his breath. Paul ignored him and listened as Tim went through everything on the agenda. His words were accompanied by the wheeze and rattle of the ancient radiator, though Paul would've been hard pressed to repeat any of it.

Leave her.

The words burned through him like a bushfire. Was it a threat? That had been his first conclusion, which was why he'd broken nearly every rule in the road code to get to the hospital. The relief at seeing Jenna safe and well had been overwhelming. And then to find out they were having a son.

My son.

Nicole's message had taken on a whole new meaning then. It now said to him that someone was trying to come between him and his innocent child. Unacceptable. He'd sent Nicole half a dozen messages since yesterday, but she hadn't responded to any of them. Which meant he needed to take matters into his own hands.

It's what he should have done from the start. Waiting for Nicole to come to him could only end badly. He needed to find her and tell her how it was.

The meeting finally came to an end and Tim's secretary was immediately in his ear before they both hurried off.

'No rest for the wicked,' Alison said sidling up to him as they looked at Tim's retreating back. 'And if his workload is anything to go by, he must've been very wicked in the past.'

'I suspect the most our beloved Head has ever done is get a speeding ticket. Even then it was probably because he was rescuing a sick kitten,' Paul said as they walked over to the kitchen counter. Alison usually ate an entire second breakfast before class and he could use more coffee.

'Good point. And great news we finally have a new science teacher. I won't miss doing science club. Give me English essays any day of the week. Have you met her yet?'

'Yeah,' Paul said absently as he spooned in some instant coffee into a cup. 'Seems like a good fit for the place. Plus it's great to have more women in the sciences.'

'It should make the press back off now. They can go find some new scandal to dissect. I wonder how Eric's doing?'

'Not good,' Paul said as the science teacher's dishevelled appearance came into his mind. 'Chloe kicked him out and he's staying with his sister. But when I bumped into him, it looked like he was spending most of his time in the King's Head.'

Alison shuddered. 'That place is a dump. Did you try and talk to him?'

'He wanted me to have a drink, but that seemed like enabling,' Paul said, trying to ignore the fact he'd given his former colleague thirty quid to ease his own guilt. Not to mention the pills he'd swallowed this morning. 'I should have done more, but there's been a lot going on.'

'Don't beat yourself up. Eric made his own choices, and he obviously doesn't want to face up to them,' Alison said.

Paul winced, thinking of his own bad choices. 'Hey, I want to say thank you for helping out Jenna yesterday. She said you were amazing.'

'I wouldn't go that far,' Alison said in a bemused voice. 'She was a bit overwhelmed, imaging the worst that could happen. She seemed rattled that you couldn't make it.'

'Yeah, I know. I feel like such a turd for letting her down.'

'So what happened? She said it was a staff emergency.'

Paul put down his coffee cup and rubbed his brow. That was the problem with being friends with someone from work. He sighed. 'I went to meet Nicole. I wanted to make it clear that the past is the past, and that Jenna's my future.'

Alison's pale amber eyes widened. 'Shit. You *saw* Nicole? That's why you missed the scan. This is huge. How did it go? What's she like? Has she changed?'

Paul held up his hand to slow her down. Neither of them had a class first period and he nodded for her to follow him into his office.

'So?' Alison said once they were safely behind his door. 'Tell me everything. The suspense is killing me.'

He rolled his shoulders and began to pace the small office. 'There isn't much to tell. She never showed up. Which means I missed Jenna's scan for nothing.'

'Do you think the timing was intentional?'

'We both know Nicole well enough to guess the answer to that,' Paul said in a dry voice. 'And there's more. She had this delivered to me.' He held out the letter and Alison let out a long breath.

'Christ. You need to go to the police.'

'No,' he said, his voice sharper than he'd intended. Going to the police wasn't an option. Not yet, anyway. 'I need to talk to her face to face. She isn't responding to any of my messages, though. Has she given you any idea where she is staying?'

Alison steepled her fingers together and pressed them up to her chin. 'Paul, I'm the last one to give advice, but do you really think that's a good idea?'

'What choice do I have? You saw first-hand how rattled Jenna was when I didn't turn up. Which is why we need to talk. So I can draw a line under the whole thing.'

'What if it makes matters worse?' Alison said, still clearly troubled at the idea of helping him.

'How could they be worse? She's tried to come between me, Jenna and my son.'

'Son?' Alison let out a gasp and her entire face softened. 'I'm so happy for you both. Jenna said she hadn't been sure whether to find out the sex or not. A baby boy. That's so wonderful.'

'Now can you see why I need to talk to her. She's been a shadow lying over me for far too long. I want it to be over.'

'Okay,' Alison finally answered as she took out her phone and scrolled through the screen. 'Last week she invited me to join her and a bunch of her old friends for a girls' night in. I didn't go because it would've been weird, but she did send me her address.'

Paul stiffened. 'You've had her address since last week? Why didn't you tell me?'

'Because I like Jenna and I didn't want her to think I was

encouraging you. Which for the record, I'm not. I think it's a bad idea for you to see her,' Alison said.

Paul swallowed. 'Sorry. And I do appreciate you looking out for me and Jenna, but I promise I won't do anything stupid.'

'I hope not,' Alison agreed before finally looking up at him. 'Ah, here it is – 23a Gibson Terrace. It's a second floor flat.'

'Thank you.' Paul let out a breath and some of the tension in his chest was released. He had an address. Now Nicole wasn't in control. They could finally talk about what had really happened two years ago, and then he could do what he'd been longing to do for such a long time.

Ask Jenna to marry him.

23

I decided to go blonde today. No, I didn't dye my hair, I used a wig. It was so liberating. I wouldn't say I had more fun, but I certainly had more freedom. This bloody village is so God damn small that everyone knows my business. And they all love Paul. It's totally gag-worthy how many people stop me in the street, wanting to tell me how great he is. I mean, yeah sure, he does a good job. But being a teacher is hardly rocket science. Yet they treat me like I'm an accessory.

We got into an argument about it the other night and Paul said it was hardly fair I blamed him for what other people said, and that I was trying to pick a fight with him. But that's bullshit. If he would misbehave a little bit, loosen up and relax like a normal thirty-two-year-old, then people wouldn't put him up a bloody pedestal. I told him that and, instead of complaining, he told me I was adorable when I got grumpy.

A word to the wise. Don't call me grumpy or adorable. I'm neither one of those things. Though he might have a point about me picking a fight.

Guilt is a terrible thing. It sneaks up on you in the night, waiting silently at the edge of your awareness, until it's safe to start whispering. But most of the time I know it's fine.

Besides, Gwendolyn said I needed to face my shadows, so maybe this is my way of doing that? All I know is that there's a corner of my mind that isn't satisfied by how bloody good and perfect Paul is. It needs something darker, dirtier to give it a voice. To bring it into the light.

After the wedding I'll have to break it off with X, but until then it's fun. A lot more fun than sleeping with Paul with his control and vanilla sex.

This affair is my last chance to explore the darkness before I lock myself into the cage of matrimony. Besides, it might help me bring myself to let Paul touch me again.

Wait. What?

Jenna, who'd stopped bothering to take photographs of the diary, and had taken to bringing the entire box downstairs to examine Nicole's possessions and read more entries, sat up from the lounge chair as her eyes scanned back over what she'd read.

This affair.

I'll have to break it off with X.

So Nicole *had* cheated?

Jenna leaned down and scooped the diary back off the floor, as she feverishly scanned the page for a name. Nothing. She turned the page and let out a groan as the tell-tale sign of tiny, jagged edges sat between one page and the next.

Someone had ripped out the vital page.

Jenna upended the box before she could stop herself. As well as the pale pink cardigan she'd borrowed, there were three skirts, a bra and a pair of spiky shoes, several necklaces and a couple of bags of make-up. But no missing page.

Disappointment caught in her throat as she glanced at her

watch. Paul would be home in half an hour, which meant her reading session was over. It only took a couple of minutes to pack everything away and carry it up to the attic. She'd been up there so many times in the last fortnight that the dusty floor was now almost entirely filled with shoeprints.

She frowned as she climbed back down. Who had Nicole been sleeping with? Were Bridget's suspicions about Daniel correct? No wonder her neighbour seemed to have a love/hate relationship with Nicole. It explained a lot.

She longed to ask Paul if he knew about the affair, but she could hardly admit to reading the diaries. And what did Nicole mean about not wanting Paul to touch her? Had she been cold to him? Distant?

Jenna's heart ached for how that kind of betrayal must have hurt him. Especially since he'd lost his parents at such a young age, and she'd seen how personally he took rejection. It was why he was such an amazing Deputy Head, because he worked so hard to make sure all the parents, teachers and students felt accepted and valued.

Then she stiffened as she thought of how ill she'd been feeling during her first trimester, and how angry she'd been at him for keeping Nicole's appearance a secret. Was he feeling rejected now? By her?

When she reached the kitchen, an old Elvis song blared out from her phone and Lucy's name flashed up on the screen.

Jenna winced. She wished she'd never left the panicky message while she'd been at the hospital because her sister would dissect it in excruciating detail. But the longer she left it, the worse it would be. Sighing, she picked up the phone and went out into the garden.

'What's up?'

'You tell me,' Lucy said as Jenna reached the rosemary bush.

'Why didn't you call me back last night? Mum and I have been worried about you. I can't believe Paul let you down like that.'

'He didn't let me down, he got stuck in a meeting and felt awful about it.'

'I bet. And before you bite my head off, hear me out. If Paul's so committed, then why doesn't he propose?'

'Can we please drop it?' Jenna gritted her teeth and gathered up a handful of the aromatic herb. 'Besides, you haven't even asked me what the sex of the baby is.'

There was silence down the other end and Lucy let out a reluctant chuckle. 'Okay, sorry. You're right. It's time for me to stop being an overprotective big sister, and start being an aunt. So, tell me. Am I going to have a niece or a nephew?'

'Nephew,' Jenna said, her animosity fading. It was hard to be mad when the scan had gone so well. 'Paul and I are having a baby boy.'

Her sister let out a very un-Lucy-like squeal and the next ten minutes were spent talking about baby showers and breast-feeding, while Jenna walked back into the house and put the rosemary on the bench. Wafts of garlic filled the air as she opened up the oven door and took out the lamb. The meat had a hint of red, while the buttery potatoes were done to perfection.

Beep. Beep. Beep.

The familiar sound of the garage door made her smile as she took her sister off speakerphone and held it up to her ear.

'Hey, I've got to go. Talk soon.'

'Will do, and don't forget to tell mum about the baby,' Lucy instructed as Jenna finished the call. She hurried into the lounge where she kept her lipstick. She'd started adding an extra coat in the evenings, but then she laughed as she looked down. She was dressed in sweats, so it hardly mattered. She put the tube down as the clip, clip, clip told her he was walking down the hallway.

She was about to turn away from the mirror when she noticed something pink reflecting back at her. Jenna's throat tightened and she spun around to where a cardigan was sitting, neatly folded on the lounge chair. Jenna clamped her hand over her mouth to stop from gasping as she hurried over to it. For the first time, she didn't marvel at the softness of it, she simply scooped it up and threw it under the chair. As she picked it up a note fluttered to the ground in Nicole's all-too familiar handwriting.

Stop playing with my things.

Her mind whirled. Had she left the front door unlocked when she'd gone out into the back garden? It was entirely possible. Paul was the one who worried about security, not her. And he'd been right to worry.

Nicole had been in the house.

And in my mind. Nausea churned in her belly as the full irony hit her. She'd been so worried that Nicole might try to seduce Paul that she hadn't realised *she* was the one being seduced. She'd been the one obsessively reading her diary and taking her advice. *I even dressed like her.*

And she'd mistrusted Paul.

Had Nicole somehow manipulated her?

'There you are.' He strode into the room, a bunch of flowers in his hand. His gaze swept over her and the smile on his mouth shifted. 'What's wrong?'

'Nothing.' Jenna managed to get the words out of her dry mouth as she crumpled the note up and shoved it into a pocket. She didn't want to see the worry lines that had been permanently etched between his brow return. Not to mention she didn't want to admit she'd been reading the diary or going through Nicole's things. From now on, she'd make sure she locked the doors.

His smile returned as he took her in his arms. 'Good, I've missed you and our son,' he murmured, pressing his face into the curve of her neck.

'We've missed you, too,' Jenna said, trying to drag her eyes away from the pink cardigan barely visible from under the chair. She'd clearly underestimated how dangerous Nicole could be.

* * *

'Don't tell me you've found room for more potted plants in the house?' Paul asked as he stepped out onto the patio. At one end was a table and chairs and the other end had a small potting table that he'd built for Jenna. She was leaning over it now with a bag of potting mix and a glossy peace lily. Next to it was a large ceramic pot that he recognised as coming from the garden centre where she liked to shop.

'Don't worry, I'm not turning the place into a jungle.' She looked up at him and smiled. The smooth hairstyle she'd taken to wearing was gone and her hair was pulled back in a messy ponytail, while there was a smudge of soil on her nose. She looked gorgeous. 'It's for Alison. I wanted to take her out to lunch to say thank you for helping me at the hospital, but she had to wait in the house for the electrician, so I'm going round there. She won't let me bring any food, so this is the next best thing. It's a pity you can't come.'

'I know. But I'm sure you two will have plenty to talk about without me in the way,' Paul said. He'd been mildly surprised when Jenna had said she wanted to see Alison today, but he'd soon realised it was a blessing in disguise since he would be free to confront Nicole.

'It will be nice to spend more time with her,' Jenna admitted as he walked over and kissed her. He gently rested his hand on her belly and felt the taut skin, which enclosed his son like a protective shield. It's exactly what he was doing. Being a shield to protect Jenna and their child from Nicole's deluded machinations.

Jenna left the house an hour later and he waited until her car had turned out of the street before he set the security system and climbed into his own car. The address Alison had given him was on the other side of town in an upmarket apartment block that had been recently completed.

It was exactly the kind of place Nicole would pick to live in.

He parked round the corner and lifted out the huge bunch of flowers he'd ordered. Unlike the wilted ones from the corner shop, these came from an upmarket florist and had cost far too much money.

Jenna wasn't the type of person who ever checked his credit card statement, but all the same he'd used cash, not wanting her to think he was giving flowers to someone else. The heady perfume caused his throat to tighten as he walked up to the three-storey block and craned his neck.

There were three apartments on the second floor. Was she standing at the window of one of them right now? Watching him? Did she feel smug that she'd come back and tried to come between him and Jenna? She'd always liked to be in control.

The pathway was flanked by a well-maintained garden and led up to a slick glass doorway and a discreet intercom system. He scanned the directory.

Nicole Williams. Apartment 4.

The letters began to dance in front of his eyes and memories pushed at his skull: of the first time he'd gone back to Nicole's apartment; of her slipping out of her impossibly expensive dress until she was wearing nothing but a couple of scraps of lace. Back then he'd been mesmerised by her. Her beauty and charm had concealed her ruthlessness, her need to win at all costs.

He'd made excuses for it. After all, just because she didn't have scars running up and down her arm like he did, it didn't mean she didn't have her own wounds. But they were better hidden. She hadn't told him much about her past. Only little snippets. He couldn't blame her. He'd been the same.

No one who'd experienced what they had wanted to revisit it more than they had to.

But it had to stop. For Jenna's sake. And for his son's.

He pressed her buzzer. Once, twice, three times. But there was no answer. He hadn't really expected there would since he'd gone onto her social media page last night and discovered she was going out with friends to see a movie. He'd timed his visit to coincide so that when she came home, he would be waiting. Then she wouldn't have a choice but to speak to him face to face.

He would finally find out what happened that night. *And* let her know that if she kept trying to play her games he really would go to the police.

He fumbled with his school lanyard and slipped it round his neck, while tucking a pencil behind his ear, hoping he looked like a stressed delivery agent. Then he pressed the intercom for apartment three.

'Yes?' a woman's discombobulated voice answered.

'I have some flowers for Nicole Williams,' Paul said. 'But no one's answering. I was instructed to leave them by the door if no one was at home. But they didn't mention that I couldn't get in. Any chance you can buzz me up?'

There was silence from down the other end of the intercom and then the woman let out a pained sigh.

'Fine,' the woman said before the door made a clicking noise.

Paul let out his breath and turned the handle before the neighbour could change her mind.

The reception area was overly ornate with marble floors, a huge gold-framed mirror and dull lighting. There were locked mailboxes and Paul stopped at Nicole's, peering in through the slit to see if any envelopes had piled up. It seemed empty, which meant Nicole had been collecting her mail.

There was a lift at the far end, and he quickly walked over to it. It was a short ride and when the doors opened it was to another marbled hallway with four doors along it. One opened up and a woman with short blonde hair poked her head out to watch him. It was obviously the person who'd let him in.

He gave her a cheery smile. 'Thanks, you're a lifesaver.'

'Yeah, well, don't thank me. The woman who lives there has a terrible temper. Last time one of her deliveries got returned to the depot and the whole bloody floor knew about it. Leave them over there, by her door.' The woman pointed and then waited until Paul had put them down on a nondescript doormat and made his way back to the lift. Seemingly satisfied, the woman disappeared as soon as the doors closed shut. Paul went back down to the ground floor but didn't walk out of the building. He hurried over to the stairwell.

He climbed back up to the second floor and carefully opened the fire door. There was a shallow recess and he stepped into it. He longed to walk up to Nicole's door now and pound on it, but the neighbour had already seen him, and he didn't want to risk her hearing him. He settled down to wait until she left.

An hour passed and his stomach grumbled from lack of food, and he was almost wondering if the whole thing had been a bad idea when the door from number three swung open, and the blonde woman stepped out.

Paul pressed himself back into the recess and waited until she stepped into the lift. He waited another ten minutes to make sure she hadn't forgotten anything before he finally ventured back up to Nicole's door.

He side-stepped the flowers and took the small kit of tools he'd purchased yesterday. It had been surprisingly easy to get them, as had finding a YouTube tutorial. Though practising on his office door was a bit different to being fully exposed in a hallway where he didn't live.

Paul's hands shook as he lifted out the smallest file and inserted it. Two minutes later the door clicked. Grim laughter caught in his throat as he turned the handle and opened the door. He paused only to pick up the flowers before he stepped inside.

There was an open plan kitchen and a small dining table to one side and a couple of leather sofas facing a large television, while to the front was a long window that looked out to the sweeping views of the nearby hills.

Nicole's familiar scent was everywhere but the place felt sterile and empty. Panic pounded in his chest as he stalked into the bedroom and looked around. There was a bed in the centre, but no sheets were on it. He opened the wardrobe, and it was empty except for a piece of paper on the carpet.

He snatched it up.

Do you really think I'd give Alison my address?

He dropped the flowers to the floor and swore under his breath. This was getting beyond a joke. He yanked his phone out and pulled up his messages. He quickly stabbed the screen.

Why won't you meet me?

The reply was almost instant.

I told you. Leave that bitch and then we can talk.

Paul ground his teeth.

That isn't going to happen.

Ping. Another response came in.

We'll see.

24

THE HORROR CONTINUES
by Aaron Richards

While the name suppression continues on the eleven-year-old girl discovered locked in a tiny cellar cupboard, the horrors keep coming. It has now been revealed that the child, who was in the foster system, had been missing from her appointed family for over two months. The family in question didn't report the child missing for fear of losing the payments and had simply hoped she had run away.

The chilling social media posts made by the defendants, Stefan Taylor and Sharon Willis, tell a different story. In a now-deleted post, Taylor said they'd bought a brown van with a distinctive snake painted on the side. The same van had been seen by multiple witnesses in the days leading up to the child's original disappearance. It is believed that they used the van to abduct the girl and take up residence some eighty miles away. The child was next seen with shorter hair and using a different name. She was enrolled to attend a local primary but only ever attended twice.

Neither the original disappearance or the child's lack of attendance at either the original or new school was followed up, and questions are now being asked. But it's obvious that the system has once again let down a child who relied on them for protection and care.

25

'You're so sweet,' Alison said as she clutched the peace lily and ushered Jenna into the house. It was a narrow two up, two down and the front room was brightly furnished with an emerald-coloured sofa and a club chair in red velvet. The walls were white but there were several splashy prints on them.

'You're welcome. My way of saying thank you for last week.' The truth was that after discovering the pink cardigan in the house, Jenna hadn't been able to think about anything else.

If Nicole had left her a secret message, who was to say that she hadn't been in contact with Paul as well? Had Jenna been right about why he'd missed the scan? It would explain the terrible nightmare he'd had last night. She wasn't even sure if he remembered it, but he'd spent most of the night thrashing his legs and moaning, as if he was trying to outrun something that wouldn't leave him alone.

And that was why she had started digging. She'd searched again through Bridget's social media feeds to see if there were any messages or photos she hadn't seen and had done the same with anyone else she could think of. She hadn't had much luck, and so she'd done a general search, but apart from a LinkedIn profile and a few newspaper articles, she hadn't been able to find anything about Nicole.

Jenna still wasn't quite sure how Alison could help her, but she had to try.

'It was nothing,' Alison said before wrinkling her nose. 'I'm not sure whether I should admit that Rob gave me an orchid a few years ago and I managed to kill it.'

Jenna laughed. 'Don't worry. This isn't nearly as difficult to care for as an orchid. It needs a little bit of light and water, and you'll be fine. By the way, this is a gorgeous room.'

'Thanks,' Alison said. 'I forgot you haven't been here before. Sorry we couldn't go out to lunch. It's nearly impossible to get a tradesman who will make house calls on the weekend, I didn't want to run the risk of missing him.'

'Tell me about it. We had a leak in the bathroom six months ago and we waited weeks for the plumber to show up. Nightmare.'

'I bet,' Alison agreed as she walked through to a small dining room that led onto an equally bright kitchen. 'Now, would you like a cup of tea or coffee? I've made a quiche for lunch but it's still in the oven.'

'A herbal tea would be lovely, thanks.'

'Great. Sit down while I boil the kettle. Paul would have my guts for garters if I kept you standing. I've never seen him so protective.'

'Really?' Jenna beamed as she climbed onto a wooden stool tucked under the breakfast bar while Alison busied herself in the kitchen.

'Yes, it's sickeningly sweet,' Alison chuckled as she filled the teapot and scooped in some leaves. She swirled it round a couple of time and carried it over to Jenna. 'So, are you going to tell me the real reason you're here?'

'T-to say thank you,' Jenna protested but Alison raised a brow as if to say she wasn't buying it. 'Am I that obvious?'

'Let's just say that if we were playing poker, I'd have all your money by now.' Alison grinned as she passed over a china mug and held up the teapot so she could pour. 'Is it about Paul?'

Jenna clutched the cup and let out a sigh. 'Now I feel like a terrible person. I basically invited my way into your home, and I had an ulterior motive.'

'Don't be so hard on yourself. Paul and I go back a long way, and if I can help you, I will. Though, for the record, whatever's bothering you is probably something you should talk to him about.'

Jenna swallowed. 'It's complicated.'

Alison nursed her tea in her hands. 'Let me guess. Nicole.'

'You're right. I *am* bad at poker.' Jenna put down her tea.

'If it's any consolation, I've been expecting you to ask me more about Nicole ever since you and Paul hooked up,' Alison confessed.

'You have?' Jenna said in surprise, wondering how many hours of anguish she could've avoided if she'd been more direct. Alison gave her a reassuring smile.

'Don't worry. I only thought it because that's what I'd do if my new partner had a glamorous ex-fiancée. So, what do you want to know about Nicole?'

'I'm trying to figure out what kind of person she is. Everyone seems to have a love/hate relationship with her. And then there's the fact I can hardly find anything about her on the Internet.'

Alison raised an eyebrow. 'You've gone looking?'

Heat bloomed in Jenna's cheeks. 'Now I sound like a crazy

girlfriend. I swear I'm not. And it's not like I check Paul's phone or anything. It's just—'

'It's okay.' Alison cut her off with a small smile. 'Been there, done that. The first year after Rob left, I swear I spent more time on his feeds than on my own. But a word of advice. That way madness lies. Try to forget she's back. I'm sure she'll disappear in a few days and things will settle down.'

Jenna swallowed, wishing it was that simple. 'She left a message for me the other day, and there have been a couple of other times when I think she's tried to contact me.'

'What kind of message?' Alison said in a sharp voice. 'Did she call you?'

'Not exactly. She came into the house and put one of her pieces of clothing on the chair, along with a note. *Stop playing with my things.*'

'Hell. Jenna, are you serious? She broke into your house and threatened you? Please tell me you told Paul.'

Jenna flinched. 'Not yet. I didn't want him to worry. But then I wondered if she's been doing the same thing to him as she's doing to me? Has he said anything to you?'

Alison pressed her lips together, clearly unhappy. 'The pair of you need to talk. I know you think you're protecting him, and he clearly thinks he's protecting you, but has it ever occurred to you that's what Nicole wants? To separate you?'

So Nicole *had* been in contact with Paul.

Her stomach dropped and she pushed the tea away but, before she could speak, the doorbell rang.

Alison gave her an apologetic grimace. 'Sorry, that's the electrician. I need to show him the power socket in the cellar and then I'll be back, so we can figure out this mess once and for all.'

Jenna gratefully nodded her head as Alison disappeared out into the hallway. She could hear them talking about circuit breakers and lighting before there were more footsteps as she led him into the cellar. A few minutes later, she reappeared.

'Okay, he should be down there for at least an hour.' Alison pulled up a second stool and sat. 'Have you told anyone else about what's happened? Paul mentioned you're close to your neighbour, and that you have a sister. Surely one of them must've suggested going to the police.'

The police? Jenna swallowed. Going to the police would make everything so formal. And what real proof did she have? Plus there was Paul's job. After the Eric Chambers scandal, she knew Paul and Tim had been doing everything they could to keep Hepworth off the radar. How would it look if the Deputy Head suddenly got a restraining order against his ex-fiancée?

'Paul would hate it,' Jenna said as her phone beeped. She glanced at the screen, in case it was Paul but an unknown number flashed up along with the message.

Someone's been sleeping in my bed.

Jenna frowned as she tapped on the message and a photo appeared.

It was of a bedroom. It was dark but there were shafts of moonlight pouring through the window onto two sleeping figures. They were both concealed by the covers but on the bedside table was a familiar light as well as several library books.

She let out a scream. It was her bedroom, and someone had been standing in there watching her and Paul sleep.

'What is it?' Alison said, her gaze going from Jenna's face to the phone. 'Oh, shit.' She snatched the phone up and turned it off, before she reached for Jenna's hand. 'Okay, I'm going to take you over to the sofa so you can lie down, and then I'm calling Paul. Whatever Nicole's playing at has gone on long enough.'

26

Paul finished the call and put down his phone. Jenna was curled up on the sofa. Her face was pale and drawn but she'd stopped crying now. Christ, what a mess.

At least Alison had forced them to both talk about what had been happening. Each had been equally shocked to discover Nicole had come into the house on more than one occasion. Jenna had also shown him the diary and the box of clothes, none of which he'd known was there. The diary had been painful to read. Full of Nicole's endearing but infuriating personality.

And she'd had an affair.

That part had been a complete surprise. Sure, Nicole flirted with everyone who crossed her path but being physical with people wasn't what she liked. It was the psychological victory.

After Jenna finished talking, Paul told her as much as he could, without including the visit to the grave and the lost memory of what really happened the night she 'disappeared'. But as soon as he knew what was real and what wasn't, he would tell her the rest. It was the least he could do.

It had been enough, and Jenna had wept openly as she'd clung to him.

God, if anything had happened to her...

He joined her now and threaded her fingers through his. 'The security company have reset the keypad codes and will change the locks tomorrow. I've also hired a plain clothed security guard who will keep an eye on the house twenty-four hours a day. Their speciality is discretion so there is a good chance we won't ever see them.'

Jenna nodded, tightening her grip on his hand. 'Is it really all necessary?'

'I hope not,' he said, suddenly weary to his bone. 'But I'm not taking any chances. I need to keep you and the baby safe.'

'We need to keep each other safe,' she corrected. 'We're a team, which means we have to be honest. No more secrets. Promise?'

'Promise,' he agreed, getting to his feet. 'No more secrets.'

'Oh, my God, you have more security than the Palace.' Lucy stepped into the house on Saturday. Her sharp eyes seemed to take in the extra window locks and new keypad that was embedded into the wall. Jenna wondered what she would say if she could see the barely visible John, who silently watched their house from a variety of different cars. Jenna had only seen him twice the entire week, but he'd been sending Paul comprehensive reports each night.

'There have been a few break-ins in the area.' She reached for her bag. It had been a week since Nicole had sent her the photo of them sleeping, and since then neither of them had heard from her. Jenna wanted to think that it was at an end, but Paul still had a haunted expression. Like he was waiting for the other shoe to drop. And so, while he'd gone to Hepworth each day, Jenna had agreed to work from home, but when Lucy had called, insisting they needed to go shopping, Jenna found herself wanting to.

She needed to see more than the four walls of the house.

'Which is why you should consider moving. You need to start thinking about school catchments,' Lucy said in a prim voice, which Jenna ignored. 'Anyway, let's go. I don't want to get caught in traffic.'

'Okay, let me tell Paul that we're off.' She nodded for her sister to wait while she went upstairs to the second bedroom that Paul used as an office.

On one side of the narrow hallway was the master bedroom and the soon-to-be nursery that was filled with cardboard boxes, waiting to be unpacked and their contents assembled, and to the side of this was a small room that acted as an office for them both. Paul was sitting at the desk, a pile of school reports by his elbow, while his face was fixed to a monitor that showed the camera feed for their front and back doors as well as down the side of the house.

'Hey.' Paul looked up. Dark smudges ran under his eyes and his skin was wan. Not surprising, considering his lack of sleep. Even the nights he did nod off, he was soon thrashing around, plagued by the nightmares he didn't talk about.

'Hey. Lucy's here so we're going to take off.'

'I still don't think this is a good idea.'

'I know, and that's why I love you.' Jenna pressed a warm kiss to his brow. He wrapped his arms round her waist and rested his head on her growing stomach. The tension in his body lessened. They'd spent the last two nights discussing it, and Paul eventually conceded that Jenna couldn't stay cooped up forever. 'I promise I'll be careful.'

'You better. Tell Lucy to take no prisoners.'

Jenna smiled. She pitied the person who crossed her sister. She gave Paul another kiss and then walked back downstairs to where her sister was waiting.

* * *

'So, where next?' said Lucy two hours later as they walked out of the small café at the far end of the shopping mall. Jenna clutched a bag of maternity clothes. This time, she'd let Lucy help her and not rely on Nicole's diary entries.

'I still wanted to look at a drone for Paul's birthday. He says he doesn't want anything, but you should see his face light up every time he sees one.'

'What is it with men and gadgets?' Lucy complained, but for once there was no sting in her voice as they threaded their way through the Saturday afternoon crowds to the large outlet store on the second floor.

A harassed sales rep was dealing with someone holding a giant television, complaining that it didn't work, so Jenna and Lucy wandered up and down the aisles looking for anything resembling a drone. But without someone to advise them where to look and which model to buy, their search was next to useless. She craned her head to see if anyone could help, but two other staff members had now joined the argument, and suddenly Jenna felt tired.

'You know what? Let's just go. I can order one online, and it's far too busy in here.'

'Agreed. Plus half the customers stink of body odour. It's like they don't bathe.'

'Shh,' Jenna chided her sister, knowing it wouldn't make any difference.

'What? It's not rude if it's the truth,' Lucy replied as they stepped outside the store. 'Now, we probably have time to—'

'Excuse me,' a female voice said, and the two sisters turned to where a security guard stood in front of them. She was at least five foot nine, with red hair tied back into a knot and thick arm muscles pressing against the blue shirt. 'Can you please come with me?'

'Come with you?' Lucy blinked. 'Why would we want to do that?'

'Please come with me,' the woman said, her gaze never leaving Jenna's. 'We need to search your bags. You've been seen shoplifting.'

Some Kids Never Stand a Chance
by Aaron Richards

Police are now getting a clearer picture on the history of the unnamed child who was rescued from her cellar prison almost two months ago. It is believed that she was first put into the foster system when her parents both died in a tragic house fire that left them so badly burned that they could only be identified by dental records. A credible friend of the family revealed that an aunt had offered to take the child in, but authorities had dismissed it as being an unsuitable residence. The child in question is still being cared for in a protected environment with counselling and support available to help her come to terms with her short but tragic life. And it's too soon to say how this trauma will affect her in later years…

Paul wheeled the lawnmower into the shed and wiped his brow. His legs were covered in grass and his T-shirt clung to his back. A car exhaust backfired on the street, and he stiffened. Damn. Was he going to jump at every single noise now? The lack of sleep hadn't helped. Every night, he was scared that if he drifted off Nicole would somehow find her way into the bedroom and take another photograph.

Or worse.

The first time she'd hit him was a year after they started dating. They'd been out with friends and had started bickering in the taxi on the way home. He couldn't even remember what it was about. One of those silly things like he'd picked up the wrong milk. But after they were inside, it had suddenly escalated, and Nicole had turned on him and slashed her long nails across his face.

He knew what Nicole was capable of, but he'd chosen to ignore it. And now Jenna was paying the price.

He stalked to the kitchen for a glass of water and downed it in one. Feeling better, he sat down as his phone rang.

Jenna's name flashed on the screen, and he snatched it up.

'Everything okay?'

'Not exactly,' Jenna said in a small breathy voice. He stiffened. He knew he shouldn't have let her go out. Even with Lucy for company. If Nicole had tried to confront her, he would—

He cut himself off. This wasn't about Nicole, it was about Jenna. 'What's going on?'

'I'm at the police station. You've got to come here straight away. They've accused me of shoplifting. I didn't do it. I promise you I didn't do it, but they don't believe me.' Her voice choked.

Police? His vision blurred and jagged memories pushed in his mind, sending waves of pain through his skull. *Not now.* He gripped the table and forced them away.

'Which station are you at?'

'The one at the shopping centre. They've got some sort of police area with security guards where they bring people.'

'Stay put and I'll be with you as soon as I can.' He ended the call and grabbed his jacket and keys. The Saturday afternoon traffic wasn't too bad, and he put his foot down, praying to the traffic gods to give him the green lights he needed. They obliged and he was there within twenty minutes.

He gritted his teeth as he stalked into the shopping mall, the bright lights stabbing at his eyes. He headed for the information desk. A woman with long grey hair pointed to the lifts and told him to go to the third floor and turn right by a shop selling sunglasses.

Pushing past a few casual shoppers, he finally reached it. It was down a stark hallway with a plain white door. He tried the handle, but it was locked. He banged several times until someone came and let him in.

'I'm Paul Henderson, you have my wife here.'

'Come this way,' the security officer said, leading him into a small room.

Jenna was sitting on a plastic chair, her face devoid of colour. There were several reusable bags on the table, their contents spilling out. Paul scanned the room.

'Where's Lucy?'

The officer grimaced. 'She's next door demanding to see the security footage.' As he spoke, Paul could hear a raised voice, which was answered by Lucy's glacial tone. He felt sorry for anyone who had to face her in court.

Paul sat down next to Jenna, and she leaned into him. She wasn't crying but her cheeks were damp. 'What exactly happened?'

'They said I stole some headphones. But I wasn't even in that section of the store. We were looking for a drone. For your birthday. But it was too busy so we decided to leave. As soon as we walked out the door, they stopped me.'

Paul turned to the guard. 'Did you see her putting them in her bag?'

'No, but as she left the store, I could see that something was sticking out of the back of her shopping bag. On closer inspection it was the headphones.'

'Yes, but I didn't put them there,' Jenna said in a frustrated voice. 'If I wanted headphones I could have bought my own.'

'You think we haven't heard that one before?' The guard raised an eyebrow. 'The headphones were in her bag, and she left the store without paying for them. That's theft, anyway you cut it.'

Unless it was a set up.

Paul's skin crawled as the most obvious explanation flashed into his mind.

Nicole.

Next to him, Jenna stiffened, as if reading his mind.

'Look,' he started to say but before he could, the door swung open and Lucy walked back in, her phone in hand.

'Ah, Paul, you're here. Good. You can help Jenna pack her up purchases. We're leaving.'

'What?' The guard's jaw went slack. 'I don't think so.'

'Actually, Bill.' A muscular woman walked in behind Jenna. 'There's been a mistake, and we owe Miss Reynolds an apology.'

'What do you mean? Did you find out how they got into my bag?'

'We sure did,' Lucy said in a calm voice as she tapped her phone. 'The camera footage clearly shows someone walking up behind Jenna and slipping them into her bag. It's too blurry to properly identify them so no charges will be pressed. I took a photo with my phone of when it showed this happening on the video.'

'Can I see the photo?' Paul said, trying to hide the panic in his voice.

'Sure.' Lucy pressed the screen and Jenna leaned closer to him. His hand slid into hers and he gave her a reassuring squeeze as the black and white image came up. It was grainy, though a partial face was visible through the blur of pixels. And it wasn't Nicole.

He leaned closer and frowned as he turned to Jenna, whose eyes were no longer filled with tears, but with confusion.

The face was one they both knew well. It was their next-door neighbour.

Daniel.

29

'As your lawyer, I'm not happy about ignoring this,' Lucy said an hour later as she pushed away her empty teacup and got to her feet. 'You should be taking this evidence to the police and pressing charges. If it wasn't for the footage you could've ended up with a record, which might have greatly affected your chances of getting the baby into a good school.'

Jenna bit back the hysterical laughter rising in her throat. Even with everything going on, her sister was thinking about schools.

'We at least want to talk to Daniel first. And Bridget. They're our friends,' Jenna said as she squeezed her sister's hand. 'But thank you so much. You were pretty amazing back there.'

'All in a day's work.' Lucy shrugged as she picked her car keys off the table. 'But I mean it about pressing charges. If you're not happy with Daniel's answers, let me know.'

'We will,' Paul said as he put an arm round Jenna's shoulder. Heat raced down her spine and she pressed into him, stealing his warmth and energy. Her whole life seemed to be turning into a surreal movie. One that she had no control over.

They waited until Lucy's car disappeared into the distance before turning to each other.

'I still don't understand any of this,' Jenna said.

'There's only one way to find out. I need to go and talk to him.' Paul pressed his mouth onto her brow.

'You're not going alone.' Jenna pulled away from him. 'Whatever's going on involves me too.'

Paul's mouth tightened, like he was going to argue, but then he let out a breath. 'You're right. No more secrets.'

'Thank you.' She gave him a grateful look. Not that he'd agreed for her to go with him, but that he was no longer shutting her out. Her biggest fear was that barrier of reserve he'd always had would reappear.

They locked the house and slipped through the gate that separated the two houses. The front door was shut but classical music drifted through, which meant at least Daniel was home.

Jenna pressed the door chime and several seconds later she could hear footsteps and Eddie's excited bark. The door opened up and Bridget appeared. She was dressed in her regular gym gear, but her face was wan.

'Oh, hey. Did we have something planned?' She rubbed her brow, as if willing for a memory to appear. Paul shook his head.

'No, but we need to talk. Is Daniel here?'

'Daniel?' Bridget clutched at the doorframe, not moving. 'Now isn't really a good time—'

'This is important,' Paul said in a firm voice, honed from years of teaching.

'Why? What's going on?' Bridget's eyes widened and her grip on the door increased.

'It's okay.' Daniel appeared behind his wife, his shoulders slumped, as if he'd been waiting for something like this to happen. 'Let them in, Bridget. You might as well all hear it at the same time.'

Wordlessly Daniel strode down the hall and into the well-decorated lounge. Jenna had been in there hundreds of times before and she'd never seen so much as a drink coaster out of place, but now it looked dishevelled. Newspapers were stacked on the side of the lounge and the giant fiddle leaf fig was drooping, as if it had been neglected.

It was clear that something was going on between the couple, but Jenna could hardly spare it a thought. She had too many things of her own going on. Like why Daniel would want to get her arrested for shoplifting.

'Anyone want a drink?' Daniel poured himself a glass of whisky.

'For God's sake,' Bridget bristled. 'Jenna's pregnant and Paul isn't drinking. Not to mention it's only four in the afternoon. Tell me what's going on? You've been acting strangely for weeks.'

'Weeks?' Paul's face tightened and he clenched his fists. Jenna caught her breath. She'd never seen him look so mad before and her pulse thumped, hoping that this didn't escalate any further. 'All this time it was *you*?'

His voice was like a dart and Daniel visibly flinched.

'Oh, God.' Daniel drained his glass and dropped down onto the lounge, knocking the stack of newspapers to the floor. No one touched them. 'I'm so sorry. I didn't want to do any of it.'

'Do what?' Bridget's voice went up an octave as she studied Daniel's face before turning to Paul and Jenna. 'Someone please tell me what's going on.'

'Jenna was arrested for shoplifting today,' Paul said, his voice glacial and his eyes never leaving Daniel's slumped figure. 'Thankfully the video footage showed us what really happened. Daniel was in the store, and he put something in her bag. That's why we're here. Do you have any idea what stress can do to an unborn child, and to the mother? Jenna's four months pregnant.'

'Shoplifting?' Bridget blinked looking from Jenna to her husband. 'That's impossible. Why on earth would Daniel do that?'

'I'm so sorry. Sorry for all of it,' Daniel moaned, ignoring his wife's questioning gaze.

'What else?' Paul was statue still, and Jenna almost put her hand on his wrist to see if he had a pulse.

Swallowing back a shudder, Daniel finally looked up. 'Bridget had a key to your house and the security code. I used it to put a letter on the hall table, and to take a necklace. There was also a cardigan... I was meant to put a parcel in there as well, but Bridget found it and delivered it by mistake. Sh-she made me do it.'

'She?' Bridget blinked, as if her husband had suddenly started speaking a second language. 'Who are you talking about?'

'Nicole,' Jenna said, the words dragging across her throat like gravel. 'He's talking about Nicole. But I still don't understand why?'

Bridget didn't seem to have heard. Instead, she continued to stare at her husband, pain slipping into the lines round her mouth, tightening them until her face was a mask of hurt.

Her voice came out as a whisper. 'You've spoken to her and didn't tell me? How could you do that to me?'

'To you?' Paul widened his eyes. 'I think this is bigger than the fact he had an affair with my ex-fiancée. It's about the fact he systematically tried to break up me and Jenna, and I want to know why.'

Daniel barked with laughter and stood up. His eyes were bright and were tinged with mania. 'You think *I* had an affair with Nicole? That's rich.'

Paul went to open his mouth but shut it again. Jenna didn't blame him. They both stared as Daniel marched over to the drinks' trolley and poured out another whisky. He drowned it in one and then slammed it down.

Finally, he spoke. 'Do you want to tell them, my lovely wife? Or shall I?'

'Tell us what?' Paul growled.

Bridget wrapped her arms round her waist and started to rock. 'Daniel wasn't the one to have an affair with Nicole. I was.'

30

Silence spread through the room like a contagion. Bridget stared at the wall while her husband glared at her, pain written across his face. Jenna was motionless, shock written deep in her eyes.

Paul blinked, his mind trying to fit this new information into the fractured narrative in his mind. The pieces swirled together, trying to lodge themselves into the missing gaps.

Certain memories played out. Of them going out to dinner for their anniversary. They'd then come home, tipsy, and made love in the back garden under the stars. Yet when he recalled it again, they'd come home and argued. About something silly, and Nicole had stalked out of the house, not reappearing until the morning.

Her eyes had been bright, and the Cheshire Cat grin had told him wherever she'd been, it hadn't been alone.

Had she been with Bridget?

'Go on,' Daniel's voice was rough. 'You might as well tell them what happened.'

Bridget shot her husband a bitter glance before squaring her shoulders. 'I thought I loved her. It was three years ago. Daniel and I had been trying for a baby for so long, and every month it was like I was being mocked. Not just by my period, but by the whole world. Daniel's family, my friends, the media. Babies were everywhere.' Her voice choked and she looked towards the ceiling, as if trying to stop the tears from flowing.

'Nicole happened to come over one afternoon. She wanted my cousin's phone number. She's a freelance florist and Nicole was interested in using her for the wedding. Anyway, she found me crying and before I knew it, I'd told her everything. But she didn't feel sorry for me. She burst out laughing.'

'Because she was a bitch,' Daniel said with a growl.

'No,' Bridget snapped back at him. 'Because she knew that babies weren't the be all or end all. That we're more than wombs. Plus, if I wasn't pregnant then it meant we could drink cocktails. It was such a relief to let my hair down and relax. That night as she left, she ran her finger along my cheek and said that she always thought I'd make a sexy drunk. Then she kissed me.'

Paul clenched his knuckles together. Where the hell had he been? At work? At home, sitting in his study while Nicole played seductress? Or had his memory been playing tricks on him again?

Bridget didn't seem to notice.

'I didn't see her for a week. I think she was away on work, but that kiss was *all* I could think about. It was like a virus that invaded my entire body, leaving no room for any other thoughts. Any other feelings. She arrived back on the Saturday and that afternoon she called and asked me to come over. When I got to the house she was upstairs in the bedroom.' Bridget paused. 'She was in lingerie. I – I thought she must have been waiting for Paul. Maybe she wanted to get a second opinion on the outfit. But then she—'

She broke off and lowered her head.

'Did she ever say anything about me? About the wedding?' Paul asked. Next to him, Jenna flinched.

Bridget was quiet. 'It wasn't like that. We didn't talk about you or Daniel. It was about us. It was beautiful.'

'Until she dumped you,' Daniel said in a bitter voice.

'That's not what happened,' Bridget said, but it wasn't clear who she was trying to convince.

'So how did it end?'

'I still don't know. About a month before she moved to Australia, she sent me a text saying it was over. And that was that. Every time I tried to speak to her, she shut me down. Like I didn't exist.'

Paul ran a hand through his hair. It was such classic Nicole that he almost felt sorry for Bridget.

It was Jenna who spoke next. She turned to Daniel. 'So how do you fit into any of this? Why did you do it?'

Daniel began to pace the room. 'Four weeks ago, she sent me a text, saying that she needed my help. I told her to go screw herself. The affair almost destroyed our marriage and the day she left for Australia was the greatest day of my life. Hearing she'd returned was a kick in the gut. Especially since Bridget and I were finally getting our life back together.'

'What did she have over you?' Paul said. It was a guess, but the look Bridget and Daniel shared confirmed it.

'There was a tape. Of her and Bridget together. It was... explicit.'

Bridget let out a strangled gasp as she stared at her husband. 'She said no one would ever see it. I thought that when she left, she would've—'

'Destroyed it?' Paul raised an eyebrow. It showed how little Bridget really understood Nicole. Acid burned in his throat as he turned back to Daniel. 'So you terrified Jenna because you were worried the world would see the tape?'

'I'm so sorry.' Daniel came to a halt, his breath ragged. 'I'm a surgeon and this town is small. We couldn't afford the scandal. But... I told Nicole it was a bad idea. Then, when you changed the locks, I thought it was over. But she wanted me to do one last thing. She promised if I did it she would give me the tape.'

'Why didn't you go to the police?' Jenna whispered. 'Or tell us?'

'Because he didn't want me to know about it,' Bridget said. She looked haggard and Paul almost felt sorry for her. He knew what it was like to be under Nicole's hypnotic pull. That had been him for a long time. Swept up in her energy, unable to walk away even when you knew you should.

'Why did you lie about Daniel and Nicole having an affair?' Jenna suddenly chimed in. 'You clearly knew it wasn't true.'

Bridget bowed her head. 'I was angry at her for leaving me. I didn't want you to think she was a nice person.' She was silent for a long time then she turned to her husband, voice choked. 'Did you see her?'

Daniel's jaw clenched. 'Christ, Bridge. Nothing's changed, has it? You promised me it was over, but look at you. The bloody mention of her name and you're right back where you were. Why don't you get it? She wasn't some great love. She got a new job in Australia and left you behind. I'm the one who stayed. Not her.'

Bridget buried her face in her hands and Jenna hurried over to comfort her.

Paul studied Daniel, who seemed to be running the gamut of emotions, from shame to anger to bitterness. 'Did she say why she was doing it? What the hell she thought she'd achieve?'

Daniel looked up, giving Paul a pitying smile. 'I thought that was obvious. She wants you to leave Jenna.'

* * *

Paul leaned back in his study chair and glared at his watch. It was two-thirty in the morning and his eyes were gritty with fatigue. Jenna had fallen into an exhausted sleep as soon as she'd finished her dinner. Not that she'd eaten much. She'd spent most of the meal pushing her food round the plate, her eyes bright with unshed tears. There hadn't been a lot of conversation between them, mainly because Paul had no idea what to say to make it okay.

Because it *wasn't* okay.

Jenna was good and sweet and kind and didn't deserve to be dragged into any of this.

Even in sleep, her face was still racked with the sting of Bridget and Daniel's betrayal, and while he'd also been shocked, it was less painful, because he knew what Nicole was capable of.

She wants you to leave Jenna.

Frustration pounded in his brow as he tried to work out how far Nicole would go.

Would she expose him? Or take it out on Jenna? But without knowing what had really happened between them, he couldn't judge what her next move would be. All because of his wretched memory. The irony was that his memory always became worse when his insomnia was bad.

He stood up, restless tremors running up and down his legs, making sitting impossible. If he wasn't so worried about leaving Jenna on her own, he would've gone for a jog to try to shake some of the unwanted energy out of his system. As it was, he was stuck in the house. He stalked across the room, his eyes landing on the leather-bound diary sitting on the shelf.

NW was engraved on the cover.

When Jenna had confessed to finding the box of clothes and the diary, Paul had only been able to read a couple of pages before putting it aside. It had been too overwhelmingly 'Nicole' and every word was like a jab in the ribs. As if she'd written them knowing he might one day read it.

He swallowed and walked back to his chair. If he was going to be awake, he might as well do something useful. He turned to page one and read.

> *Gwendolyn says that it's not uncommon for two children of trauma to be attracted to the other's shadow. She thinks we find comfort in the shared darkness.*
>
> *Maybe she's right. When I rage, when I flirt, when I sulk, he never judges me. He understands. Sometimes I think he's the only person who has ever truly loved me. And how do I repay him? By cheating on him.*
>
> *But he's so God damn good all the time. Sometimes I want to punch him in the mouth. To see how far I can push him. Gwendolyn says it's not Paul I'm trying to push, it's myself.*

As he turned page after page, it was clear Nicole had become a lot more comfortable at pouring out her opinions onto the page. The voice became clearer, almost razor sharp in her assessments. Even her affair.

If he'd found out at the time, he might have been devastated. Back before he knew what she'd done. Before he thought he knew what *he'd* done. But now it hardly registered. Jenna had shown him what proper love was like. Kind, gentle, compassionate.

He continued to read.

> *Gwendolyn also asked me how I'd feel if it was Paul who'd cheated? That's simple, I said to her. I would kill him.*
>
> *She thought I was joking. Which shows what a wildly average therapist she is. Because if she hasn't learned by now*

that I never joke, then she's doing a pretty bad bloody job of
trying to help me.

Paul shut the diary with a snap, but Nicole's words still
blurred in front of his eyes.

Kill him.

How could he have been so stupid? All this time he'd been
trying to figure out what had happened between them. What was
locked inside the vaults of his memory? But it turned out it didn't
really matter. All that mattered was that Nicole didn't believe in
having friendly exes. She didn't believe in letting anything stand
in the way of getting what she wanted.

Which meant that if he wanted to keep Jenna safe, he needed
to make sure she was far away from him.

He glanced at his phone. Four thirty-one. As soon as Jenna
was awake, he'd explain what needed to happen. Then he could
end things once and for all.

* * *

'I hate this.' Jenna stood at the bottom of the stairs. Her face was
forlorn and there were bags under her eyes. Paul gathered her up
into his arms, her warmth taking away some of the heaviness that
had settled over him since they'd discovered Daniel's role in their
lives.

Jenna hadn't been happy when Paul suggested she go and
stay with Lucy for a couple of days. Hell, he wasn't happy,
either.

'I hate it, too. But it's not you that she's trying to hurt, it's me.
So, as long as you're not nearby then you'll be safe.'

Jenna was silent. Only because they'd already thrashed it out.
She was worried that giving Nicole what she wanted would only

make things worse. And he agreed, but he also knew it couldn't go on like this. It needed to be over.

This terrible tension that stopped him from crossing back onto the side of the street he wanted to be. The one with Jenna. The one where they could get married and raise their son.

And then there were the police.

Jenna had floated it. He hadn't been able to explain the real reason why he couldn't go to the police. In case he'd done something that was as bad as murder.

He shut his eyes, once again willing the swirling fog to recede, but his only reward was bitter bile rising in his throat as his temples throbbed.

'Are you going to text her?'

'No.' He shook his head. 'I'm sick of letting her play games. Besides, she'd probably stand me up again. I'm going to find out where she's staying and confront her. This time on my terms.'

'Promise me that you'll be careful,' Jenna said. 'And that you'll come back to me. Paul, I couldn't bear if—' she broke off into a soft sob and he cradled her face with his hands.

'Hey,' he whispered, his eyes holding hers. 'There's nothing she can do to come between us. Remember, we're a team.'

'No secrets,' Jenna said, managing to give him a wobbly smile.

'No secrets,' he agreed and kissed her hard. The drive to Lucy's house was subdued and, while Jenna's sister didn't seem satisfied with the reason for the unexpected stay, she finally stopped questioning them and Paul drove away. He had work to do.

* * *

'You look like crap.' Tim passed over the jar of instant coffee. 'I thought you weren't drinking for the entire pregnancy.'

'I slept badly.' Paul took the jar and tipped it straight into the cup, not even bothering with a spoon. His prescription had run out last night and so he'd been forced to resort to codeine to help keep himself focused. His head was pounding, and his hand was shaking. The last two days had been a never-ending hunt on the Internet, trying to find where Nicole was staying. He'd even called up several of her friends that he vaguely remembered. But none of them knew the address. They said they'd only seen her once or twice, always at clubs, always being the centre of attention.

Typical Nicole.

She still hadn't responded to any of his messages, though her social media continued to be updated with her apparently carefree life. It hadn't been conducive to a good night's sleep, and every time he did drift off he'd be consumed by the same dream where he was lying in the ground with Nicole shovelling dirt into his face, and he'd wake up drenched in sweat.

At least Jenna was safe. An extra security guard was now discreetly fixed outside Lucy's house and there hadn't been any sign of Nicole, or anyone else watching the house. He hated that the only time Jenna had been in danger was when she was near him.

I'm nobody. Nothing.

Yet until he knew the truth about what had happened so that he could go to the police and get a restraining order against Nicole, he couldn't let Jenna come home.

'Well, make sure you get some rest,' Tim said before catching sight of his secretary. 'That's my cue. I'm interviewing for the rest of the day, but I purposely gave you the first slot tomorrow. The board will be fresh then and desperate to be dazzled, so make sure you bring your A game.'

'I will,' Paul said, trying not to grimace. He'd forgotten about the interview. It was almost comical at how bad the timing was.

Still, by tonight this whole thing would be over and then he could concentrate.

'Wow, you look rough,' Doug said in a cheerful voice as he walked over to the bench and poured a cup of tea from the large pot that had been brewing.

Alison gave Doug a sharp look then waited until he'd wandered off to join a group of teachers who were discussing VAR.

'He's such a heathen,' she said, by way of an apology for the music teacher. Then she let out a sigh. 'But he's right. You don't look like you've slept in a week. Has Nicole...' she trailed off, as if unable to predict what else Nicole might have been capable of.

He didn't blame her. Alison had never been a fan of Nicole. If only he'd listened to her sooner. He toyed with telling her about Daniel and Bridget and about the fact Jenna was staying with her sister, but he thought better of it.

'No, it seems like the whole thing has blown over.'

The worry in Alison's eyes faded. 'Thank goodness. Especially with the interview looming. Have you heard anything about the other candidates?'

He shook his head. 'No. It wouldn't be ethical if Tim had told me. Did you hear back from Penny Rivers? Was she shortlisted?'

'She called last night to say she was travelling up this morning. I think her interview is this afternoon. But don't let that faze you. She's a great administrator but a terrible fit for Hepworth. The board will see that. What time's your interview, I've forgotten?'

'Ten o'clock.'

'Well then, lunch will be on me. We can celebrate.'

'I like your optimism.'

'Rubbish,' she said in a no-nonsense voice. 'You're the best person for the job, and there is no way the board will miss that. Do you want me to write you a letter of recommendation?'

'Not necessary, but thanks all the same,' he said, grateful for the support. He'd never really considered Daniel or Bridget close friends, but still, what the pair of them had done felt like a betrayal. It was nice to know that at least one person was in his corner. 'So, are you going to give me the next update on Rob? You know Jenna grills me every night on how you two are going?' he deflected, and the worry in Alison's eyes faded.

'Great. He's got one more week in his current job and then he'll be down here for good. I'm still pinching myself.'

'It's Rob who should be pinching himself,' Paul said, trying to keep the tiredness out of his voice. He was happy for Alison. She deserved it but he couldn't help wishing he did as well. His future with Jenna and his son was so tantalisingly close. But like the fog of his mind, there was something dark and innocuous that was standing between him and what he wanted. It was like his crappy childhood was determined not to let him leave the pain behind. He shook away the dark thought.

He was going to get to the truth, no matter what the cost.

31

Paul staggered out of Boots, clutching his prescription tightly in his hands, the pills rattling as he walked. The day had dragged on, filled with meetings and classes and a detention for two girls who thought it would be funny to set their blazers on fire. The pounding in his brow had reached the point where every sound was a crescendo of pain. That's when he'd called his doctor and made an emergency appointment.

The late afternoon sun stabbed at his eyes, and he put his hands up to shield it, wishing he hadn't left his sunglasses in the car.

'Paul, hey,' a voice called out through the blur of bright glare, and Paul blinked as Eric Chambers came into view. Some of the colour had returned to his cheeks and he'd lost the unkempt look of someone who was wearing the same clothes they'd fallen asleep in. His shirt had been neatly ironed and his hair was combed, though the hand that he held out to Paul shook slightly.

Still, compared to last time they'd met it was a vast improvement.

'Good to see you doing better,' he said truthfully as they

shook hands. Eric's mouth twitched with shame and his cheeks coloured.

'I kept trying to figure out if I'd actually spoken to you, or if it had been a dream. It's all such a blur.'

Paul gave him a sympathetic nod. It was something he knew only too well. 'I take it you've given up the booze?'

The other man nodded. 'I'm still living with my sister, but Chloe and I have been talking again. She's still worried because I've tried to give up before, but I think this time it's different. The therapy is definitely helping. Turns out I was using alcohol to mask my pain.'

Paul had to stop from rolling his eyes. Eric's therapist sounded as ditzy as the one Nicole used to see. For all he knew, it was the same woman. Dishing out platitudes and sound bites with no real meaning.

It had always driven him nuts that Nicole had—

He stiffened.

Nicole had talked about what Gwendolyn said. It was even all through her diary. Which meant she must have told the woman all about her home life. About what was going on between them.

Eric tilted his head, as if trying to work out what he'd said to cause such a long pause in the conversation. But Paul hardly noticed. If he could find out what had really happened between him and Nicole, then he'd also be free to go to the police. To put an end to her campaign to separate him and Jenna.

In other words, he could have his life back.

And all he needed to do was find a copy of what they'd discussed.

* * *

Gwendolyn Marsh kept a small office in a rundown post-war building on the eastern side of the town. Personally, Paul would've preferred to go to her house rather than run the risk of her office having high tech security. Still, it couldn't be helped. It was almost eleven at night and he'd been sitting in his car for the last hour, making sure there was no one still in the building. The same collection of files he'd used to get into Nicole's old apartment were sitting in his lap. At this rate, he would be a career criminal before the end of term.

He had toyed with trying to make an appointment to see her, but he quickly realised how futile it would've been. It didn't matter how weird the practitioner was, he couldn't see them eagerly sharing details about their conversation with ex-patients from almost three years ago.

Which was why he'd decided to break in. But as well as running the risk of getting caught, there was always the chance the woman hadn't even kept records of each session. Yet after a week of almost no sleep and no leads, he couldn't ignore it.

He sucked in a breath and climbed out of the car. He'd slung an old cloth cap over his head and flipped the collar of his jacket up to hide some of his face. Definitely not dodgy.

The five-storey office block had been built in the sixties and was an ugly concrete structure that was out of keeping with the rest of the area. He suspected the rent was probably cheaper because of it. He hoped the security was equally cheap.

A nearby streetlight bulb flickered, and he took full advantage of it, stepping into the shadows of the night as he slipped into the doorway. Despite the ugly exterior, the doors were made of heavy wood, which on any other day he might have admired. Someone had added a card swipe that restricted access and he swore. If he tried to shove his slim files into that, he'd probably end up electrocuting himself.

Swearing, he kept walking, turning left to inspect the side. There were no windows on the ground floor and those higher up were small and impossible to open.

He continued walking and stepped into the service lane out the back. The road was narrow and again there were no reachable windows. He followed it down past a series of skips and heavy-duty collection bins that were filled with cardboard until he reached a loading bay with a huge roller door that was pulled down for the evening. There was another electronic swipe card on the wall, but at the bottom of the heavy door was a bolt with a padlock to hold it in place.

Paul let out a hopeful breath as he checked there were no cameras or passers-by. The moon was half concealed by a sweep of clouds, and even though there was an overhanging security light, it didn't work, which meant someone would have to go out of their way to see him.

He dropped to his knees and slipped the small torch out of his pocket and laid it down on the ground so that it shone on the old-fashioned padlock. His hands shook as he wriggled it to one side so that he could slip the first of the slim files into it. Unlike the door of Nicole's old apartment, it didn't pop and release immediately, and by the fifth attempt he was about to leave and go home to collect a hacksaw to file through the thing when all of a sudden the pressure on the lock released and he was able to twist it round.

A surge of adrenaline raced through him, but he pushed it down as he carefully eased the bolt out and stood back up. His knees hurt from pressing into the concrete and his muscles were stiff from lack of movement. And he still didn't know if removing the padlock had released the door.

He reached for the handle of the roller door and twisted, half expecting it to stay locked in place, but it twisted round and, when he lifted the door up, it slowly rolled. The noise was like a sudden jolt of thunder, and it rang out in the quiet night.

Shit. How long had it been since the damn thing had been oiled?

His original plan had been to push the door the entire way up, but the sooner he stopped the noise, the better, so he came to a halt as soon as there was enough room to roll under.

Once he was in, he pulled the door back down, in case anyone came past. Then he got to his feet and inspected the area. Like the outside of the building, the loading bay was also made of concrete. It was filled with boxes and cartons and a workbench that ran along one wall. But all he cared about was a door. He used his torch to inspect the wall until he finally spotted it in the far corner.

He hurried over and opened it up. It led to internal stairs that were dimly lit by flickering bulbs set into the wall. His heart pounded wildly, the fear of being caught only balanced by the need to make sure his family was safe. Gwendolyn's office was on the third floor, and once there he carefully opened the stairwell door and stepped into a narrow hallway.

The utilitarian carpet appeared original and muffled his foot-steps as he inspected each doorway until he found the one that said Gwendolyn Marsh, Lifestyle Coaching Services. He swallowed down his resentment at how easily people gave themselves titles and knocked on the door.

As he expected, there was no answer, and this time he didn't bother to pick the lock. He used his shoulder to push the door in. The poor hardware hardly even protested as the door swung open and he stepped inside.

There was a small waiting room, which he strode through and into the office. It was plain enough with a wooden desk under the window and a two-seater sofa and several chairs clustered in a circle at the other end. An ancient computer was sitting on the desk, so old that Paul suspected most of the kids at school wouldn't even recognise it. Hell, if he wasn't mistaken it still used floppy disks.

Which hopefully meant Gwendolyn was old school. He walked over to the huge shelving unit that ran the length of the wall. The top half was filled with books, several framed photographs and far too many crystals. He ignored them and concentrated on the cupboards below. He opened them up to reveal an entire row of cardboard document boxes, all carefully marked in alphabetical order.

He stared at them.

The first time Nicole had mentioned she was starting therapy, he'd been surprised. Weren't they the couple that laughed over new age practitioners who used crystals and threw around words like self-awareness, as if it could somehow come close to touching the bloody mass of bleeding pain that most people carried around deep within them?

But she'd laughed and told him that it was because she wanted to improve her relationship with some of the work colleagues she'd ostracised in the past. And that there was no way she was going back down memory lane. It was purely to improve her career prospects.

And I believed her.

His hand shook as he pulled out the box with W on it. He flicked it open to reveal a stack of manila folders with names written on the front, along with the date. He lifted each folder out one by one until he finally came to the one he'd been searching for.

Nicole Williams, born 25th November 1983.

He sucked in a breath. This could help him remember what had really happened. His heart pounded at the idea he'd finally be able to push aside what he now believed to be the *false* memory of Nicole's death. Then there would be nothing standing between him and Jenna. It's what he wanted.

He put his torch in his mouth so he could have enough light, and then he opened the folder and began to read.

32

August 25th

Summary of session with Nicole Williams, aged 32.

The patient came to see me because she had problems sleeping and didn't want to use medication. However, as she talked about her current levels of work stress it became obvious that the problem went further back. At first, when I asked probing questions, she was reserved to the point of glacial but after two sessions of sitting in silence, she finally began to open up.

As a child, she'd experienced her parents both dying in a car crash. She was soon put into a foster family but, as her rage became more physical, she was sent back to a residential facility called Arlington House where she suffered numerous psychotic breaks, resulting in memory loss. Though she did recall a dream she always had. About waking up in an empty grave—

What the actual fuck.

The folder fell from Paul's hand as his vision swam.

What Gwendolyn had written down wasn't Nicole's past, it was his. The parts of it that he'd dared share with her. The parts that no one else knew. Not even Jenna.

But why? What possible motive could she have had to see a therapist and pretend she was him? Was she trying to find out what was going on inside his head, like he was trying to do with her? Or, and this one seemed more likely, was she simply trying to hold something over him? Prove he was crazy?

Memories pressed against his skull, jagged and hard, but he pushed them back into their cage as he picked up the fallen folder. His eyes skimmed over the rest of the narrative until he reached the end.

My conclusion is the patient is suffering from deep childhood trauma, which has caused memory suppression in order to not just survive, but to function. My recommendation is that we use a variety of CBT techniques to deal with the trauma rather than continuing to ignore it.

Stabbing razor blades pressed against his temples as he turned the page to the next sessions. On and on it went. Nicole skilfully blending all the tiny pieces of him into an ongoing narrative, with her as the main actress. And that's what she was, an actress.

He continued to read.

The patient longs for a child but her fiancé won't consider it. She explains it's why she first started her affair with the woman next door. To get him back for refusing to give her a child. When I questioned how it would be payback when he wouldn't know about it, she became defensive. Even more defensive when I suggested that by having a same-sex relationship she also didn't run the risk of getting pregnant by anyone else. She abruptly left the session.

His knuckles turned white as he clenched one hand into a fist, while using the other one to keep turning until he reached the final entry.

It was short, less than a page long.

Nicole missed her last session, which is of concern to me. Her mind has built a cage around the trauma, but she doesn't seem to realise that it's not a cage, it's a dam. And every time she has a blank in her memory the dam becomes more unstable. Unless she deals with the past, her psyche will become more shattered until it's impossible for her to know what's real and what's not. It's my belief that it's safest for her if these issues are resolved before trying to get pregnant.

Thick mist descended across his vision, and he quickly thrust his head down between his knees, determined not to faint as a wave of emotions swept through him like a torrent.

He'd come here to get more insight into Nicole and what had happened in their final days together. But he'd been forced to read about her cruel betrayal of him. Appropriating his own story as hers. But why? Was it to get insight about him so she could manipulate him even more? Or was it something else?

His breath became shallow as he scanned for the dates. Her first visit was six weeks before she told him about the abortion. Which meant she'd probably been pregnant while sitting in this very office, pretending to be him.

So she could find out what kind of father I would be?

What kind of monster she was living with?

Another violent wave of raging emotions washed over him, leaving him panting.

Once the onslaught passed, he got back to his feet and put away the file, keeping Nicole's folder in his hand. The room began to spin, and his head pounded as shards of memories tore at him.

Him and Nicole slow dancing on their second anniversary of dating.

Nicole tear-stained after she'd been overlooked for a promotion because she wasn't a man.

Of how they listened to Bridget and Daniel bicker from over the fence.

Of him dragging her dead body through the bush.

Of the last time he ever saw her when she threw the engagement ring at him before stalking out of the house and calling an Uber.

He put a hand to his temple. He knew all the memories weren't true, yet they continued to flood his mind. He staggered back down the hallway and had to stretch out a hand to stop himself from falling.

I'm nobody. Nothing.

He was gasping by the time he staggered down the street. A car hurtled by, the headlights blazing like twin suns. Paul raised his hands to shield them as pain exploded in his head. A low buzz started, and he dug his nails into his flesh as the car flashed past him.

Nicole found out the truth about him and killed his baby.

What if Jenna did the same thing?

No. She would never do that. She was kind and sweet and good.

And yet she read Nicole's diary without telling me. She wants to go back to full time work. She told Alison things she'd never told me.

Not true. He tried to blur out the images in his mind of Jenna wearing a red dress like Nicole's. Of the gleam in her eyes when she said his income might not be enough to support the baby.

Another set of headlights blinded his vision and the world seemed to spin. He fumbled for his pills and swallowed two more.

He needed to make it stop. Make it all stop.

The pounding continued and he hurried along, eyes scanning until he found something advertising beer. Crimson mist blurred his vision and he wiped his eyes so he wouldn't stumble as he pushed the door open.

The King's Head was a dump. The last time he'd been there, it was filled with old men, and a few students who liked the cheaper pints and the free pool tables. As he stepped inside, he could see it hadn't improved with time. The interior was a dark burgundy, and the low hanging lights only added to the gloom.

A few men propped up the bar and there was a group of middle-aged women sitting in the corner playing cards. No one looked at him as he reached the bar, his head a throbbing minefield of Nicole's betrayal.

She found out what kind of man he was, and then aborted his child.

And now she's telling Jenna to do it too.

No. He had to make it stop. To put his finger back in the dam round his thoughts. He'd been a fool to think he could extract only one memory at a time. It had never worked like that. His mind had told him long ago, it's either all or nothing, and right now Paul wanted nothing.

'What can I get you?' The man behind the bar looked up from yesterday's crossword.

'Whisky,' he gasped. 'And make it a triple.'

33

'I'm not happy about your blood pressure.' The nurse frowned as she swivelled away from the computer to face Jenna, who'd rolled her sleeve back down. 'It's very important we get it back down. Have you had any extra stress in your life?'

You mean apart from discovering Paul's crazy ex is back in town and trying to break us up. Or that I'm a grown woman living with my older sister. Or that I secretly ate three Twix bars even though I promised myself I wouldn't.

She shook her head. 'Nothing out of the ordinary. Is there something I can take to make it go down?' she asked, knowing it was the first question Paul would ask her. He'd been hyper-focused on the pregnancy from the moment the pink line had shown up, and she knew how much it was killing him to not come with her to the appointment.

'Watch the salt intake and make sure you exercise.'

Jenna winced. She'd only been for one jog in the last two weeks. A mantle of guilt slipped over her shoulders. Was that why it had happened?

Her son wasn't even born yet, and she was already a bad mother.

The nurse gave her a list of things to try and gave Jenna a dismissive wave of her hand. Jenna swallowed and slowly walked to the car park, wishing Paul was next to her, his large hand tight round hers.

He would tell her she wasn't a bad mother. That, considering what they'd been through, it was a miracle her blood pressure wasn't higher. And that it didn't matter because, by his very nature, he'd make everything all right again. But he wasn't with her, which is probably why she had high blood pressure to begin with.

It was all Nicole's fault.

She'd taken away the magical moment of the last scan, and now this.

Jenna swiped her phone open and pressed Paul's number, but the call went through to voicemail. Again. She'd tried to call before she went into the nurse's office but there hadn't been any answer. He was probably preparing for his interview, which would be starting in half an hour. She'd already booked the whole day off work, so maybe she'd swing by the school at lunchtime and find out how it had gone. It wasn't like Nicole could do anything to them in the grounds of Hepworth.

Feeling better at the decision, she climbed into her car. She'd promised Lucy she'd pick up some dry cleaning and she had a few errands of her own to run, so she headed out of Rugby and turned onto the A14 dual carriageway.

Thankfully she'd missed most of the commuter traffic and the roads weren't too busy. She turned on the radio but quickly switched it off as the news blasted out. Hearing about underpaid NHS workers and the ailing economy always made her depressed, so she tended to not listen to the news at all. Paul always teased her, calling her his own personal ostrich.

'What's so bad about that?' she'd always reply, to which he'd simply answer her with a kiss. The truck in front of her slowed down, and Jenna did the same, for the first time looking into the rear vision mirror as the car behind her only stopped in time to avoid hitting her.

Adrenaline fizzed through her and she wriggled her body, trying to shake it off as the truck once again increased its speed. Jenna followed suit, as did the car behind her. Her hands tightened on the steering wheel, sweat making them moist, and when the junction which would take her onto Harborough Road appeared she let out a relieved sigh.

She indicated and turned off, but then she glanced in her outside wing mirror. The same car was still behind her, so close that if she slowed her speed even a little bit they'd surely crash. Then it indicated as if it wanted to overtake her, and it almost clipped the back of her car as it drew level with her.

The driver's face was concealed by a hood, and they were staring straight ahead, almost like they didn't know she was there. Her hand shook as she pressed down on her horn. The blast made her jump, but the car didn't move forward, it stayed level with her even when she tried to drop back.

Her heart pumped in her chest as the road narrowed down into a single lane. Still the other car didn't move ahead. It pressed closer and closer to her, before the sound of steel on steel rang out as the left side of her car scraped along the barrier. She pressed her horn again, trying to make the other car go away but still it pressed her, forcing the side of her car to continue scraping the barrier.

She clung to the steering wheel as the metal safety rail gave away all together, and Jenna's car went crashing through it, flip-

ping twice before coming down with a tangle of metal and shattered glass.

Jenna screamed and screamed, and then the world went
black.

* * *

'Can you hear me?'

Jenna forced open an eye. Her head was pounding.

'Yes,' she croaked.

What had happened? She tried to move but her arms and legs
were trapped.

'I'm Alan, a fire officer. You've been in an accident and we're
going to get you out of there as soon as we can, but we need you
to not move. Can you do that?'

'I think so,' she whispered, unsure of how she felt. 'My head...'
her voice fell away.

'What's your name?' the officer asked.

'Jenna.'

'There's an ambulance here waiting to take you to hospital,
Jenna, as soon as we've got you out of there.'

Ambulance? Was she badly hurt? She couldn't tell. And what
about—

'I'm pregnant,' she managed to say, though her voice sounded
slurry.

Alan's grip on her hand tightened and he paused. 'That's good
to know. Stay perfectly still.'

She wanted to say okay. But this time, when she opened her
mouth and tried to speak, nothing came out. Pain erupted in her
leg and her vision blurred. An image of what had happened
flashed through her mind. The white car. It had got so close,

waiting to overtake at a time when all she could do was veer off into the barrier.

'Jenna, it's Alan. Are you still with us?' The words came from a long way away. Down a tunnel. She tried to answer but her tongue was thick, and her body was on fire. But she needed to be okay. Paul would be worried about her. And their son. Oh, God. *My baby.*

She managed to blink her eyes, and another burst of pain shot through her body.

'We're going to cut you out now. It will be noisy, but all you have to do is stay as still as you can.'

Noise exploded as the high-pitched screech of metal being cut rang out. She had to will her body not to move away from the monstrous sound. She pushed her mind out of her body. Taking her and the baby somewhere safe while unknown people worked on the damaged car. Did Paul know they were here? That they needed him?

Someone needed to call him.

After what seemed like an eternity, they finally cut her free and stretchered her to the ambulance. Jenna drifted in and out of the darkness, and her final thought before she succumbed completely was.

Please save my baby.

34

Something was jabbing at his skull. Paul raised a hand to swipe it away. Whatever it was could go and get fucked. The jabbing continued, this time accompanied by a shrill ringing noise that ricocheted through his entire body. He opened his mouth to protest out loud, but his mouth was dry, and his tongue was thick with what tasted like curry.

Groaning, he forced an eye open.

The lounge was a mess. His clothes were strewn around the floor and the remains of a half-eaten Indian takeaway were discarded on the coffee table. The jabbing in his skull continued and he pressed his hand to his brow.

How much had he drunk last night?

Brrrriiing.

The noise came again and this time he realised it wasn't part of his hangover, it was the doorbell. His eyes flew open. Shit. What time was it? He fumbled for his phone and stared at the time: 12.32. Shit. Shit. Shit.

There were thirty missed calls on his phone and the doorbell rang again.

'Coming,' he managed to say as he got to his feet. A wave of nausea swept over him, and he swayed unsteadily as he ran a hand through his hair. He staggered into his jeans and pulled on last night's shirt, which stank of booze and sweat.

Had he missed any classes this morning? He racked his mind for the timetable that was always in his head, but there was a gap there. Wait. No, it wasn't a gap. He'd blocked out his diary because of his interview.

Brrrrriing.

'Coming,' he said again, this time louder. His throat was tight and dry from too much nicotine. Had Tim sent someone to come and find him? He was going to have to do some fast talking. He glanced round the room at the curry. Food poisoning? Yeah, that would work.

He would explain what happened and get them to reschedule. Tim would understand.

He gingerly walked to the door, his head pounded with every step. He cracked it open, and the bright light stung his eyes. He lifted a hand to shield them before focusing on who was there. He'd been half expecting Doug, or even Alison, but there were two uniformed police officers.

'Mr Henderson?' the female officer said.

'Yes,' he confirmed, rubbing his hand across his chin, trying to wake himself up. Had Tim sent the police? It didn't seem likely. The Head wasn't one to panic, and even if Paul hadn't shown up to school, he'd assume there was a good reason for it.

'We'd like to come in, if we may,' she said, taking a step towards him.

'Is that necessary?' he said, thinking of the mess in the lounge. 'Can you tell me what this is about?'

The woman exchanged a look with the other officer, who shrugged. 'There's been an accident involving your partner.'

The swirl of alcohol threatened to rise up into his throat and the world started to spin.

Jenna? This was about Jenna?

'W-what happened? Is she okay?' He gripped at the door-frame, desperately trying to force down the nausea.

'It really would be better if we could come inside,' the other officer said. 'You don't look well. We tried Hepworth first, but they said you hadn't turned up for work.'

'Food poisoning,' he managed to say as he nodded for them to follow him inside. He led them through to the kitchen, which was thankfully clean. 'What's happened to Jenna?'

'This morning she was in a car accident. She and the baby both survived but they're in hospital.'

Sour bile reached his throat. Oh, God. He bolted from the room, into the downstairs toilet. He made it just in time. Stomach acid burned up his throat as he puked. Once it was finally over, he rinsed his mouth out and splashed water on his face. He didn't dare look in the mirror, knowing only too well that he must look like shit.

He walked back into the kitchen. One of the officers had boiled the kettle and handed him a cup of sugary black tea.

'You're out of milk,' he said before nodding for Paul to sit down. He did, and after swallowing the hot, sweet tea his head stopped swimming so much.

'How did it happen?'

'Her car went through the barrier on the turn-off near the A14. It flipped twice and she had to be cut out.'

He began to shake. The road was well known for causing accidents. It should have been three lanes and not two, it was so busy. From the day it was built it couldn't take the volume of traffic, especially the lorries.

'How badly hurt is she?'

'The doctors said she is in a serious but stable condition,' the female officer said. 'She has a crushed pelvis, several broken ribs and a broken leg. We'll know more shortly.'

Serious but stable? That was bullshit. It was the kind of medical speak that doctors trotted out to families to try and keep them calm. Serious was serious.

Paul unsteadily got to his feet. 'I've got to get to the hospital now.'

'Not yet. We have a few questions we'd like to ask.' The male officer stood up. He was broad chested, like a front row rugby player. 'Could you please sit down?'

Paul stared at the chest blocking his way. Why would he want to wait? Jenna was seriously hurt. Which meant so was his son. She'd be scared. Alone. *Dying?*

'Can't they wait until later?'

'No,' the female officer said in a flat voice. 'Do you own a white late model Toyota?'

'Yes. Why?'

'We understand from a witness that your partner was run off the road by someone in a white Toyota. The car subsequently drove off.'

Run off the road?

Oh, shit.

His legs began to shake, and he sat back down.

Nicole. More bile rose in his throat. He'd been so sure that Jenna would be safe as long as she was away from him. That Nicole was trying to ruin his life by stopping him from being happy. He hadn't thought for a minute she'd go after Jenna. After the baby.

'Surely you don't think it's me?'

'We'd like to take a look at your car.'

He swallowed. Where was his car? He'd driven last night to

Gwendolyn Marsh's office, but he had no recollection of driving home. How had he even ended up here? Shit. Had he driven it while he was drunk? Shame filled in the narrow cracks between his hangover and Jenna's accident. Of all the bloody stupid things to do.

The officers both stood, their gazes unreadable.

'Okay.' He reluctantly led them back to the hallway and through the internal door that led to the garage. The female officer snapped on the light and the other one pressed a second switch that raised the garage door. Sunlight flooded in and Paul's headache returned with force.

Both officers walked over to the car, each dropping low to examine the paintwork on the left wing. Paul followed them over and gagged. Yesterday his car had been in pristine condition, but now there was a several thick scratches running along the wing and a large dent.

'How did this damage occur?'

Paul swallowed. 'I'm not sure.'

'When was the last time you drove the car?'

What could he say? That he didn't remember if he drove home last night? That he didn't know what time it was? That he broke into an office block to illegally read his ex-fiancée's patient files?

Sweat beaded on his brow. Could the officers see it?

'I met someone for a drink last night. I'm not sure what time I came home.'

'And where were you this morning between nine-thirty and ten o'clock?'

Again there was no good answer. He couldn't say passed out on the sofa. But what could he say? 'I was probably throwing up,' he said weakly.

'And is it true that you and Jenna Reynolds were estranged?'

'What? No. Absolutely not. Why would you ask that?'

'Because, according to Miss Reynolds's sister, Jenna's been staying with them for the last week.'

Paul's mouth went dry. There was a logical explanation, but he couldn't say it out loud. He couldn't say any of it out loud without making the situation worse. Besides, why should they believe him?

'It's complicated,' he said by way of an answer. 'Please, I've got to go and see Jenna, she'll want me there.'

The officers exchanged another look. Hell, did they teach them telepathy these days? Finally, one of them nodded. 'We will escort you to the hospital as forensics will need to take a look at your car. But first, I suggest you shower.'

Paul managed to shower and dress in fifteen minutes. He also swallowed a couple of painkillers before joining the officers in the kitchen. They stopped talking the moment he reappeared and nodded for him to follow.

He sat in the back of the police car. The doors were locked as if he was under arrest.

'What else do you know about the accident?' he asked, as they took off down the road in the direction of the hospital.

'No more than we've already told you. The car was forced off the road and ended up on its roof. The other vehicle didn't stop and continued driving towards the Harborough Road. The fire brigade had to cut your partner out and she was taken to hospital.'

'And you say there was a witness who saw Jenna being run off the road by a white car?'

'Yes.'

'Did they get the number plate?'

'No, they couldn't see the licence plate as they were behind, having come off at the same junction. but they did identify it as a white late model Toyota.'

He dropped his hands into his head.

If Paul ever cheated on me, I'd kill him.

Nicole's words in her diary floated into his mind. He'd been so stupid to take them literally. There was always more than one way to skin a cat. And why kill him physically, when she could do it so much more brutally by killing everything and everyone that he loved?

35

'She has a broken leg and minor burns,' a grim-faced doctor said as Paul sat down in a small reception room, flanked by the two officers. 'But our main concern is the internal bleeding. She has three broken ribs, which is what probably caused the damage. We're taking her into surgery in half an hour.'

The painkillers had kicked in and Paul was able to nod his head without his vision swimming. 'What about the baby?' he said, voice still hoarse from smoking too many cigarettes the previous night.

'Stable.' The doctor gave a faint smile for the first time. 'Your son is definitely a fighter.'

'Can I see her now?' Paul said and the doctor's smile faded.

'You can have ten minutes.'

The doctor got to his feet. An obvious dismissal, and one Paul had used numerous times when dealing with problematic parents. Was that what he'd become? A problem? The officers continued to flank him as they led the way to the Emergency Department and through to a cubicle, which had been curtained off at the end.

'You can see your partner and then we're taking you to the station for further questioning,' the other officer said.

He opened the curtain slightly and his breath caught in the back of his throat. Jenna was lying there, red welts across her face and her leg in a half-open plaster cast. She was still as a statue, but as he stepped toward her, her eyelids fluttered.

And then he was next to her. His hand pressed into her hand, hardly daring to breathe. 'I'm here. It's okay, Jenna. I'm here.'

She made a tiny noise at the back of her throat but didn't open her eyes.

'Don't try and talk. Everything is okay. The doctors have to operate, but you're fine. And so is the baby.'

At the word, Jenna's hand moved against his. Emotion swam through him, and he pressed a light kiss on her face. Her hair was framing her brow, lank and tired.

This was all his fault.

He should've gone to the police and told them about Nicole when she first started threatening them. There were so many things he should've done. But he'd been scared. He'd been trying to protect himself, and Jenna had paid the price.

I'm nobody. Nothing.

He stared at her limp hand lying in his. The delicate ring her parents had given her was gone, but he could still see the mark where it should have been. Unlike her wedding finger. There was no mark to show that an engagement ring had ever been there. He knew she was desperate to get married and it was what he wanted, yet he'd refused to consider it.

And now she might die without even knowing how he felt.

He pressed another kiss into the side of her brow but this time she didn't move, and he realised she'd lost consciousness again. Crimson mist passed across his eyes as the memories tried to crash out, but he dug his fingers into his thigh, so deep that he could feel blood rising to the surface.

If the memories surfaced, he might forget this moment.

He might forget that Jenna was lying in a hospital bed fighting for her life. She didn't deserve to be forgotten. So he gritted his teeth and made sure the dam round the past remained intact.

Too soon, the curtain around the cubicle was pulled open and the two officers swam before his eyes.

'If you're ready, we need to head back to the station for questioning.'

Paul took one last look at Jenna and slowly got to his feet. What did it really matter? If Jenna died then he didn't care what happened to him. It didn't matter if Tim decided to fire him, like he'd done to Eric Chambers.

Whatever way he looked at it, Nicole had won.

* * *

'Could you please tell us your movements last night?'

Paul clenched his teeth and toyed with the lukewarm coffee he'd been given three hours ago. Since he'd arrived in the station, he'd already been interviewed by the two officers, then they disappeared, and another woman had entered. She wasn't in a uniform, but the neatness of her suit suggested she wore it with the same regularity as a beat copper.

She had introduced herself as a Detective Constable Pip Adams and had proceeded to ask him again and again what had happened. By the fourth time, Paul could barely remember what he'd said.

His stomach growled and he reeked of last night's whisky as it made its way out his pores. The woman stared at him expectantly, but he was no longer sure what to say.

What if he hadn't broken into Gwendolyn's office and then gone to the pub and spent the night drinking whisky?

What if he really had gone home and in the morning he'd woken up and trailed Jenna as she drove to her nurse's appointment? After all, he knew the time. He could've sat in his car and waited for her to come out before following her. Then he could've tailgated her before driving up alongside her, forcing her off the road.

Had he watched her face morph from confusion to horror as the car had finally broken through the barrier? Had he kept driving as if nothing had happened?

But why?

He loved Jenna. And she was carrying his son.

I loved Nicole once.

And my parents.

His brain pounded. What did it mean? He loved Nicole but he'd built up an elaborate fantasy that he'd killed her. Was that happening again with Jenna? But it couldn't be, because if it was a fantasy, he wouldn't be sitting in a police interview room.

He stared at his hands, watching blood drip down onto the concrete floor.

It wasn't real.

But that didn't make it any less true. He had blood on his hands. His parents had died in a car accident, which had been his fault. Had something like that happened to Jenna as well?

'I'm waiting for an answer, Paul,' DC Adams reminded him, but he couldn't be bothered. What was the point? No matter what he said, they would blame him. Maybe it was for the best? Jenna would be better off without him. He was tarnished by his past, whereas she was pure and good.

The officer made a grunting noise, as if to suggest she was running out of patience, but before she could speak, there was a knock on the door, and the female officer who'd come to the house poked her head and nodded.

Christ. More telepathy.

DC Adams stopped the recording equipment to suspend the interview before leaving him alone in the room. He shut his eyes. They wouldn't even tell him how Jenna's operation had gone. Was she still in surgery? Was she out and looking round the room, wondering where he was? The police had promised they'd contact Lucy and Jenna's parents so they could be with her. But he should be as well.

The scrape of the door broke his meditations, and he opened his eyes. This time the detective was accompanied by the two officers.

'We've been speaking to the barman at the Old King's Head, where you spent several hours last night,' the female officer said.

Paul swallowed. He remembered ordering the first triple whisky, but then everything else was blank. His palms were wet and there was a good chance he was going to throw up again.

'You were being very vocal about your dislike of your ex-fiancée. And then this morning she is run off the road in a car matching your description. Also, forensics have finished comparing the paint. It's a match.'

His head began to spin. 'No, you've got it all wrong. Jenna isn't my ex-fiancée. We're together. I love her.'

'And yet you were living apart. Miss Reynolds's sister said that things had been tense between the pair of you for some time, and that the last time she'd visited, you were on edge.'

Despair filled him as DC Adams fixed him with a glacial stare. 'Paul Henderson, I am arresting you for the attempted murder of Jenna Reynolds and her unborn child...'

36

Jenna was having the most delicious dream. The sky was a delicate shade of duck-egg blue that faded into white as it fell down onto the shimmering water of the lake. She was lying on a picnic rug close to the shore while Paul played with their tiny son, lifting him up before the waves could swirl at his ankles. The little boy squealed with delight and Jenna's heart swelled with love. My family.

Then the beeping started, and Paul turned to her, his face sad. 'You have to go now, love.'

Jenna frowned. Go? Why would she ever want to leave her husband and son?

But he's not your husband, a small voice whispered. Remember? He didn't love you enough to propose. Or to stop the car from running you off the road.

The beeping increased and her eyes fluttered.

'She's awake,' a familiar voice whispered. 'Jenna, it's okay, we're all here. Mum and Dad are outside.'

Jenna shut her eyes trying to think. She knew the voice. She was sure of it.

'It's okay. You've been in surgery but you're out now. The doctors are happy but listen. You have to make sure you fight. Do you hear me?' the voice said.

So familiar. Was it her sister? She thought she had one.

Who are you? she wanted to ask, but her throat was dry, and her mouth wouldn't move. Everything hurt. She wanted to go back to the lake. To Paul. And her baby.

'Fight,' the voice repeated but Jenna hardly heard as she let the cool water sweep her away.

* * *

The metal bedframe dug into Paul's back, and he twisted, trying to get comfortable. He should've called his solicitor to arrange for him to get out on bail so he could see Jenna. She would tell them the truth. But it all seemed so pointless. Plus he only had one phone call and he hadn't wanted to waste it.

So he'd called the doctor.

The surgery had gone well but Jenna hadn't regained consciousness. He said that the next twenty-four hours would be critical. The baby was still safe but, if anything happened to Jenna, it would be almost impossible to keep a twenty-week foetus alive.

Once he'd finished the call, he'd been escorted to his cell, where his shoes, belt and phone had been taken from him. And, after a meal he couldn't eat, the lights had flicked out. Though sleep refused to come to him.

He thought longingly of the prescription he'd picked up the day before. Hell, had it only been a day ago? It seemed like a century. He stopped trying to chase sleep and opened his eyes, staring up at the concrete ceiling that so many inmates before had looked at.

Had this been Nicole's plan all along?

But he already knew the answer.

Yes, it was.

She'd figured it out and opened the door, and he, fool that he was, had walked straight into it.

And there hadn't been a thing he could do to stop her, because she'd held all the power. She knew what had happened before she left, and he didn't.

All because he'd been too scared to remember.

We all have to face our demons.

That's what Alison had said about Eric Chambers, but she could've been talking about Paul. He'd tried to do everything he could to stop Nicole, except the one thing that he really needed to do.

Remember what happened.

And now it was too late. Jenna was paying the price, and therefore it was only fair that he paid it as well. He belonged here.

The room began to spin, and the walls narrowed in. His head pounded and suddenly the uncomfortable bed was gone, and he was lying in the grave and the faceless woman was standing over him, shovel in her hand.

His mother.

Nicole.

Elma, his foster mother.

The faces winked in and out like dying stars as dirt caught in his throat.

But for the first time he didn't protest. He'd always known it would end like this.

The clang of metal rang in his ear and Paul woke with a start. He groaned and rubbed his eyes. The grave was gone, only to be replaced by the cell walls. He couldn't decide which was worse.

Someone brought in a breakfast tray and said he had thirty

minutes to eat and wash himself before being collected for more questioning.

He managed to swallow several bites of the dry toast and used the sink in the corner to wash as best he could. He was sitting on the edge of the bed when a different officer appeared in the doorway.

They handcuffed him and then led him down a series of corridors into a different interview room. DC Adams was waiting for him. She was wearing a different suit, but it looked like it had been bought from the same store. He didn't bother to say hello.

'I hope you slept well,' she said, without a hint of sarcasm in her voice. She didn't seem to expect an answer because she quickly coughed and held up a piece of paper. 'Today we'd like to talk to you about your relationship with Nicole Williams.'

Paul's pulse hammered so loudly he was surprised no one noticed. They seemed to be studying his face. Looking for a reaction. But what kind of reaction did they want?

'What do you want to know?'

'Were you engaged to her?'

'Yes, though it was a long time ago,' he said, unsure where the line of questioning was going.

'We've spoken to your neighbours. Bridget and Daniel Milton. Daniel admitted that Nicole Williams had blackmailed him with the sole purpose of splitting up you and Jenna Reynolds. Is this correct?'

The air rushed from his lungs. He hadn't expected that. The detective continued to study him.

'That is correct.'

'And why didn't you to come to the police after you found out from Daniel Milton what was happening?'

Paul bit down on his lower lip. That really was the question. He was usually pretty good at reading people, but he couldn't get much from the detective's calm gaze. 'I'd hoped that it had been a mistake. That she wasn't really trying to come between us. And then, after Daniel told us what happened... I assumed that would be the end of it.'

It wasn't quite the truth, but it was as much as he was prepared to offer. DC Adams scribbled something down on her pad, and then stared at it for several moments before looking at him again.

'How long have you known Nicole Williams?'

Paul swallowed. 'We met at university, so almost twelve years before we split up.'

'And would you say that she was dangerous?'

At this, Paul's mouth dropped open. 'Why do you ask?'

DC Adams paused, as if deciding what to tell him. Then she leaned back in her chair. 'We have reason to believe that Nicole Williams was the one who ran Jenna off the road.'

Paul's head began to swim. He knew it was Nicole, but she'd framed him so perfectly. Was this another fragmented memory? 'I don't understand.'

'Lucas Creswell has come forward and cleared your name.'

Who the hell was Lucas Creswell?

Paul's confusion must have shown on his face and the detective smiled. 'Yesterday, when we went back to your house, we noticed you had a monitored security system, so we contacted the company for video footage. Not only did they provide it, but they informed us you'd also hired a security guard to monitor your house, as well as Miss Reynolds's sister's house. The guard has provided a detailed statement, which the video footage has confirmed. You left your house last night at ten o'clock and returned at three in the morning. Then, a woman with long dark hair was seen entering the code into your security system and going inside. She drove away in your car several minutes later and returned it at eleven-fifteen.'

Paul's head spun. The invisible security guard who'd done such a good job of blending into the background that the only reason Paul knew he was there was via the detailed reports and the large bill he'd agreed to pay.

'But how did she get the code?'

The police officers exchanged a glance. 'Hacking home surveillance units isn't as difficult as it seems. Of course the security company will never admit that,' the detective finally answered. 'He tried to call you numerous times, but you didn't answer, so he followed her once she returned to your house but lost her when she drove into a shopping centre car park and disappeared into the crowd.'

'So what happens now?' Paul's head spun as he stood up.

DC Adams gave him an apologetic smile. 'You're free to go. But Mr Henderson, from now on if you have any contact with Nicole Williams, or believe she has been in your house, you are to inform us immediately. This is now officially a police matter, and we don't take kindly to anyone who withholds information in an open investigation. Do I make myself clear?'

'Crystal,' he said as the officer stepped towards him and unlocked the handcuffs.

'Good, here is my number, call me straight away,' the detective said in a softer voice while handing him a card. 'Now, would you like to go home or head straight to the hospital? Your car's still impounded while forensics are working on it, but one of our officers will drive you.'

'Hospital,' Paul said automatically as he rubbed his wrists. Once he had collected his possessions, he walked outside the building to wait for the squad car. The morning sun was warm and after being confined for twenty-four hours, he revelled in its

heat. There was still no sign of the car, so he turned on his phone
added the detectives phone number to his contacts and checked
all the missed calls and emails. He was about to email Tim when
a message came in. From Nicole.

What the hell did you tell them?

Paul stiffened and peered around. Had she seen him come out
of the station? Then annoyance took over.

We talked about the fact you tried to kill Jenna. Did you think the
police wouldn't find out?

If they catch me, I'll tell them the truth.

Good. It's about time they knew.

Paul typed as some of the pain in his neck dissolved. It was
the trump card Nicole had been holding over him. It's what had
let her get away with so much. There was a pause, as if she was
considering what to say.

Paul... don't do anything stupid.

The only stupid thing I've done is let you call the shots.

He stopped typing and held up his phone. If she was watching, he wanted her to know what he was doing.

I'm sending this to DC Adams.

He hit send and copied the detective into the entire thread. He stared at the screen for several minutes, waiting for a reply, but there was none. Nicole still hadn't replied by the time the squad car pulled up and Paul climbed in. He looked round one final time, still not able to see Nicole anywhere. Not that it mattered. Now the police were involved, he knew Jenna would be safe while he did the one thing he should've done right from the beginning.

Face his demons.

37

Gwendolyn Marsh wasn't as old as the name suggested. He'd been expecting someone in their eighties with wild grey curls and a preference for mohair. Instead, she was a smiling middle-aged woman with a tapered waist and generous hips. Her eyes twinkled as he entered, and she gestured for him to sit down in the chair by her desk.

Even the room seemed different in the daylight. Though that might have had something to do with the fact he was no longer breaking and entering. It had been three days since he'd been arrested and Jenna was finally out of danger, which meant it was safe to leave the hospital for his first appointment.

'Paul Henderson, I was surprised to see your name. From what Nicole once told me, you aren't a fan of my profession.'

That was an understatement.

And he still wasn't one hundred percent sure this was the right decision. Especially since, thanks to Nicole's lies, Gwendolyn had already been fed parts of his life. Would that change things? Probably. He should've picked another therapist, but in her notes, Gwendolyn had said she knew how to help. Plus, if he put it off any longer, he'd back down again.

Was that such a bad thing? After all, he'd lived with his own kind of mental torture his entire life, maybe it wasn't so bad.

Bullshit.

He cut himself off. Doing things the old way was what had almost got Jenna killed. From now on, he was doing it by the book. He rubbed the back of his neck. The pressure had become intolerable the last few days.

'I've had a few bad experiences over the years.'

'And what makes you think this will be any different?' she asked in a melodic voice.

Jenna's face swam in front of him. He'd come so close to losing her. To messing everything up. He sucked in a breath. 'Because I want it to be. I'm tired of carrying around the past. I know what I want in my life, and I'm prepared to work hard to get it.'

Gwendolyn didn't speak for a long time, but finally she nodded. 'That's as good a reason as any. Now, why don't we start by telling me where in your body you feel your past?'

Paul blinked. 'Where do I feel it?'

She nodded serenely. 'Don't think, just answer.'

As she spoke, the intense weight at the back of his neck increased, like a blade was hovering above the bone, waiting to cut him down. Paul swallowed. 'My neck.'

She smiled and her whole face transformed. He felt like he'd passed some test, despite not even knowing the rules. She stood up and walked round to the back of his chair and put her hand several centimetres above his neck. Without even touching it, she hummed, and some of the fiery heat dissipated.

'Oh, yes. It's definitely there,' she agreed, her musical voice was soft now, like a lullaby. 'Now, let me explain what our work together will look like. Nothing you believe is true. You are not the things that have happened to you. You are separate from your past. And, as we travel back to the root of your pain, we will find the key. That key will let you unlock the memories you've hidden away. Is that okay?'

Paul's heart pounded in his chest, but Gwendolyn's words had made his limbs feel languid and relaxed like a fly caught in a hot room. He swallowed and thought of Jenna again.

'Yes, that's okay.'

'Good.' She beamed at him as she reached for a giant sage stick on her desk and struck a match. The heady scent of burning herbs filled the air, and Gwendolyn lowered her voice some more. 'Now, I'd like you to close your eyes. We're going to take a trip...'

* * *

'Is it true you got arrested, sir?' Jeremy Lewis asked as Paul stood in the playground. The day was overcast, and he thrust his hands into his coat pockets. It was his first day back at work, but news had travelled quickly, and the students had lots of questions, all of which Paul had tried to answer patiently.

'I'm afraid it is. And it's not something I'd recommend,' Paul admitted as a gaggle of other students joined him. 'The food's horrible and it's a pretty scary place.'

'So how come they arrested you if you didn't do it?' someone else demanded.

'Because the police have a job to do,' he said as the bell chimed out, signalling the lunchbreak was over. 'Now, let's get moving. I don't want to give anyone a detention on my first day back.'

'You wouldn't,' they all chorused, and he repressed a smile. They were right. He'd never used detentions as a way of disciplining students.

'That's true, but there's nothing to stop Mr Barnes from giving you one,' he said, which immediately sent them all scattering. He stayed where he was and waited for Tim to reach him. They'd spoken on the phone several times and again this morning when Paul had first come back to work.

Each time, Tim had assured Paul his job was safe, and that no decision would be made regarding the Deputy Head position until after his interview, which had been postponed.

It had been a huge relief, since looking for a job right now might have been one challenge too many. Jenna was still facing weeks in hospital, and he'd booked in several more appointments with Gwendolyn. They hadn't found the so-called key to his past yet, but the intense pressure in his neck had dissolved, leaving behind only the faintest of twinges.

'Are the kids still giving you the third degree?' Tim said, finally reaching him.

'That lot weren't too bad. None of them asked if I got a tattoo.'

'A tattoo? You were only there one night.'

'I blame television,' Paul said and rolled his shoulders.

'You're probably right. Anyway, I've had a phone call from the police. They've had plain clothed officers watching the school all day and there haven't been any sightings.'

'Good to hear,' Paul said. He'd had a similar call to say that the officers watching Jenna's hospital room hadn't reported anything. It certainly helped the knot that was still in his stomach.

'Also, I want to let you know that we've decided not to reschedule your interview.'

Paul's jaw flickered but he nodded his head. 'That's understandable. In your position I'd do the same thing. After what happened with Eric—'

'No, you misunderstand,' Tim said. 'We did have a preferred

candidate but when they had to pull out, the board unanimously agreed to offer you the position. It's what they should've done from the start.'

'That's... unexpected,' Paul said, not quite sure how to take the news. He was delighted, but compared to almost losing his family, it didn't have the same effect that he would've expected. Tim seemed to read his mood and nodded in approval.

'There's plenty of time to talk about it later. For now, you need to concentrate on Jenna and the baby. Let me know if there's anything I can do.'

'I'm fine. The police have assured me that it's best if I stay out of it and let them get on with their job.'

'I wish they'd hurry up.' Tim blew out a column of air. 'How's Jenna doing? Any improvement?'

Paul brightened. 'Yes. The doctors have said she's out of danger and so is the baby. I'm heading there soon.'

'Great. Give her my love and tell her everyone at Hepworth is rooting for her,' Tim said before spotting a group of girls still standing in the quad. He sighed and marched over to them. Paul walked back to his office to collect his things. At the end of the hallway, he caught sight of Alison and Doug. They waved him over, but he gave them an apologetic shake of his head and tapped his watch.

Besides, his head was whirling.

The job he'd fought for was going to be his.

They seemed to understand, and he made a mental note to catch up with them both tomorrow to say thank you for the lawyer they'd organised, unbeknown to him, in case he'd needed it. He'd spoken to Alison briefly on the phone, but he owed her a proper explanation.

Especially since she'd been the one who'd wanted him to go to the police in the first place.

The trip across town was slow, mainly because he'd been checking his rear vision mirror the entire time, as well as making sure to travel the B roads. He doubted Nicole would come after him on the road, but he didn't want to take any chances.

It was almost three by the time he stepped out of the lift onto the long ward where Jenna was being kept. As he passed the waiting room, he could see Lucy having a phone call with someone, but at the sight of him, she waved. He returned it and walked into Jenna's room.

She was perched up on several pillows and her face was covered in bruises, but some of the colour had returned to her face and the dazed expression had left her eyes. The baby journal was sitting on the table that was positioned across the bed, and it was opened up to display a half filled in page.

At the sight of him, her entire face broke into a smile, and she put down the pen.

He was a lucky bastard.

He strode across the room and gently kissed her, resisting the urge to drag her into his arms. According to the doctors, she was still a month off being dragged anywhere. He held her gaze as he sat down, his fingers lacing into hers.

'How was your day?' he asked.

'Full of doctors and needles and trying to digest what was meant to be a rice pudding,' she said, a tiny smile dancing round her mouth. 'And you?'

'Oh, much the same, minus the rice pudding and needles. Actually, you can scrap the doctors as well.' He leaned forward and pressed his lips to the back of her hand. 'But lots of kids. They all wanted to know what it was like to be a master criminal.'

Jenna let out a horrified gasp. 'They don't think that's what you are, do they?'

'They'd like to,' Paul said with a grin. 'I'm pretty sure my street cred would go up if that was the case. Unfortunately, I was a big disappointment to them. I didn't even get a tattoo.'

A smile tugged at her mouth. 'Now I know you're joking. What was it really like?'

'It was actually okay. The kids were very gentle with their questions, and Tim spoke to me today. Looks like I'm going to get the job after all.'

Jenna let out a little squeal. 'I knew it. That is amazing. How do you feel?'

'Actually... pretty calm. I'm happy, but it doesn't seem as important as it once did.'

The last part was due to Gwendolyn. He'd already had three appointments and it was amazing how detached he felt from how he'd once been. The memories with Nicole hadn't returned yet, but other ones had. Like the night his parents were killed. And she'd helped him see that even though an eight-year-old child might think it was their fault, he was no longer that child.

Gwendolyn thought it was definitely a step in the right direction.

'Good. You always did work too hard,' Jenna said. 'Plus it means you'll have more time to play with your son.'

'And my son's gorgeous mother,' Paul said as he slipped his hand into his pocket and dropped to his knees. It meant he was now only eye level with the hospital bed but considering how much he'd messed things up when he'd given Jenna the gold necklace, he didn't want her to be in any doubt.

'I'm not gorgeous—' she broke off as her hand flew to her mouth. 'No. Paul, you can't be... I mean... we're in the hospital. And I'm a mess.'

'You're not a mess, you're a survivor,' Paul said, his voice catching in his throat. 'I'm so sorry this has taken such a long time. I thought I had to wait... until... well, it doesn't matter. I thought the time wasn't right. But I've finally learned that there's no good time or bad time. There's only now. And what I want more than anything is to be your husband. Right now. So, Jenna Reynolds. Will you do me the honour of becoming my wife?'

As he spoke, he pulled out the box he'd been carrying around in his pocket for the last three days. Tears glistened in her eyes as he handed it to her.

'Don't cry. You might hate it,' he said.

'Impossible,' she said, the tears now rolling down her cheeks as she snapped the box open. Inside was the antique rose gold ring with a flat diamond inside it. It was one she'd been admiring in an antique store near her work. 'You remembered.'

Paul gave her a half smile. He might not remember everything yet, but that was one thing that had stuck in his mind. 'So, what do you say? Are you ready to become my wife?'

'Yes.' Jenna beamed as Paul slid the ring onto her finger. 'Yes, yes, yes.'

38

Jenna stared at the ring on her finger. It had been a fortnight since Paul proposed and she still hadn't been able to drag her gaze away from it. Being stuck in a hospital bed meant she didn't have that many other things to do. But still... it was the most perfect ring in the world. The downside was that the happiest day of her life had only come about because his crazy ex-fiancée had tried to kill her.

'You're doing it again,' Paul said, walking back into the room with a cup of tea. He carefully put it down on the table across the bed and then kissed her on the forehead.

'Doing what?'

'Reliving the accident.' He sat down on the corner of the bed and took her hand.

'Not all of it,' she promised as she looked round the room. It was full of cards and flowers that her visitors had given them, once the happy news of the engagement had been released. 'The best parts.'

'Good, because Gwendolyn said that the more we focus on the past, the more of a prisoner we become.'

'I see,' Jenna said, trying to repress a smile. For as long as she'd known Paul, he'd hated the idea of therapy but the fact he'd started going to the same counsellor as Nicole had been quite a shock. 'Did she say anything else?'

'As a matter of fact, she did.' Paul picked up the baby journal and turned to the page where they were meant to record the father's history. It was as blank as the day Bridget had given her the book. 'She said it was time I told you a bit more about my past.' Jenna sucked in a breath as his eyes met hers. 'My mother's name was Evelyn...'

* * *

Twenty minutes later, the page was half full, and while Paul wanted to keep going, the lines round his mouth suggested it was better they did it in stages. She took the pen from his hand and kissed him.

'That's enough for now,' she whispered, but before she could kiss him again, DC Adams poked her head round the door.

'Hope I'm not interrupting,' she said. Since Paul had been released, the detective had come in several times to update them on the search for Nicole. But so far it had been fruitless.

Next to her, Paul stiffened, and Jenna caught her breath. 'Has there been any news?'

The detective stepped into the room and closed the door. 'I'm afraid so. We found a credit card in Nicole's name but when we went to the address—' she broke off and licked her lips. 'There had been a fire.'

Jenna gasped and Paul's face drained of colour. 'Was... she there?'

DC Adams ran a hand across her face. It was obvious she

didn't like having to deliver bad news. And somehow Jenna knew that was exactly what this was going to be.

'There was a body, but it was so badly burned we could only identify it by dental records.'

'Nicole's dead?' Paul's voice was hollow. 'Are you sure?'

'Absolutely sure. Forensics said the fire was started intentionally. The coroner will have to give a final verdict, but it appears to be a case of suicide.'

Suicide? Jenna's chest tightened as conflicting emotions tore through her. Relief at knowing they were finally safe, but also guilt. What had driven Nicole to kill herself? Was it because she knew the police were closing in, or because she'd accepted Paul was lost to her?

A lump formed in her throat. How could the same woman who'd written the diary with such charm and wit have taken her own life? Stop it. She caught herself as the years of training kicked in. Most people who attempted suicide were fighting invisible battles that no one else could see.

Next to her, Paul's face was chalky white, and his hands were shaking. 'Are you okay?' she whispered, hating how inane the words sounded. How utterly useless it was to try to sum up the entirety of a human life in three little words. Yet somehow he seemed to comprehend what she was really telling him, and he let out a shuddering breath.

'It's a lot to take in,' he finally said before they lapsed into silence.

After several more minutes, DC Adams coughed. 'I've got to deal with the paperwork but, if you have any questions, call me, and I'll be back in touch as soon as we've got the final ruling from the coroner.'

It wasn't until she'd left the room that Paul finally turned to her. His eyes were dazed. Jenna wasn't surprised. She'd worked with enough families who'd lost loved ones to suicide, and it was always the same expression. Guilt that they couldn't have done more.

She reached for him. His hand was cold, like he'd had it in the freezer for several days.

'It wasn't your fault,' Jenna said in a soft voice. He finally let out a breath and looked at his hands, as if something was there. Then he blinked and turned back to her.

'You're right. It really isn't,' he said, eyes filled with awe. He must have caught her confused expression and he gave her one of the half smiles that set a swarm of butterflies loose in her stomach. 'For so long I felt responsible for how we broke up. As if it was something I'd said... or done. Now I realise it wasn't me. Part of me wants to feel happy, but—'

'Hey.' Jenna cut him off, sensing that the words were starting to choke him. That the terrible burden of the break-up was obviously something he still carried with him. 'It's okay to have mixed feelings about this. What she did to us was terrible, but she was still a person, and she must have been in a huge amount of pain to have taken her own life. You're allowed to be sad.'

'I'm not sure how I feel,' he admitted before resting his hand on her belly. 'Actually, that's a lie. I'm relieved it's finished and that you and our son will be safe. That's all I've ever wanted.'

Then he leaned over and kissed her, and Jenna tried to stop herself from shivering. Up until this moment she hadn't realised that she and Nicole had actually been at war. And that now it was finally over.

39

'Seriously, you're still on mineral water?' Tim complained on Saturday afternoon. They'd all been at the interschool athletics day and after the Hepworth team had won a resounding victory, a few of the teachers had retired to the local pub to celebrate. Paul had gone along more as the sober driver than anything else. And besides, Jenna had only been home a couple of days. So, he had no intention of being hungover.

'Yep,' Paul agreed as Doug appeared. 'Here's to Hepworth.'

'Screw that. Here's to you being an engaged man,' Doug interjected as he held his glass up and took a long gulp. Paul had told his colleagues about his proposal, and they'd all been thrilled. He'd also told them about Nicole's death, and while they hadn't looked devastated, they'd refrained from celebrating.

He was pleased. Jenna was right. He still had very mixed emotions. The fact that Nicole had tried to kill Jenna and destroy his life made it hard for him to mourn her. But knowing he hadn't been the one to kill her had also lifted a weight off his shoulders. Gwendolyn thought that now Nicole had passed, he might be more successful in finding the key to the elusive memories.

Though they were getting closer and, two days ago, during their session, he'd remembered an incident with Nicole two weeks before she left.

It had been innocuous. They'd been cooking dinner and she'd complained about the way he'd cut the onions. It hadn't been a fight, just a bicker, but that night he'd slept on the sofa, which made him think there must have been more to it. However, when he tried to press his memory further, the mist had gathered in his mind, and he hadn't tried to push it.

Like Gwendolyn said: *The key will come when it comes.*

'You must be so excited about Jenna coming home?' Doug said as Tim drifted off towards the dartboard. He was already swaying from drinking too much in the heat of the day.

'Absolutely. She's almost six months pregnant now and the nesting gene has fully kicked in. I think from now on I'll be setting up cribs and painting walls.' Paul put the drink back on the table. The warm day had already caused the ice cubes to melt, and condensation trickled down the glass.

'And you will love every second of it,' Doug teased as he stood up. 'I'm going to get another drink. Want one?'

'No.' Paul shook his head and got to his feet. 'I'm going to push off. I don't want to be away from Jenna for too long.'

'Oh, yes,' Doug leered, but Paul ignored it. He really was juvenile at times.

'Promise me that you'll get an Uber home.'

'Yes, boss.' Doug gave him a salute and sauntered over to the rest of the Hepworth teachers who were gathered round the dart board. He thought about going over to say his goodbyes but thought better of it. It would drag things out. Better to disappear and make his apologies on Monday. The bar was busy, and he pushed his way through the crowds and out the door. It was still ight outside but there was a shimmery haze of the night to come, and the heat of the day was finally fading.

His car was parked over in the far corner but, before he could reach it, Alison swayed into sight.

'You weren't going to leave without saying goodbye, were you?' she said. Her eyes were unfocused, and her cheeks were full of colour, like she'd stepped out of a sauna.

'Guilty,' he admitted as she came to a halt in front of him, staggering slightly to the left. He raised an eyebrow. 'Are you okay?'

Alison's cheeks turned red, and she giggled. 'Sorry, I think I'm a little drunk. I didn't get a chance to eat lunch.' She lurched a little then steadied herself. 'Okay, a lot drunk.'

'Come on, I think I'd better drive you home.'

'That's crazy, you live in the opposite direction. I'll ask Tim for a lift,' she slurred as she turned to wobble back toward the pub.

'Whoa. That's a terrible idea.' Paul gently reached for her arm, thinking about what had happened to Eric. And while she was right about them living in the opposite direction, he could hardly leave her like this. 'Let me drive you home. That way I know you'll be safe.'

A grateful smile flashed across her face as her voice went husky. 'You're a very lovely man,' she said with a hiccup before leaning heavily against his shoulder, her arm hanging against his jacket. Christ. How had she managed to get so drunk so quickly? Paul steered her into the passenger side of the car and helped her put the seatbelt on.

'Least I can do,' he said as he pulled out into the afternoon traffic. He turned to ask her if Rob would be back at the house to look after her, but she was already asleep, snoring softly as her head lolled to one side. As long as she didn't throw up before he got her home.

* * *

'How many visitors have you had?' Lucy looked round the lounge
at the overflowing vases, the clusters of balloons and the huge
collection of engagement cards that lined the window. It had
been two days since she'd finally been released from hospital
and it seemed like a never-ending stream of people had passed
through the house.

'A lot,' Jenna admitted as her sister settled Saffie into the
chair, along with a colouring book and several stuffed animals
that had seen better days. 'At this rate we won't need an engagement party.'

'Nonsense,' Lucy said in a brisk voice as she handed Saffie a
container of chopped up carrots and celery. 'I've already started
planning it. We thought sometime in July would be good. Then
you can have the ceremony the following year. Plenty of time to
get your figure back.'

Jenna opened her mouth to retort but couldn't decide what to
unpack first. Besides, no matter how much Lucy liked being in
charge, the engagement party and wedding would be what she
and Paul wanted, not what her family wanted. At the thought of
him, she smiled. Ever since she'd come home, he'd been waiting
on her, hand and foot.

He'd even tried to cancel attending the athletics tournament,
but Jenna had insisted he went. *It wouldn't look good if the new
Deputy Head appeared flaky*, she'd teased him. *Besides, Lucy will be
here with me all afternoon.*

And so he'd kissed her soundly on the lips and promised to
be home as soon as he could legitimately get away.

'What's this, Mummy?' Saffie suddenly asked.

'What's what?' Lucy said turning to her young daughter who
was holding up Jenna's baby journal. Then she frowned. 'You

shouldn't be touching that. It belongs to Aunty Jenna. Remember what we said about touching other people's things?'

'Yes, but I wanted to look at the drawing. Why's it so funny?'

'Drawing?' Jenna frowned as she leaned over to see what her niece was talking about, but before she could, Lucy snatched it out of her hands and shut it, her face draining of colour. 'Lucy? What's going on?'

'Nothing,' her sister said a little bit too quickly as she pulled out her phone and flicked it onto a YouTube clip before handing it to her daughter. Saffie immediately let out a squeal of excitement before becoming lost in the show. Jenna's throat tightened. Her sister *never* let Saffie have screen time during the day. Especially not when they were in public.

'Give me the journal,' Jenna said in a tight voice as her eyes locked with her sister's. Lucy let out a slow breath before finally handing it over. Jenna turned the pages, not quite sure what she was looking for until she came to the page that was dedicated for any memories about their marriage. Yesterday the page had been blank, but now there was a drawing in there. It was a stick figure lying flat on the ground with a knife protruding out of their chest. But the thing that was the most chilling was the words written underneath.

He'll never be yours.

* * *

'God, this is so embarrassing,' Alison mumbled as Paul helped her walk up the short pathway that led to her house. 'I feel like such an idiot.'

'Don't be daft,' Paul tried to reassure her as she fumbled with her house keys. After failing several times to get them into the lock, Paul took them out of her hand and let them both inside. 'Besides, at least you had the good sense to leave before anyone could see you.'

'Yes, except I would have probably gone back if you hadn't rescued me,' she said with another groan as she walked through to the kitchen. He'd been in the house a couple of times, but the walls had changed colour since then, and there was a new bench top and appliances, making it look like something out of a magazine. 'I think I need to drink my body weight in water, then have a cup of tea. Do you want anything?'

'I should probably get going,' he said, then winced as she took a glass of water and made a hiccupping noise, as if she was going to be sick. 'Is Rob around?'

'No. He's away for the weekend.' She shook her head and hiccupped again. 'But I'll be fine.'

It was doubtful. 'Okay, I'll stay for a cup of tea,' he reluctantly agreed and reached into his pocket for his phone. He'd better text Jenna to let her know he was going to be a bit late. Then he frowned as he reached into his other pocket, but both of them were empty. He sighed and rubbed the back of his neck. He must've left it in the car.

'A cup of tea coming up.' Alison beamed as she navigated her way to the kettle, with the same intense concentration that Paul imagined Scott had while trying to navigate the Antarctic.

'Here, let me help.'

'Nonsense. I'm fine,' she said as some of the colour returned to her cheeks. She pulled out two mugs from the cupboard and spooned some tea leaves into a teapot before filling it with hot water. Then, without giving it time to brew, she poured it out, splashed in some milk and handed it over. It looked like the colour of sand.

He reluctantly drunk some. It tasted as bad as it looked, and he was about to push it away when there was a heavy scraping noise outside. He jumped.

What was that?

Alison blinked and tilted her head. 'You okay?'

He frowned. 'Sorry. That noise startled me. Did you hear it?'

She gave him a confused look. 'I only heard a car backfiring.'

Heat stung his cheeks. 'Sorry. I still hear a noise and forget that Nicole's not alive any more.'

'It's okay. After everything you've been through, it's not surprising you're a bit jumpy.'

His body swayed and he clutched at the bench as a wave of bone-wearying sleep washed over him.

Alison's eyes widened and she hurried to his side. She was saying something. His name? But he couldn't focus.

'Sorry,' he tried to say, but his tongue stuck to the top of his mouth, and he made a squeaking noise. This wasn't right.

Alison said something else, but it was like she was in a fish tank. Or was he the one in the fish tank? He couldn't tell. And his legs turned to lead.

Alison was beside him now, her face filled with concern. 'No. No. No. You have to be okay. You have to be okay.' She kept saying it over and over again like a lullaby. Then she let him go, her own face going slack. In the periphery of his mind, a flicker of worry went through him. Was she drunk? Or was the same thing happening to her that was happening to him? Then her eyes shut, and she slid off his chest and onto the floor.

Paul wanted to stand up, to make sure she was okay, but moving was impossible and even opening his eyes was too hard. He let out a pained groan and the blackness overtook him.

* * *

'What do you mean, you can't find him?' Jenna clutched at her phone. 'But he must be with you.'

'I'm sorry, Jenna, but we haven't seen him since about five. He should've been home by now,' Tim Barnes said. There was noise in the background, and it sounded like he was still out somewhere. 'Knowing Paul, he's gone back to work. He's determined to get as much done as he can before the baby's born. I'm sure he'll be home soon.'

'I guess,' Jenna said, though it still didn't explain why he wasn't answering his phone. She thanked Tim and asked him to call her if Paul turned up. She rolled her shoulders, wishing she could stand up without every part of her body aching. She'd already called the police about the picture, but while DC Adams had been polite and understanding, she clearly thought Jenna was wasting their time.

It was probably true.

She toyed with calling them again when her phone pinged with an incoming text message. It was from Paul.

Crazy traffic. Can you believe I'm stuck behind two hundred sheep? Love you and I'll be home as soon as I can.

The tension in Jenna's shoulders disappeared as she eagerly replied to him.

You poor thing. Drive carefully and I'll see you soon.

She sent Lucy a quick text to say that Paul was okay and then leaned back into the sofa, suddenly feeling exhausted. As soon as he was home, they'd work out how the terrible drawing had appeared in her baby journal two days *after* Nicole's body had been found.

40

Paul woke with a start. His mouth tasted like a sandpit and his head pounded. He slowly opened his eyes and peered around. The room had concrete walls, one of which was covered in newspaper articles. Where was he?

He shut his eyes and prodded his memory. He'd been at Alison's house, and he'd fainted. No... he hadn't fainted. Something had knocked him out. Was it drugs? He frowned, trying to recall. He'd had a drink and then everything had gone blurry. Alison had tried to help him but then she seemed to pass out too.

Shit. Was she okay? He craned his head, trying to ignore the stab of pain that ran up his spine. There was no sign of her anywhere, but it was clear who was behind it.

Nicole.

How was she still alive? The police said they'd matched her dental records? Somehow she'd fooled them as well. Panic seized him. Where was she? Was Jenna okay? And Alison?

Still feeling groggy, he tentatively got to his feet and looked for a way out. It seemed like the room, perhaps a basement, had once been used for storage, but it was now empty apart from a single bed, a small table and a cupboard. There were no windows, and the only door at the top of some stairs had an electronic security lock on it.

He tried it all the same, but the reinforced steel door didn't even budge.

'Let me out,' he hollered, hitting the wall with his hand. Nothing happened, but he tried again, and again. Ten minutes later, his mouth was dry from lack of water, and his hand stung.

Breathe, he instructed himself. He needed to stay calm and keep looking for a solution. The wall that ran adjacent to the door was covered with neatly cut out newspaper articles. Would they give him a clue about where he was?

He walked over and studied them. *Young Girl Found Locked in Cellar.* He scanned the article. It was about an abduction over twenty years ago where an eleven-year-old girl had been found in a cellar cupboard. She'd been beaten, starved and tortured.

He vaguely remembered the headlines, but he'd been too caught up in his own private hell to pay much attention to anyone else. Another article said *Cellar of Horrors* while a third screamed *Social Services Slip Up Again.* He read them all one by one and then rubbed his brow.

Why where they on the wall? Unless the girl had been Nicole?

His throat tightened. Nicole had often shared small parts of her dysfunctional upbringing, but there had been no mention of a cellar. Then again, she'd never been one for sharing too many details of her life. Even with him. He thought of Gwendolyn. Was that why Nicole had used his trauma and not hers when she'd visited the therapist? Was she too scared to even tell someone in confidence?

He rubbed his head, willing his sluggish mind to think, but it was no good. The effects of the drug were still in his system and his stomach growled from lack of food. Fatigue pinched at the edge of his mind. No. He had to stay awake. He had to get away. To make sure Nicole didn't hurt anyone.

But despite his best efforts, his eyelids fluttered, and he dropped back down onto the bed and into the darkness.

The next time Paul woke, there was a low hum of music and the overhead light had been turned off, which meant the room was only illuminated by a desk lamp in the far corner. He rubbed his eyes, trying to bring his scattered thoughts back together. The humming increased and the hairs on his arm prickled.

The humming wasn't from a radio.

There was someone in the room.

Paul sat up straight, his body weak from lack of movement. Over in the corner was a figure. It was a woman with long black hair, wearing a white dress. It was cut low at the front with pale lace barely covering her breasts. A wedding dress.

Hot bile tried to push its way up his throat and a grim realisation hit. He knew that dress. It was the one Nicole had planned to wear when they walked down the aisle together.

As he stared at her, she gave him a wide smile, and Paul frowned. His vision was still blurred, but there was something wrong with her mouth. It wasn't quite right. Nor was her nose. Then the figure stood up and walked towards him, hips swaying in time to the humming. As she got closer, her amber eyes were wide with happiness.

'Alison?' he croaked. 'What's going on? Why are you dressed like that?'

'Do you like it?' Alison said, smoothing down the front of the dress. 'Personally, I think it's a bit slutty. But then that's Nicole all over. Not to mention the fact she wasn't fit to wear white. The number of affairs she had while you were together... well... it was disrespectful.'

Paul blinked as Alison carefully lifted off the black wig and put it down on the table before using her fingers to massage her scalp.

'Where's Nicole?'

Alison laughed. 'Please, you know exactly where she is. We both do.'

What?

His mouth was dry, and his body was shaking from lack of food as he tried to follow what Alison was saying. He stood up and tried to step towards her but, too late, he realised his legs were bound together with thick rope. He fell back onto the bed, then struggled into a sitting position.

'Sorry.' She nodded to his feet. 'It's not really how I planned to start our life together, but it's a precaution. You've been through so much, and that bitch has brainwashed you. But don't worry, it won't be forever.' Alison started humming again. It was an Irish folk song, and it made his skin itch.

His temples pounded as he tried to wriggle his ankles, but the rope held tight. 'Why are you doing this?'

She stopped humming and looked at him, amber eyes wide. 'You know why, Paul. It's because we're meant to be together. I've known it from the moment we met. We could both feel it, but you were with that narcissistic cow. She never understood you. Neither does Jenna. Not like I do. Because we're the same. I know what happened to you when you were young, but I would never hold it against you. Because I understand. I went through things too. They locked me in a cupboard, starved me, hurt me,' she said as she held up her arm. It was bare in the wedding dress and running all along her forearm and inner wrist were silvery scars. 'See, we even share the same pain.'

Had she gone completely mad? His neck ached, as if it was carrying a thousand tonnes of weight. All the pain that had disappeared came back in a flood. He gritted his teeth.

'You can't keep me here. Jenna's expecting me home. When she discovers I'm missing, she'll go to the police.'

'That's exactly the sort of thing she *would* do,' Alison said darkly, eyes flashing. Then she shrugged as she held up a phone. 'But it's okay. I've taken care of it. She thinks that you're stuck in traffic.'

'You broke into my phone? How?'

'Far too easily. Your password was very basic,' she said in a chiding voice. 'After we're married, I'll show you how to do an encrypted one. Better yet, I'll do it for you. There are all kinds of crazy people trying to steal your online information. No point leaving the back door unlocked.'

'Please, you have to let me go.'

She laughed. 'Of course I will, silly. I haven't gone to all this trouble to hurt you. Is that what you thought? I'd never hurt you. I love you. Everything I've done has been for you.'

'But how? I saw the photos, and all the newspaper articles. And Daniel.'

Alison broke into a jittery laugh. 'Do you have any idea how many tutorials there are on YouTube? Doctoring a couple of photos and hacking into some websites? As for Daniel... Jesus. I never understood why Nicole wanted to have an affair with Bridget, but at least she had some backbone. Daniel is as spineless as they come. He was practically pissing his pants when we met. I don't think he looked at me once. Pathetic.'

'And was it pathetic when you tried to murder Jenna and my son?'

At the mention of Jenna's name, Alison's face darkened. 'That bitch had it coming. You were doing so well until she got herself knocked up. It's not good for you. See what happened with Nicole? How much you suffered because of what she did?'

Paul shut his eyes, trying to centre his thoughts. But none of it made sense. And why wouldn't she stop humming? He forced his eyes open.

'Come on, Al, this is all a joke, right? You don't love me. We're friends. Besides, what about Rob? Things are going so well with you both.'

She burst out laughing. 'I love how you always see the best in people. It's what makes you such a great teacher. Unfortunately, Rob didn't understand anything. He came down here once and saw my things. All the gifts you'd given me, and he said all kinds of mean things. That I was sick. That he was going to tell you about my collection.' She smiled fondly. 'So I had to stop him.'

Paul swallowed, trying to get some moisture into his dry throat. 'How did you stop him?'

She titled her head and looked at him, amber eyes wide like a child. 'There's only one way to stop someone, Paul. You should know that. I killed him.'

'When?' Paul's voice was barely a whisper as his temples pounded.

'Two and a half years ago.'

'You said he moved to the Isle of Wight.'

A guilty flush stained her cheeks. 'I hated lying to you, my lamb. I really did, but I always knew I'd tell you one day.'

Shit.

Alison had killed Rob over two years ago and all this time she'd been walking around, acting like he'd broken her heart? He shuddered before realising he'd been doing the exact same thing. Bile rose in his throat. Was he like her?

'How can you talk it about so calmly?'

She blinked, as if confused by the question. 'Because it *is* calming. People are painful to be around. All they do is talk and judge and hurt. Things are so much quieter once they're dead. It was like that with my parents. They hated me. Always jabbing hings in me. Cutting me. But as soon as I lit the fire, it all topped,' she said in a dreamy voice.

Paul shivered, thinking of the article on the wall. How the bducted girl had been an orphan whose parents had died in a ire. So badly burnt that they could only be identified by their lental records.

The same thing that had happened to Nicole.

Except Alison said Nicole had never been back. Did that nean she'd burnt Nicole's bones after digging them up? Another hought slammed into him. If Nicole hadn't been alive, then he still didn't know how she'd died.

The room began to spin, and he leaned forward, trying to end off the tingling sensation running through his body. I can't faint. I can't faint. He jabbed a nail into his leg and his circulation slowly returned.

'What happened to Nicole?'

'You still don't remember? Poor lamb. But it's okay. I remember. I saw your true self that night, and you saw mine. That's when I knew for sure that we were meant to be together.'

'Saw what?' Anger rose up in him. All this time he'd been looking for answers, looking for the truth, and Alison had known it all along. She'd somehow been part of it. 'If you know what happened, you need to tell me.'

'It's better if you find out for yourself.' Alison gave him an understanding smile as she got to her feet. She was taller than Nicole had been, and the wedding dress was too short, making her look like an overgrown schoolgirl as she walked towards him and sat down on the bed. Her shoulder brushed his, and it felt like a thousand tiny spiders were skittering along his arm, while her musky perfume cloyed in his throat.

She reached into her pocket and pulled out a slim box. She opened it up to reveal a syringe. He tried to move away, but she

had him pressed against the wall. She hummed as she presse
the needle into his arm.

Darkness tried to pull him down. 'Stop.'

'Don't fight it,' she advised. 'Let it take you. While you sleep,
need to prepare. I have a loose end to tie up.'

He frowned, her words distant. 'None of this makes sense.'

'I know, my lamb, but it will. When you have the key.'

* * *

The cool air prickled his skin and night insects darted in and out of hi
vision as Paul crawled along the rough ground. Stones jabbed at hi
knees and hard soil broke his fingernails. He needed to go faster. If he
stopped, it would be over. But he was so tired. Suddenly the night sky
shimmered, and the blazing hot sun appeared, beating down on his pale
skin. Sweat poured from his brow and the heat bounced off the ground,
burning his palms. Don't stop. Don't stop. He chanted the words over
and over again, but his aching muscles began to scream.

He dragged himself into a clearing and over to where a pile of sun-
dried soil had been heaped. Next to it was a shallow hole. Just large
enough for a body. Just large enough to sleep. A worm slithered over his
hand, but he hardly noticed. So tired. He half fell, half rolled into the
shallow recess and the stabbing sensation behind his eyes retreated as
his aching limbs settled against the dirt bed.

'You poor lamb,' a voice crooned, soft and low like a lullaby. He
forced one eye open to where a woman was standing over him. Her
long hair pulled to one side, her beautiful face covered by a tiny
widow's veil. Alison.

'What do you want?' he croaked. But she didn't answer. She leaned
forward and handed him an ornate key.

Paul stiffened. He was asleep but he was also aware. And this wasn't his dream. Where had the key come from? He paused. He knew that word. He was meant to do something with it.

He let his body sink back into the grave so that the veil of sleep could surround him, and then he reached for the key.

The metal was warm in his hand, and it seemed to whisper to him. Stand up. Stand up. He climbed out of the grave and brushed away the dirt. Then he looked round, but he was no longer in the woods. There was a cage. It was familiar.

It was the one that always stood on the other side of the swirling mist. When he was younger, he sometimes ventured there, but it never ended well. Not for anyone, so he always stayed well away. But today he could see a heavy wooden door with dull bolts going through it, reinforcing it so nothing could get in and out. And by the handle was a small lock.

The key in his hand warmed up, and pain seared through his hand from the unexpected heat. He needed to drop the key... or put it into the lock.

Just for one moment, so he could see what was there. Then he would shut the door and it would be okay. The burning sensation in his hand increased as the key turned bright red. It was now or never.

Paul slowly put the key into the lock and watched as the wooden door swung open and he could finally witness his life.

41

Nicole was standing in the lounge, her hand resting lightly on her flat stomach. The coffee table was full of papers as well as an array of magazines scattered over the floor.

Her eyes were damp, like she'd been crying. Paul frowned. Nicole never cried. Not even when they'd been skiing, and she'd broken her arm halfway down an advanced run.

'What's wrong?'

'Dust in my eye. That woman we get to clean the place needs to be sacked,' she snapped, sounding more like her usual self. Paul sighed. The woman was a mother of one of his students who had recently separated from her husband and was desperate for work. Besides, it was Nicole who was the messy one. For someone who always looked so meticulous, she had an ability to leave a trail of destruction in her wake.

'I'll talk to her,' Paul said non-committedly as he began to stack up the papers. 'How are you feeling?'

'Fine,' she said, turning away from him. 'It was stomach cramps. Stop fussing.'

Again Paul sighed. He was hardly fussing. She'd been

doubled over for most of the night and had taken painkillers before going into the spare bedroom to sleep. She claimed it was because he kept her up with his nightmares.

Hiding his guilt, he bent down and stacked the wedding magazines into a neat pile. A letter fell out and fluttered lazily to the floor. He absently picked it up and put it with the pile of letters he'd already sorted. Then he stiffened as his eyes scanned the content.

Surgical abortion.

The words stared out at him.

Dear Nicole Williams,

We are writing to confirm your appointment to have a termination on Tuesday the fifth of March...

He read the rest of the letter as something cold and dark raced through him. Tuesday the fifth of March was yesterday.

'What have you done?' The words were raw and jagged as they came out of his mouth, pain stabbing at his temples. A child? They were going to have a child?

He was going to be a father?

Have a family?

The two things he wanted more than anything... and before it had even had a chance to be a seed in his mind, it had been taken away from him.

'What are you—' Nicole broke off as she spun round and saw the letter in his hand.

Her beautiful face was bleached of colour, and she took in a shuddering breath and steadied herself. 'Oh... that.'

Bone-chilling mist swept across his vision and the pressure on his neck felt like a guillotine about to come crashing down on him.

'That? You're speaking like you went to the store to buy some bloody milk. You killed our baby.'

She glared at him, eyes defiant. 'Don't say it like that. I didn't kill anything. You have to see that the timing is all wrong. I'm trying to get my career back on track, and I can't do that in a bloody maternity dress. It wasn't alive. I terminated a pregnancy, it's different.'

The scars on his arm burned and his vision blurred. His whole body began to rock, and he wanted to punch something. Someone. His fingers curled into a fist and his breathing quickened. Nicole glanced down at his clenched hands and gave him a telling look.

'Seriously? You don't even kill flies and now you're going to hit me?'

Paul's heart hammered and the rage boiled. It had always been like this. Brewing in him like a volcano. Ever since the first time his father had beaten him. The lava was his pain and rage and fury at being voiceless for so long.

I'm nobody. Nothing.

No. He slammed the cage back down round the anger that was always threatening to consume him. Long ago, he'd made a choice to not make his pain or abuse turn him into an abuser. Even if the urge was always there to lash out.

The doctors and therapists never understood what he was doing.

They kept trying to push him to open up. To unlock his past and take away the cage.

But they didn't understand that the cage was what kept him safe.

It kept them all safe.

The mist lifted, and he took a step back towards the wall until he had calmed down. 'No, Nicole. I'm not going to hit you. But we are going to talk about this.'

'I beg to differ,' she snapped and turned to stalk away. But one of the glossy wedding magazines was still on the ground and her stiletto heel slid across it, sending her tumbling straight into the coffee table before crashing to the ground.

No.

Paul stared in horror as Nicole lay in a crumpled heap on the ground, her leg twisted at an awkward angle beneath her. There was no blood, but her face was pale, and her eyes were shut. So peaceful. Like she was sleeping.

No. No. No.

Paul couldn't move. His legs were rooted to the ground as he stared at her, waiting for her to sit up and complain about the cleaning lady again. Somehow blame her. Or him for leaving a magazine on the ground. But she hadn't shifted.

Brrrrring.

The doorbell went, but still Paul didn't move. He'd learned long ago, when people had hit him, or put their hands where they shouldn't go, that the best thing was to stand perfectly still. It didn't make it stop, but it somehow hurt less because he wasn't fully there.

'Paul?' a voice called out. Alison? She worked with him at the school, and they were friends. He racked his brains. Had she been due over? Maybe it was to see Nicole? The pair had taken to spending Saturday mornings together shopping. 'Is everything okay, the door was unlocked, and... holy shit. What did you do?'

He looked up. She was in the room now, staring at Nicole's unmoving body, and then back to him. He could see it in her eyes. She thought he'd killed Nicole. That he was capable of that.

That's what they'd all think. They'd go back over his history and discover how his parents really died. They'd decide he was a

murderer. The perfect storm about to happen, and this wonderful
life he'd finally built for himself would disappear.

But what else could he do?

His throat was dry, and his hands tingled, like they were too
big for the rest of his body. Alison stopped staring and hurried
over to him, her arms gently leading him to the sofa.

Finally he spoke. 'We need to call the police.'

'The police?' She looked at him like he was a first grader
who'd asked something ridiculous. 'No, my lamb. We don't want
them to bother us. They can never understand what it's like to be
us, and you can't let one mistake define who you are. You taught
me that. Now, you sit here, and I'll make some tea. Then we'll
work out a plan of what to do. I know a really great place to take
the body...'

42

Jenna needed to pee. After receiving Paul's text message, she'd managed to stop Lucy from insisting on coming back over and caring for her like she was an invalid. Even though, as it turned out, she kind of was. And she'd hoped that Paul would be home by now. Still, he wasn't too far away. He'd sent her several more text messages updating her on the slow-moving sheep, and she was sure he'd be there soon.

Except not soon enough to help her to the bathroom. She groaned as she tried to roll herself into a standing position, but in the process, she managed to send her engagement ring flying up into the air and down the back of the sofa.

She'd lost weight while she'd been in hospital and Lucy had told her to wear the ring round her neck until it fitted her again, but she hadn't been able to bear it. She awkwardly shifted so that she could slip her hand down to retrieve it, but her ribs were painful, and the swell of her belly stopped her from twisting properly.

Gritting her teeth, Jenna rolled herself off the sofa, careful not to knock the coffee table with her plastered leg. She should prob-

ably wait, but the idea of not having her ring on when Paul came
home was unbearable. Besides, how much damage could she do
by lifting up the ugly linen squab? She used her shoulder to half
lift, half push the large cushion to one side and let out a sigh of
relief as her ring lay nestled above the cloth that covered the
springs.

She gratefully picked it up and this time slipped it into the
pocket of her cardigan. When she was settled, she'd do as her
sister suggested and thread it onto a necklace. The one with the
daisy that Paul had given her a few months ago. Smiling, she
started to move the large cushion back into place when she
noticed a tiny piece of paper sticking out from between the teeth
of the zip.

Curious, she reached over and tugged the zip. The paper tore
as she eased the zip open, the teeth giving way one by one. Once
they were past the trapped paper, the cushion opened easily and
she pulled back the cover to see a handful of papers sitting on top
of the thick foam.

She picked them up and her throat tightened as she stared at
Nicole's familiar handwriting.

March second. My lover's name is Bridget...

Jenna let out a little gasp. It was the missing pages from
Nicole's diary. But why had they been hidden away in the cushion
of the sofa?

Her hands shook as she carefully searched the rest of the
cushion before zipping it up and replacing it. She inspected the
second one as well, but there was nothing there. Once she was
certain, she settled herself back down onto the sofa, this time
barely noticing how uncomfortable it was. All she cared about
was why Nicole felt she had to hide the pages.

My life is ruined. Funny, if you told me three months ago that my entire future would be destroyed, I would've laughed. 'Please, bitch,' I would've said. 'I have everything. The perfect fiancé, the perfect lover, and I'm about to interview for the perfect job, which I'll get.'

Until a week ago.

I still don't know how she found out about the fraud allegations. It was a setup. Fucking Stuart Barclay screwed me over and set me up to take the fall. And the senior fucking partners believed it. They didn't want their precious reputation to take a hit, so they merely fired me and didn't press charges. Which was fine. I was going to sue their arses off for unfair dismissal, once the private investigator I hired found the trail led back to Stewart.

But I never got the chance. Instead that bitch blackmailed me. At first she wanted money, but then she became more outrageous. Go to therapy, but don't tell the truth, pretend you're Paul. I want you to know how fucked up your fiancé is.

I knew what she was doing. She wanted me to leave him, so that she could swoop in and take care of him. I only went along with it while I figured out a way to get her back. But then she found out about the abortion.

God, the way she looked at me. Like I was something on the bottom of her shoe.

But it was her fault. All those therapy sessions, pretending I was Paul, and having to listen to Gwendolyn talk about how trauma from the past needs to be healed or it will destroy everyone... well... I'm not going to lie. It scared me.

What if Paul did suddenly snap and hurt our child? That's probably what she intended me to think all along. All I know is that Alison Temple is a psychotic bitch who's ruined my life.

The pages fell from Jenna's hands. Was that why they'd been hidden? To stop Alison from finding them? Why didn't she destroy them, instead? Or was it a safeguard so Paul would learn the truth?

That Alison had been blackmailing Nicole? Threatening to ruin her life if she stayed with him? Scaring her into having an abortion because she feared that Paul was crazy? Was that why Nicole had left? To get away from Alison?

More importantly, if Alison was the real threat, that meant they were all still in danger. She reached for her phone and called Paul, but it went straight to voicemail. Now what was she meant to do?

43

Paul's head was spinning but he bit into the side of his mouth. Mild pain erupted, enough to force back the hangover from whatever drug Alison had given him.

Had she known he hadn't killed Nicole?

Had she overhead their conversation? Watched the accident unfold? Images of her standing in the garden, peering into the lounge, took hold in his mind. She could be doing that to Jenna right now.

He still had so many questions, but there was no time to look for answers. If Alison was capable of killing her parents and Rob, and calmly helping him bury Nicole's body, then she was capable of hurting Jenna and his son.

After all, she'd already tried once.

I have a loose end to tie up.

Adrenaline surged through him. He had to get out of there. He had to keep Jenna safe.

The rope was still round his ankles, and his hands had been dragged behind his back, tied together with something. His

whole body ached from sleeping in such a terrible position and
he longed to roll his shoulders.

Soon. He could do that soon.

He didn't bother trying to stand. He wriggled himself across
the bed and slipped down to the floor. He rolled onto his
shoulder and used the momentum to turn himself over. Hard
concrete bit into his skin and dust motes flooded his nostrils. He
coughed and this time tried to breathe out as he rolled again.

He was panting and, when he craned his neck, the workbench
was still another three metres away. Despair filled him, but he
pictured Jenna alone in their house, scared. Vulnerable. He
grunted and flipped himself over again. And again. Again.

Sweat poured off him and he reeked of body odour, but he
finally reached the bench, even though he was lying prostrate
below it. He gritted his teeth and managed to get up onto his
knees. From there he pressed his chest against the leg of the
bench and forced his aching thigh muscles to hold his weight as
he got to his feet.

His eyes scanned the scatter of hardware receipts and plastic
jars filled with nails and screws. Swearing under his breath, he
leaned forward and knocked one over, but the lid stayed in place.
Swallowing his impatience, he used the bench to steady himself
as he made small jumps to take him further along the bench.
There were no tools left lying around for someone like him to use
as a weapon.

There wouldn't be, because Alison had planned her
campaign for years. It seemed unlikely she'd be undone by a
random hammer. Fifteen minutes later, his entire body was
aching, and he dropped back down to the floor.

It was no good. There was nothing he could—

What was that?

Paul's entire body tingled as something glinted from underneath the workbench. He wormed his way under there and almost cried when he saw it. A small hole saw. The carbonised steel was about three centimetres wide with jagged teeth, designed to go onto the end of an electric drill. Either Alison had misplaced it, or a tradesman had left it behind. Either way, Paul didn't care. If he could reach it, he could use it to cut through the ropes at his wrists and ankles.

Thirty minutes later, his hands were free. Carefully he flexed his fingers and shoulders before starting on his legs. Then he went in search of a weapon. As expected, there was still no signs of any tools, but after running his hands along the exposed brickwork, he finally found a spot that had loose mortar.

Soon he was holding onto a single red brick. The concrete dust was rough against his hands, but he didn't care. It was heavy enough to use as a weapon. *If* he needed to. He started to head to the stairs, but before he could cross the room there was a scrape of metal as the cellar door slowly began to creak open.

Shit. He was closer to the bed than the stairs so he hurried as fast as he was able back across the floor, and lay down on the bed, the brick tucked closely into his side. Shutting his eyes, he let out a breath and focused on relaxing his face muscles.

'Still asleep, my love? That's okay. I'm going round to break the bad news to Jenna. Oh, and to kill her. I know you don't like blood on your hands,' Alison said, much as if she was popping out to the corner store for some milk. 'And, when I get back, we can have a bottle of champagne to celebrate. It makes me sick that you couldn't even drink because of that woman. Still, it will be over soon.' As she spoke, her voice moved closer, and soon her cloying perfume was coating him like a sticky wet substance. A fingernail traced his jawline, and it took all of his control not to flinch.

Christ. Was she going to lean over and kiss him?

A faint buzzing started in his ears and his heart pounded. How dare she touch him? Her oily hands had no business being anywhere near him. Being anywhere near Jenna or his son. His neck was stiff with the weight of the steel cage that was always there. The one that held his rage and fury.

No.

He tried to take a shaky step away from the cage. He couldn't go near it. If he did, he'd become like his abusers. And so he pressed himself back into the crimson mist, where it was safe. But something jabbed him in the shoulders, and he stumbled back towards the cage. No. No. No. At least the door would keep him safe. But before he could step back, the door swung open.

Paul stiffened and reached for the key to try and lock it again, but it was no longer in his pocket. The door was wide open now and Paul didn't have to even move as swirls of white-hot fury embraced him, like a long-lost lover. Energy surged through his veins and, as Alison's mouth pressed against his, his fingers curled round the brick and brought it crashing down on her skull.

He didn't even bother to open his eyes as her dead weight fell onto his chest. He pushed her off, and she went crashing to the floor. Finally he opened his eyes and stared at her.

She was dressed in jeans and a pink hoodie and over by the doorway was an oversized teddy bear with balloons tied to its neck. Was that how she'd planned to get into his house? By pretending to give Jenna a present before killing her?

The fury sparked again and, when Alison let out a small groaning noise, Paul calmly twisted and picked up the pillow.

His body was stiff as he dropped down to the ground and pressed it over her face as hard as he could. Her arms flayed and she let out a muffled scream. It seemed to go on for eternity but eventually she stopped moving.

He lifted the pillow from her face and felt for her pulse. There was nothing.

She was dead. Her lifeless eyes staring up at him.

He brushed his fingers across them, closing them both and then checked his watch. He'd have to wait until much later before he could bury her. Still, at least he knew where there was an empty grave.

44

Paul sat in the car and inspected himself. There was some dirt on his trousers, so he brushed it off and smoothed down his shirt. He'd already called Jenna and explained that his engine had stalled while waiting for the sheep to move, and he was now stuck waiting for the AA to arrive. He'd made her promise not to wait up for him.

Then he'd taken Alison's body through the woods to the grave where they'd both buried Nicole. But this time it wasn't a blur in his memory. There was no mist trying to ward off the events of his life. This time he remembered it all in painstaking detail.

It was probably only fair. He had killed someone, and it wasn't the sort of thing he deserved to forget. After it was done, he'd gone back to Alison's house and packed up a suitcase before finding her passport and booking some flights for her. He drove her car over to the estate on the far side of the village and climbed out, leaving the keys in the engine. By tomorrow it would be long gone. After all, why should he try to dispose of a car when someone else would do it for him?

He burnt her passport, mobile phone, and suitcase before

inally driving home. His whole body ached, and he longed for a bath. To be clean so that he could hold Jenna and forget it had all happened. He drove the car into the driveway but didn't open the garage door, worried he'd wake Jenna. He let himself in through the front door, careful to take off his shoes. But the minute he crossed the threshold, Jenna's voice echoed out from the lounge.

'Paul? Is that you?' Her voice was pitchy, like she was scared, and guilt ran through him.

'Yes, it's me. Sorry to wake you.' He half expected her to be curled up on the sofa, eyes full of sleep, but she was sitting there, clutching at a piece of paper. 'What's wrong?'

'You won't believe what I've found. It's the most terrible thing.'

Jenna opened her eyes and peered around the room. Sunlight was streaming in from the half-opened curtains and there was a rustling noise as Paul stepped into the bedroom holding a tray with her favourite teapot on. She let herself smile.

After she'd shown him the terrible diary entries Nicole had made, his face had gone as pale as hers. It was too awful to contemplate. It also meant they'd have to go to the police. Alison couldn't be allowed to get away with it. And even though Nicole had gone just as crazy, it was no excuse.

She'd wanted to go straight down to the station, but Paul had stopped her. He pulled out DC Pip Adams's card and promised he'd call her. Not long after that, he'd insisted on carrying her to bed.

'Good morning.' His cologne danced in her nostrils as he set down the tray by the side of the bed. 'How are you feeling?'

Jenna wriggled herself into a sitting position and leaned into him, his warmth spreading down her skin like liquid sunshine 'Better. Have you heard back from the police?'

He looked away for a moment, as if it was painful to talk about, then he slowly nodded. 'I'm afraid it's bad news. By the time they got to Alison's house, she was gone. Her things were packed, and her passport taken. I spoke to Tim this morning and he'd received an email from her last night, saying Rob had been offered a new job overseas and that she was going with him. She resigned immediately.'

'She's gone?' Jenna said, the words floating round the room like an echo. 'But what if she comes back? After everything she did to Nicole, what if she tries to do something to me?'

'It won't happen,' Paul said, his voice a low rasp. 'I spoke to Tim, and she hasn't only moved region, she's moved country.'

'God, where's she moved to?' Jenna's eyes widened.

'Australia.'

ACKNOWLEDGMENTS

We've been friends and critique partners for many years and had never thought of collaborating on a book before. It was an amazing experience, and we'd like to thank our co-conspirator, Christina Phillips, the third member of our writing group, for all her support and encouragement while we embarked on this.

We'd also like to thank Boldwood Books for deciding to run the contest for a psychological thriller at just the right time. To everyone at Boldwood, especially Emily Ruston, thanks for being so incredible to work with. It's been the best experience ever.

To our families, who know each other well, thanks for always being there and putting up with our incessant plotting and laughter.

MORE FROM AMANDA RIGBY

We hope you enjoyed reading *Remember Me?*. If you did, please leave a review.

If you'd like to gift a copy, this book is also available as an ebook, digital audio download and audiobook CD.

Sign up to Amanda Rigby's mailing list for news, competitions and updates on future books.

https://bit.ly/AmandaRigbyNews

ABOUT THE AUTHOR

Amanda Rigby is the nom de plume of the writing partnership between Amanda Ashby and Sally Rigby. Both authors live in New Zealand, have been friends for eighteen years and agree about everything (except musicals). They decided to collaborate on a psychological thriller which they then entered into a competition, run by Boldwood, and which they won!

Follow Amanda on social media:

twitter.com/AmandaRigbyNZ

instagram.com/amandarigbybooks

facebook.com/Amanda-Rigby-111632041134381

ABOUT BOLDWOOD BOOKS

Boldwood Books is a fiction publishing company seeking out the best stories from around the world.

Find out more at www.boldwoodbooks.com

Sign up to the Book and Tonic newsletter for news, offers and competitions from Boldwood Books!

http://www.bit.ly/bookandtonic

We'd love to hear from you, follow us on social media:

facebook.com/BookandTonic

twitter.com/BoldwoodBooks

instagram.com/BookandTonic